IF I DON'T SIX

DOUBLEDAY

New York   London   Toronto   Sydney   Auckland

IF I DON'T SIX

. . . .

E L W O O D   R E I D

This novel is a work of fiction. The references to the University of Michigan or any other institution are intended to give the fiction a sense of reality and authenticity. Moreover, any fictionalized events or incidents that may involve the University of Michigan or any other institution did not occur. Other names, characters, places, and incidents are the product of the author's imagination or are used fictitiously, and their resemblance, if any, to real-life counterparts is entirely coincidental.

PUBLISHED BY DOUBLEDAY
a division of Bantam Doubleday Dell Publishing Group, Inc.
1540 Broadway, New York, New York 10036

DOUBLEDAY and the portrayal of an anchor with a dolphin
are trademarks of Doubleday, a division of
Bantam Doubleday Dell Publishing Group, Inc.

Book Design by Leah S. Carlson

Library of Congress Cataloging-in-Publication Data
Reid, Elwood.
If I don't six / Elwood Reid. — 1st ed.
p.   cm.
I. Title.
PS3568.E4763714   1998
813'.54—DC21   97-40416
CIP

ISBN 0-385-49119-0

All Rights Reserved

Printed in the United States of America

September 1998

First Edition

1 3 5 7 9 10 8 6 4 2

FOR NINA

"I won't be bad tomorrow."

P. W. Long

"Am I a bad man? Am I a good man?
—Hard to say, Brother Bones. Maybe you both,
like most of we.
—The evidence is difficult to structure towards deliberate evil.
But what of the rest? Does it wax for wrath
in its infinite complexity?"

From Dreamsong #239 by John Berryman

ONE

But the game.

When we trot out of the locker room Habs goes apeshit, starts head-butting one of the bleacher beams. I look at Habs, eyes squinched shut, brainpan hurting him some, and think what kind of dumbfuck attacks a steel beam?

Then the screaming starts. Guys with voices like chopped cars motor out advice and threats. Women screech for their sons to Give 'em hell.

"Hey, Riley, you gonna to hit somebody?" a broad-shouldered man shouts, his face shaped like a flour sack, mouth open, yellow-green teeth. I jack my forearm into the air and this seems to satisfy him, sending him back to his steaming coffee and impatient wife, who I notice wears one of those My Son Plays for the Vikes buttons with son's picture laminated beneath. Billy Miller, our right guard.

I am not a fan of fans.

We wait under the bleachers; pumpkin-colored oak leaves and candy wrappers swirl around our feet and rattle against the snow fence. The air a mixture of smoke, rain-damp wool, and sweaty helmet. It feels like football.

Over the PA system I hear my name mentioned, then my number and some bullshit about how I'm on the honor roll. Stork looks at me and rolls his eyes as Sawicki, our starting linebacker, smacks me on the back of the helmet saying, "You gonna bust that big motherfucking brain of yours, Riley?"

I answer with a growl—Sawicki's one of those guys who run around getting everybody geeked, screaming and yelling. If I don't respond, he'll take that as a sure sign I'm not ready to play and head-butt me until I am.

I nod and rub my cleats against the rough cement as the rest of the team streams out of the narrow metal doors behind me. Coach Gil's this-is-the-end-of-the-season-and-we-are-nothing-without-victory speech rings in my ears.

My name is Elwood Riley, captain of the 1 and 7 Saint Patrick Vikings.

I am not proud of this. I go both ways, but for the money I'm a defensive tackle on a team that's got no speed and tackles like a bunch of girls. Still, we crash through paper banners held high by smooth-legged cheerleaders, while bleachers full of parents clip-clop their approval. The band blares its tubas and trombones, some drunk in a Cleveland Browns shirt screams "Go Vikes!" and for a few precious moments all of us feel bad-ass, dangerous, and ready to play for Coach. When your team is 1 and 7 you take the moments when you can get them.

On the field Coach Gil rips up grass, tosses it into the air and points east. We take the field and watch the coin toss, run like hell on the kickoff and pretty soon the flow of the game swallows me up and I'm in that flickering rush of collision. After a little flash and ingenuity (option, QB sneak, end around) Coach Gil hunkers down and starts running the ball up the gut, hoping to break their spirit. Instead, the drive stalls and we are forced to punt.

Then the Wildcats bust one up the middle, followed by another. Olivet, the Wildcats' star fullback, rumbles through our line, his breath chugging out like a diesel rattling its way across some empty road. I beat my padded hands into the grass and look out from under my facemask as the crowd goes silent and he scores.

When we get the ball back, Tyrone, our number one tailback, blows his ankle on a sweep. The band stops playing, even the tubas go mute and sag over chubby shoulders as Tyrone limps off the field. Our cheerleaders have left their pom-poms back by the Cyclone fence to flirt with non-ball-playing boyfriends. Kids smash wax cups and Frisbee them onto the field. Somebody boos and I hate the losing.

But still the game.

In the huddle, Habs says, "We're getting thrashed again. We've got no offense—where the fuck's our offense?"

Stork says, "Shut up and play ball, motherfucker. This is a test."

Habs looks at him, blood running down his arm, sixty-watt eyes dimmed to twenty, says, "You wanna piece?"

On the sideline, Coach Gil tells us to suck it up and drive—play like men. But the Wildcats continue to move the ball at will and there's not much I or anybody else can do to stop them.

When it is all over and we have lost game number eight and Coach Gil walks head-down through the crowd to the locker room, composing his postgame talk, Stork turns to me and says, "Slap some of that philosophy on me, Riley."

"Greek, Roman, or motherfucker?"

"Anything, man, but no Lombardi bullshit, just give me some words before Coach pollutes my 1 and 8 brain with one of his we-must-snatch-victory-from-the-jaws-of-defeat speeches."

I think a minute, studying Stork's sweaty face.

"Everything is only for a day, both that which remembers and that which is remembered," I say. "Marcus Aurelius."

"I like it," Stork says. "Everything, even this?" He points at the grass.

"Is nothing," I say. "In other words you are a man of the moment."

With that we hit the showers, listen to a few Hail Marys and Coach Gil's usual speech.

On Monday Stork and I cut calc class and go sit by the lake. Dead sheephead float by and we take turns trying to peg them with rocks.

"Hear from any more colleges?" Stork asks as he drags his long arms through the air, launching a rock out into the waves.

"Every day," I say.

"What's it feel like?"

"You want the straight shit or some philosophy on it?" I ask.

"I'm talking straight, Riley."

"Straight?"

"Yeah, like—you don't have to prove you've got a fucking brain to me—I know better."

I smile at him, toss a stone his way and watch his gangly body duck.

"What do you know?" I ask.

"That you're just a rockhead that talks good," he says.

"This rockhead is getting the fuck out of Cleveland," I say.

Stork sits on a piano-sized piece of cracked cement staring out at the water.

"It ain't because you run around spouting philosophy all day," he says.

"You want to know why I do that?"

"For the chicks?"

I shake my head. "Because one day in English class Pemberton called me stupid."

"He calls everybody stupid, Riley. That's what he does—walks around acting all superior when he's not getting the shit beat out of him."

"He's supposed to be some sort of genius," I say.

"What the hell's he doing here, then? If you ask me I think he's just got everybody thinking he's smart—you know the way he walks around all day reading books in the hallway, scribbling notes to himself, answering every goddamn question in calc."

"He's not a half-bad guy," I say.

"You just said he called you stupid."

"What he meant was that I didn't give a shit—that in ten years I'd be like my old man, reading the newspaper and trudging off to work every day."

"All this from Pemberton calling you stupid."

"I figured it out."

"And?"

"And now I've got colleges wanting me to play ball for them and go to school for free."

"That's because you're big and you like to hit people, not because you're some pointy head like Pemberton."

"And that's it? That's what you think?"

"No, man—what I'm saying is fuck all that, Riley—you got drive, trajectory, college, and all that recruiting bullshit. You've got to go. That's the way it is. It don't matter what you've got inside. What matters is that you can split this place, be gone, and all that good stuff."

"And you?" I ask.

Stork folds his arms and stares out over the lake toward Canada. He's a couple of inches taller than me, one of those way-tall goofy dudes who slouch through life wishing they were shorter.

"I have to play," he says. "If I didn't I'd be a queerball or a geek, take your pick. I just don't have the feet or the heart. But you can get out of here—you're six foot six inches of prime Cleveland hope."

"You staying?" I ask. Stork shrugs his shoulders and says, "What the fuck else am I going to do?"

"You could . . ."

"I could what? No, man, what happens next is I read the newspaper and trudge off to work every day, just like my old man and your old man."

"That's it?"

"Riley, I am Cleveland," Stork says.

Mom and Dad are jazzed about me going off to play ball at some big school where I'll wear smart clothes, jet around to games with ninety other guys just like me. They want to watch me on television and say things like, "That's our son, he plays football for the University of _____."

Dad was a star linebacker in high school. He was too thin, had a bad back and only okay grades so the colleges stayed away. Just an average Joe, he says. Then he met my mother, got himself a job, family, mortgage, and pension dangled out in front of him. He once told me that everything would be okay, that he'd stop thinking about what sort of player he might have been, if I could just break on through to the big time.

"I remember what it feels like to be young, fast, and full of piss and vinegar," he says.

And now? On his best days he's just a tired shoprat, worked to the bone, cored out and all that sad doomed crap.

"Son," he says, sucking in his breath. "You've got to want this for yourself."

What do I want out of all this? Answer—I want to get through it. Go to college, play ball and maybe become a stud Wheaties box jock because I'm supposed to, because I'm lucky and big and like to hit. But most of all I don't know.

Dad thinks he does.

For my twelfth birthday he made me a wooden plaque with STICK TO ITNESS painted on it after I told him I wanted to quit wrestling for the YMCA. Later that year I dropped a rock off a highway overpass onto a car.

Simon, the first kid on our block to smoke a cigarette, showed me how he dropped pennies on cars from the overpass. I tried a few times and when the coins pinged harmlessly off the speeding cars I stole a bunch of golf balls and flung them at tractor trailers. After that it was wrist rockets and BB guns. Once we shot flaming arrows at Danny, the local retard, who went around town staring into people's driveways and houses, rubbing his belly and shifting from foot to foot nervously. We never actually hit him with an arrow, but it was enough to scare him off our street for a couple of months.

But the accident that summer was all me.

Simon said he wanted to mess something up. So I picked a chunk of concrete out of a ditch, walked out on the overpass and said, "This mess something up?"

"You don't have the balls," Simon said.

I nodded and waited until I saw a Cadillac streaking toward us before I let the concrete slip through my fingers. Simon ran.

The windshield shattered and the Cadillac veered off the embankment, wrapping itself in barbed wire and sumac. There was a woman behind the wheel and I remember the way the car radio blared when she emerged from the car, blood trickling down her face, wetting her long brown hair. Then there was the scream when she saw me standing on the overpass and the way her finger trembled as she pointed at me. The air seemed to freeze as her scream filled my ears. A stillness descended on me and for a moment there were no other cars. It was me and her and the blood and I tried to run away. I ran until my lungs burned and my legs went numb with exhaustion.

Even now her scream has stayed with me like some echo that won't go away, full of fear and horribly alive. For a few moments I knew what the world sounds like when it grinds to a halt.

If it was up to me I'd disappear into the woods somewhere out West and build myself a cabin and fish my brains out. I read this story about how John Muir used to walk into the woods with just his knife and some string. When it snowed he would dance all night and sing at the stars just to stay warm. I tell my brother, Jay, about how I'm going to live off the land, hike mountains for breakfast.

"John Muir was the original bad-ass," I tell him.

"What about Mean Joe?" he says.

"Bad mother," I concede. "But Muir lived it his whole life. He just was."

"Dad says you're a ballplayer, that you read too much when you should be out lifting weights."

And there it is. What can I say? How can I tell them it's only a station in life? That I'd rather be like Pemberton, sitting around all day reading books and thinking smart things. Instead, I read philosophy books I steal from the library and keep hidden under my bed because I've got this body that for the time being won't let me do anything else except hit, hit, hit. Even I know football's a lot of bullshit, and only sometimes in those rare fleeting moments does it ever become a game. But when that happens I love the feeling of being strapped into gobs of plastic and told not only to hit somebody, but cream them in the ear hole, break their fucking ribs, and make them spit blood. Out on the field it is okay to want to hurt somebody. It is expected of you. And I like that feeling of living out on that green square with no consequences.

But in between there's practice.

There is no glory in this. We are made to suffer like cattle in box-cars (my teammates look at me blankly when I mention anything to this effect). For starters, it's hot and the coaches love it when the heat creeps up around ninety and the haze comes off Lake Erie like a curtain. Some guys drop and start crying for their mothers or complain about phantom knee injuries, bad backs or sore shoulders.

"Pimples," Coach Gil screams when he hears of an injury. "All this whining about pimples and goddamned sore pussies."

Coaches love to push the soft and gutless few who dare to drop on the field. Stork calls them bench warriors. They are weak and will eventually quit when somebody splits their chin or bloodies their nose. But every once in a while some nancy boy sticks it out and manages to make the team only to spend the rest of the season riding the pine in his lily-white uniform, waving at cheerleaders and complaining when it rains.

Letters have started to pour in from colleges, Ohio State, Penn State, Ole Miss, Michigan, even places like Denison and Grinnell, which my friends tell me are loser schools full of ugly chicks and Christians. I keep the letters in a shoe box under my bed. Jay likes the team stickers that are sent along with the letters. He goes around the house pasting them on the walls and getting hit for it.

College scouts fly in to see me practice. They wear team sweaters and tight polyester slacks and time me in the forty-yard dash with stopwatches they keep tied around their tanned gullets. They have perfect white teeth and smell of simple aftershaves and sweat. They call me son and I do the All-American crap: show them respect, look them in the eye, give them firm handshakes and stick out my chest.

On Friday nights the scouts come to the games, take notes and eat hot dogs. They look like detectives in the bleachers scribbling out observations and predictions in their small notebooks. Mrs. Kowalski, our equipment manager's wife, once told me she was in love with a particular scout who wore his tie over his shoulder when he ate. "I want a man who takes pride in his appearance. Somebody with nice shoes and some hair left on his head," she says.

When I tell her he probably won't be back she says, "I'll wait. I am patient. He'll come back for you."

Coach Gil tells the scouts when they come by to watch me practice that I'm "top shelf" stuff. They look at Coach Gil as if he were some magnificent old fossil, one of those hell-bent-for-leather types who'll drop right on the field and die someday.

Nobody loves him. His wife left him and went to Beauty College. His only son has never played a down of football, sniffs glue and hides in the wood shop all day making guitar bodies shaped like rockets.

We make fun of Coach when he stands before us spouting platitudes and shaking his fist at the chalkboard where he's scrawled the words VICTORY IS ASSURED.

One day after practice Coach Gil called me into his office and told me that coaching was the greatest high he'd ever known.

"It's better than . . ." He stopped himself, not sure what to compare it to.

My girlfriend, Heather, is all worked up about how I am going to leave her and how I don't care. I lie and tell her never. She lights up like a state fair and starts talking rings. She gets out the Service Merchandise catalog, Christmas '85, and points. Opal for starters, pre something or other. I tell her I'm cool with this "pre" idea and she lets me put my hand up her shirt and feel around until I get my fingers around one of her nipples.

She stops me and says, "I need a promise if you're going to be hopping planes every week, looking at schools."

"Promise?" I give the nipple a pinch. It's all I can think about, that and her smell. That's what nobody tells you about women—that they have these great smells: lime, fresh bread, lotion, lilacs, and sweat.

She points at the catalog again. Her mother is away at Chin's Pagoda getting loaded on gin rickeys and smashing fortune cookies with her fists until she finds a fortune she likes or numbers to play the lottery with.

"My mother says you're going to leave me. All boys want to leave."

What she means is that you have to hold on to men and not let them die, like Heather's father. Heather knows this and whenever her mom mentions her father, she looks at me as if my leaving is all the grief she needs in the world. But her father didn't leave. He died in a car wreck when she was eleven years old.

"I can get out of here," I say. I want her to know what this means, but her baby blues fog over and she's passed over into Ring Land, dreaming of our possible future.

Right now she smells like wet sidewalks and leaves.

"You won't take me with you?" she pouts.

I remind her of her one-year commitment to finishing high school and winning a starting position on the softball team. Then I look at her and she's just glowing with something I can't quite put my finger on. I want to tell her that she's too beautiful, like a postcard or cloudless sky. But I don't.

I love Heather and want her on my arm because last summer we went camping and after a glass of Boone's Farm apple wine, she let me use an old sandwich bag for a rubber. I got it halfway in before she decided the seams of the bag hurt too much and I had to settle for a hand job. I kept the sandwich bag and showed it around to some guys from school until they started calling me Ziploc Dick.

Once, after I'd explained the plot of *Of Mice and Men* to her in exchange for a solid hour of hands-up-blouse (homework makes her tense), Heather started calling me Lenny and asked if I wanted to pet her hair.

I did.

"Oh Lenny," she said.

But what I don't tell her is that I sometimes wonder if women in other states will let me lift their skirts and touch their secret thatch because I am a stud ballplayer.

"Elwood," she says. "Are you listening to me? Am I making myself clear?"

I say, "Yeah, sure go look at some rings."

"Opal," she says, pulling open her shirt and pressing her warm skin against my face. "Then you can leave."

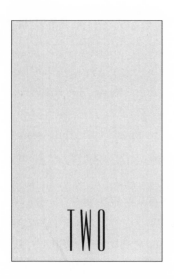

TWO

December and football season is over. All of the blacks are playing basketball and running around the hallways dressed smartly in their Viking blue warm-ups. They ask me to jump for them and laugh when I can't dribble.

"All that tall and no ball," Treg Lee says. He's their leader and can jam a basketball ten different ways with style.

I make like I'm going to blast them with a forearm shiver and they scatter, even Treg saunters past the rows of lockers, shaking his head at the crazy white boy. I want to tell him what Chairman Mao says about power, but he's too far away.

I wrestle instead. I have black bags under my eyes and I am skinny from the morning mile and rope climbing. Recruiting season has officially begun. I toss out most of the letters and start telling the shitbird colleges no when they call. Dad just sits around shaking his head. He has twenty years in at Mercury Switch and Die, hands like rotten bananas and skin the color of aluminum. Sometimes I catch him staring out windows, putting his face in his hands and rubbing his eyes as if he wants something to go away.

"This," he says, holding up the box of letters, "this is your ticket out." What he means is that he'd like to freeze-dry this moment and hold every one of my possible futures in his mangled hands. In the meantime I've got decisions to make, "About your future," he says.

A week before the big Catholic All-Meet, everything comes clear. I'm drilling double-legs with Turnell. The heaters are cranked, the windows fogged with our sweat. Turnell pulls himself off the mat, panting, places a hand on my shoulder and I shoot again. All around us, lightweights wrapped in plastic sweat suits bump and fly into each other like popcorn. Coach Rich blows the whistle and we all rush out of the room, running for the gum-clogged water fountain. I look up at my reflection in the stainless steel and know that I want the recruiting over.

After practice I go straight home and arrange my campus visits: Ohio State, Michigan, Army, and Boston.

"Which one first?" Mom asks.

I tell her Boston. Just then Dad shuffles in the door from work and I tell him how I arranged the visits.

"Army?" he says. "You know what you're getting into?"

"It's a good school," Mom says.

"Name me one pro ballplayer from Army," he says.

Mom disappears into the kitchen and I can hear pots and pans banging around.

"Got me," I say, watching Dad as he lowers himself into the La-Z-Boy recliner.

I wait for him to say something and when he doesn't I say, "I liked the recruiter."

I go into the den and sit across from him on the couch and he's just staring, lost somewhere.

After a while he says, "Sounds good to me."

And we leave it at that.

I meet Coach Borstal from Boston at Cleveland Municipal Airport.

"Riley?" he says, giving me the tough-guy handshake. "Coach Borstal."

After introducing himself to my parents and assuring them as to my well-being he turns right around and gets on the plane to Logan with me. Dad waves an oil-stained hand at me from the gate and Heather cries. Mom just stands there smoking, like she's in some movie where her son is going off to war.

On the plane Borstal orders a Scotch and soda and starts showing me brochures on the college. Green grass, tall buildings and whole-some-looking people holding books. Then he blows on about jobs, business school, the Greek system (how everybody joins), training ta-ble, and Boston's bitch of a schedule next year. He calls me a "proj-ect" and says that in a year they'll have me ripping throats out and benching 400 pounds. I tune him out until he says something about getting me a "primo summer job." Then he starts asking me about the women in Cleveland.

Borstal pointing at a stewardess: "You could crack walnuts on that ass."

I tell him I think so too and he starts smiling, his face a yellow bruise with eyes.

"Riley," he says. "You got yourself a girlfriend back home?"

"Yes," I say.

"Don't go swimming with bowlegged women," he says.

Then he goes back on the sell job, this time about how all of the "boys" are looking at pro careers or else nice fat jobs. He tells me companies just love ballplayers because they have good work habits, killer handshakes, and strong sets of values.

I know this is a bunch of bullshit, but Borstal drones on, waiting for my occasional nod or yes.

We land and drive like hell up to the college. Red brick, gray brick, lots of cars and people standing around under trees and archways with backpacks slung across their shoulders. Coach Borstal points like a ser-geant barking out orders and starts ticking off names of buildings, bars, and sandwich shops. He tells me I'll like Boston, that Boston's full of good solid citizens.

"Everybody knows their place here," he says.

I ask him what he means.

"It's not like Cleveland," he says, shrugging his shoulders.

On my right, rows and rows of neatly bricked houses each with their own tight little yards whip by the window.

"That's where the dagos live," Borstal says. Then he points to the skyline. "See that square building?"

I nod my head and follow his finger to a tomb-shaped building. "Just to the left—jungle-bunny city," he says, smiling.

I don't say anything and let him go on.

He points at another anonymous-looking row of buildings and tells me how the queers have bought up all of the brownstones and now they think they can walk around the streets holding hands and staring at flowers.

"You ever want to feel like a woman," he says, "just walk those streets and have the fags stare at your ass."

When I don't say anything for a few minutes he looks over at me and says, "What's the matter, kid?"

I don't say a word. Instead I sit there thinking about Stork telling me how he is Cleveland and how I'm getting out for this?

After a steak dinner with Coach Borstal and another coach named Powers who didn't talk much and argued about the tip, I meet a few of the guys. Most of them swollen, slow-moving linemen. Borstal introduces them by positions.

Watts, defensive tackle.

Dougie D, pulling guard.

Martino, center.

They file by and shake my hand glumly and say things like, "How you doing?" and "Nice to meet cha."

Dougie D and Watts sit on either side of me. Dougie D's one of those no-neckers—all shoulders and chest. Watts begins fidgeting with the salt and pepper shakers while Borstal rambles on about this blue-chip running back every school in the country wants.

Watts nudges me and says, "You like your visit so far?"

I lie.

"A bit overwhelming, huh?" Dougie D says. "I hated the recruiting part, so I committed on my first visit."

Watts pours salt out of a shaker and stirs his finger through it. "Don't listen to him," he says. "Take advantage of this shit, because after you sign they shitcan the red-carpet act."

"What do you mean?" I ask.

"What I mean is they own your ass and then they aren't so nice."

"Watts is a real sunny guy," Dougie says. "It's not like that."

"Bullshit, Dougie," Watts says.

"What happens now?" I ask.

Watts' broad face breaks into a smile. "We're going to get you drunk and make you sign," he says.

I laugh uncomfortably.

We go to a bar called Ham and Eggers. The bartender's name is Lou and there are dollar bills stapled to the ceiling, plastic ferns in fake brass planters and lots of paneling.

As we file into the bar I catch my reflection in a mirror and realize how small I look compared to the others. When no one's looking I reach up and pull a few bills off the ceiling and put them in my pocket.

Coach Borstal wraps his arm around me and says, "This is what it's all about."

We take a table and Coach Borstal starts telling war stories about how it was when he played. A waitress comes to our table and stares at us, her eyes widening. Before she can say anything Borstal puts a hand on her shoulder.

"Cindy," he says, staring at her name tag, "I've got some thirsty men here."

Cindy rolls her eyes at him and looks at us, blushing as she takes our order.

When they ask me where I'm from, Borstal tells them I'm from Cleveland. Everybody smiles and starts yakking in these real East Coast accents, like they're ready to break out the tweed and Yorkshire pudding.

After Coach Borstal's driven off they take me to a strip club that sits all lit up in neon and stainless steel, next to an abandoned factory. When we pile out of the car I can hear the music from the parking lot.

It's like any other naked-woman bar, rows and rows of men in rumpled suits sit sipping Gibsons and highballs while the women tease money out of them. Our size makes the bouncers nervous and they twitch and parade around in front of us like show horses, daring us to step out of line. Everybody starts ordering beers and handing them to me, calling me the new guy and "hey recruit." We take a table next to some of the businessmen who look up from their drinks to stare at our muscles for a while, before looking at their own soft guts and pink hands as they fork over five- and ten-spots to any dancer who brushes a bare calf against their faces.

I imagine that they're thinking about how nobody fights over women anymore. You tip them, open doors for them and listen when they speak. Or else you shuffle into a place like this, sip your drink and stare at tits.

Dougie D, a pulling guard from New Jersey, calls one of the older dancers over to our table. She's on the fat side of thirty, face like bread dough and she has on too much perfume to cover up the stink of beer and sweat.

Dougie D sticks a twenty in her garter and whispers to her, touching her on the side where stretch marks zigzag into her panties.

"Give him an eyeful," he says. She winks at him and places one of her sagging, tea-bag-shaped breasts in his palm. Then she looks at me, smiling.

She tells me her name is Linda and she starts grinding real slow into me until I can smell her. Behind me I can hear the guys cracking jokes, bashing their five-dollar mugs of beer together. I stare at Linda's sour-cream-colored skin and think about Heather thumbing through some stupid ring catalog back in Cleveland, her skin smelling like fresh cement and lilacs.

The guys take turns slapping me on the back and buying me drinks.

Somebody says to Linda, "Show him how we drink bourbon up here."

She smiles and places a shot glass full of Beam between her breasts. I shake my head and tell them I won't do it until Dougie D clamps a massive hand behind my neck and pushes me toward the bourbon. Linda does it a couple of more times and after a while I just lower my head and drink until the guys leave me alone.

The last thing I remember is doing push-ups in the snow while the guys count them off for me.

I wake up the next morning in my hotel room, my head pounding out the bourbon and beer, and do sit-ups until I puke.

In the bathroom I promise myself to never puke again. I tell myself that I am a man of the moment—one stoic motherfucker.

But then Borstal raps on the door to get me for breakfast.

"Good time last night?" he asks. I nod and follow him down the elevator.

Over eggs and toast he tells me how I'm going to meet the head coach and how he's going to ask me to sign right on the spot.

"He's seen your films," Borstal says. "He knows what he wants. That and you're a smart guy. Smart guys make good ballplayers."

Then he gets up in my face, sniffs my beer breath, smiles and chucks me on the shoulder.

"Good kid, too," he adds.

On the way to see the head coach, Borstal leads me through the weight room, the sauna, and where my locker will be if I choose Boston. He does his sales pitch thing again, rattling off numbers, comparing Boston's program to other programs. Of course Boston comes out number one with a bullet. I start to wonder how come they manage to lose a handful of games every year to shitbird teams like Rutgers and Maryland.

Then he leaves me with a receptionist to wait outside the head coach's office. I stare at a trash can for ten minutes before this small man with brown, watery eyes and a soft chin pokes his head out of the steel-frame doorway and points a finger at me. He ushers me into the office and closes the door behind me. I watch him walk around his trophied walls, hands on hips, mug of coffee steaming away on a large football-shaped desk.

"Jimmy," he says.

"My name's Elwood," I tell him.

He shakes his head, blinks and then smiles. I get the feeling he's done this a million times already and he'd rather be out shoveling his driveway or looking at game film.

"I'm sorry, that's my son's name. You remind me of him," he says absently.

He asks me how I've liked my visit and if I can see myself playing for him, wearing the red and gold. Then he asks me if I know what a full ride is.

"Yes," I say.

"Coach Borstal show you the facilities?"

I nod.

"Have you met some of the guys?"

"Last night," I say.

"Good," he says, plopping into his leather chair. He sighs and looks out the window at the snow as if he's thinking about a coaching job somewhere South where the girls wear bikini tops to class and people are faster because of the heat.

"This your first visit?" he says.

"I'm not sure how this is supposed to go," I tell him.

"You're doing fine," he says. "Just fine, we do this all the time here. Do you have any idea how lucky you are to be sitting here?"

I nod. "Sure," I say.

Then he pulls out a folder with my name in large block print across the top, opens it and slides a paper across the table to me.

Then he hands me a pen.

"That there, is what we call the genuine article."

"What is it?"

"It's your future," he sighs.

The paper says, FULL ACADEMIC/ATHLETIC GRANT AND AID.

"I'm not ready to sign yet," I say.

He looks out the window some more.

"If you sign now, it assures you a place on the roster. Elwood, I'm offering you a four-year full ride—do you know how many young men would kill to hear me say that?"

I tell him I know and eye him as he checks his watch.

We sit like that for five minutes, him thinking about something else and me staring down at four years of my life. I look out the window at a bank of ash-colored clouds. Snow beats against the window like moth wings, the coach sighs again, reaching across the table, to pull the scholarship away from me like it's a gun or knife I might hurt myself with.

The buzz in the room stops when I hand him back his pen and thank him.

"You'll be in touch?" he asks, fidgeting with his coffee mug.

I nod.

"We've got grad assistants manning the phones twenty-four-seven," he says. "You change your mind . . . I can't guarantee anything."

"I know that."

I put a hand on the door.

He says, "See how the other schools stack up."

"I'll do that," I say.

THREE

And I do.

It is February and wrestling season's almost over. After the All-City Meet, I fly to New York and visit Army. I walk between the granite buildings and stare down at the Hudson River, but the four-year commitment afterward scares the shit out of me. For some reason I thought it would be cool to not only go to school for football, but to really belong to something, like the recruiter said. But the sight of all the gray-faced cadets marching in straight lines, saluting, picking up trash and doing push-ups on command makes me realize I've made a mistake with this visit, that everybody and everything looks the same—like there's some big machine churning out clones and drones.

"Uniformity, discipline, and honor," says Buck, a square-shouldered assistant coach.

There are statues all over the place of rock-jawed men staring out over the land at some distant battle yet to be fought. I nod at MacArthur and Eisenhower. Then we come to General George Patton standing guard over the library.

"Patton wanted his statue placed in front of the library, because it was the only building on campus he never entered. Not once in four years," Buck says.

Just before we leave, I trail behind to stare at the statue. I reach out and put my hand on his shoulder and leave it there until the cold metal numbs my hand.

Later, as the head coach gives me this football-is-war speech, my thoughts drift and pretty soon I'm thinking about Patton standing guard on his brass pedestal.

"We're looking for commitment and guts," the coach says.

I politely turn down the scholarship, shake his hand, walk back to my hotel room, hop a plane and . . .

At Ohio State I get drunk, eat steaks in a restaurant called Buckeye's and play catch with an offensive tackle named Radcliffe Zeno who tells me to quit fucking with him when I tell him about how Zeno was the father of Stoicism and that he lived in a cave.

"Zeno said that Destiny is power which moves matter," I tell him.

Dumb-jock Zeno from Barnesville, Ohio, looks at me and says, "You memorize that shit?"

I nod.

"Why?"

"Helps me sometimes," I say.

"Man, the professors are going to love you—but if I were you I wouldn't run around the locker room spouting memorized crap— that's what the coaches do and somebody is liable to kick your ass."

The coach is this hound-faced man who waddles around the room placing his hands on his belly and clacking his dentures. He points out the Olentangy River and then the stadium and says it is cold and flat here and that it makes for good football. When I ask him what he means he says, "What else is there to do except enjoy this magnificent game of football?"

Then he drones on about tradition, how I'm from Ohio and how I should stay in Ohio. I close my eyes and try to see myself playing for him and I can't.

"What do you think?" he says, dipping his chin at me.

"I'm not sure," I say.

He shrugs his shoulders. "That's not the kind of answer I'm accustomed to hearing. I'm sorry you feel that way."

"I've got more places to visit."

"You mean Michigan," he says. "We beat them 24 to 17 last year. That's my last word."

I tell him no and he accepts my answer with a jowled indifference.

I save Michigan for last.

At Michigan everybody wears maize and blue and hates Ohio State and Michigan State. There are cars everywhere and the air tastes like aluminum.

As soon as I hit town, one of the recruiting coordinators drives me to the stadium and walks me down this long tunnel out onto the frozen field. A small patch of razor-sharp green turf has been cleared of snow. Everything goes quiet except for the rattle of empty flagpoles.

Then my recruiter, Coach Gibson, trots out from the tunnel, stops me on the fifty-yard line and asks if I can hear one hundred thousand people cheering.

I can't, but I nod and smile anyways and say something stupid like, "A hundred thousand?"

Then he takes me to the locker room. A painting of a large black eye set inside a maize and blue triangle covers the entire back wall. Gibson points at the eye and gives me this speech about the Eye of Michigan; how every player who has ever played before me will be watching over everything I do. Above the eye are the words: ACCEPT WITHOUT PRIDE, RELINQUISH WITHOUT STRUGGLE.

I recognize the quote from somewhere and finally it hits me. "Marcus Aurelius," I say, pointing at the words.

Gibson looks at me as if I've just spoken in church.

"It's from *Meditations*," I say.

"Who in the hell is Marcus Aurelius?" Gibson sputters.

"Emperor of Rome and Stoic," I say.

"Son, I can tell you, without a doubt, that Coach Roe sent us out to face the Trojans of USC in the Rose Bowl with that quote. I don't know about any Greek emperor, all I know is that we kicked some Trojan butt that day."

I nod and let it go at that.

He calms down and points out this board that hangs over the locker room doorway that says GO BLUE.

"Every player touches the sign before he takes the field," he says, pointing at the door. "Go ahead . . . I want you to touch it."

I know he's not going to leave me alone until I do, so I raise up both hands and place them flat on the brass letters, pat them once or twice.

Gibson, "Did you feel it?"

"Yeah," I say, still thinking about empty flagpoles and the cold bronze of General Patton.

Afterward Gibson takes me to see Coach Roe.

Coach Roe is a tall silver-haired guy with one of those movie star chins and cold unblinking eyes. There are stories about him yelling and screaming at recruits. I've watched him on television kicking grass at refs, tossing his headset to the ground in disgust, snapping clipboards and even smacking players in the facemask when they fuck up. For football. For victory.

Before I go into Roe's office, Gibson says, "Just look him in the eyes and shake his hand like a man—a good firm one."

I turn to go but he stops me, his wide face solemn and swollen. "One more thing—remember the Eyes of Michigan are on you."

My hands shake as I knock lightly on the door and hear a voice on the other side telling me to come in.

I push open the door and see Coach Roe standing over his trophy case staring into the glass at his own reflection. He grins at me and points at a chair.

"Mr. Riley," he says. "Somebody told me you were a ballplayer."

My throat goes dry.

"That's what you're here for, isn't it?"

My voice cracks. "I hope so."

Roe grins again and sits down behind his desk, balls his hands into fists and places them on his credenza. Then he launches into this speech: "Last boy I took from Cleveland started smoking cigarettes and bird-dogging women. Hit like a goddamn girl even though he was supposed to be Mr. Blue-Chip All-American. But he wasn't good enough to wear the maize and blue."

"What happened?" I ask.

"He quit. Shit his pants and moved back to Cleveland with some nice Polish girl and got himself a job with the UPS."

I wait, let him size me up.

"Now, I ain't saying every mother-loving ballplayer from Cleveland is soft," he says. "Being a Wolverine isn't something I can teach you. You got to be mean and stubborn as a mule, hell-bent on kicking some ass. What I'm looking for, Riley, is just a few guys who are willing to spill blood and guts, guys who want to win so bad they'd tackle their mothers and sack their sisters. What I want to know, Riley, is if you want it that bad. Because if you don't, I can assure you that there's some other flat-ass hungry kid who does."

I'm usually not big on the rah-rah stuff, all that win-one-for-the-Gipper crap, but watching Coach Roe I feel the blood go up into my ears as he pounds out the words on his desk. And before I know it my hands start to sweat and I feel like hitting somebody.

"Yes," I say, jumping out of my chair and sticking my hand out for him to shake. He lets it hang there, just grinning at me as the veins in his neck retreat back into the flab. I feel stupid and he knows it.

"Good," he says. "Now sit down and let's talk about what Michigan has to offer."

My heart's still banging away, but I sit and feign interest as he sells me on Michigan, how it's a top ten academic institution, best facilities, great place to live and study, etc. But I'm not listening, instead I want to hear more of the speech, see Roe's veins flare out again, because he's got something I can't quite place. Coach Gil never had it or if he did our team's piss-poor performance couldn't dredge it out of him. Even my wrestling coach, who motivated us with long stares of disapproval, doesn't have what Coach Roe seems to have. I know that if he asks I'm going to say yes.

This starts me to thinking about how playing for any coach is pretty masochistic stuff. For starters, all coaches take it on faith that you're a shitbird until proven otherwise. You hate them and love them. Praise is rarely offered, instead a good tackle or touchdown run is met with a nod or sometimes nothing at all. The effect of this, despite every rational thought, is to try harder. You want to get that smile or arm-swinging praise out of the coach, just to see it. So when a coach finally breaks down and offers a "Way to go, Riley" or "Nice job" you don't care anymore. You are a tree in winter, one hard bastard, a rock of hatred. That's when you become a sickdog motherfucker. A baby killer. Nobody likes you. You don't even like yourself, only what your body can do to another player. Practicing is like putting out the sun and you like it. That's the fucked-up thing about it—you like it. Other guys take the lack of praise personally and walk around all gloom and doom. They never learn to eat it and to hate. Put it this way, Mean Joe Green didn't have daffodils in his heart. He was one black angry dude. He lived to swing around the end on a full rush, busting forearm into facemask, spitting at his opponents and hating everything about them, even the way they laced up their cleats.

I know right away that Coach Roe's a master of this bullshit, a maker of men who hates the way machines do: cold and indiscriminately. The funny thing is that it doesn't prevent me from wanting to play for him. Suddenly all that crap about books and being smart doesn't seem to matter so much and I begin to admit to myself that I have wanted this all along—that here my size and ability to hit are not only wanted but respected.

So I listen to his crap about Michigan, Center of Athletic Excellence, Champions of the West and so on, thinking that playing for him would be like Coach Gil times ten.

I leave his office high on purpose and full of dreams.

Coach Gibson meets up with me in the hallway and starts yammering about how many kids have already signed with Michigan and how long it would take me to earn a starting position. He explains the redshirt policy, training table and how many frosh make the travel team.

At lunch he keeps up about the tradition at Michigan listing all of the pro players who have played for the maize and blue and who looks good for the draft this year. So far nobody has mentioned the full ride.

"Am I going to see Coach Roe again?" I ask.

Gibson stops midchew and sputters, "Hell, yes, son." Then he looks at me as if I'm retarded.

"Who else are you recruiting at my position?" I ask.

"Well, we've got a verbal from this big son-of-a-buck from Pennsylvania."

"What's his name?"

"Frank Himes—you guys ought to get along—that is if you commit."

I look down into my plate of fries, worried that no one's mentioned the full ride yet. "When am I going to . . ."

He cuts me off with a stupid story about the Rose Bowl.

After dinner Gibson takes me to see Coach Roe again.

This time he's dressed in a tight-fitting suit, his fingers wrapped in bowl rings, eyes still as pond water. A woman with black hair and liver-spotted hands sits next to him, staring at the room full of oversize bodies.

He motions for me to sit next to him.

"My wife," he says, pointing at liver spot woman.

Wife nods and goes back to staring. Waiters and busboys rush up to

Coach Roe asking for autographs on linen and menus. I watch the way they look right through his wife.

Coach Roe pushes his plate away. "Coach Gibson says you're getting a little anxious."

I nod.

He turns to his wife. "The kid likes Michigan."

All I can do is smile.

"You and me are going to have a talk tomorrow morning," he says. "Iron this thing out."

Then he sends me off with a little pat on the back, the sort you might give to a child.

I got straight back to the hotel room and call Heather to tell her about what a great guy Coach Roe is. ("Great" meaning I believe him to be a soul-eating sonofabitch.) She cries and tells me she's looking at a map of Michigan. Her complaints:

1. Ann Arbor is two finger lengths away from Cleveland. At least a three-hour drive.

2. It is too close to Detroit and she's read somewhere that Detroit is or was the murder capital of the world. Heather fears black people and believes them to be the root of all crime, mayhem, and murder. She gets this from her mother, who, when she is a bit drunk and running her mouth, refers to Detroit as Spooktown.

3. Her mother has told her several times that the state of Michigan is one of the top five cancer states. Heather's mom is obsessed with cancer. Her back and shoulders are dotted with a dozen gunshot-wound-shaped scars from where they've cut patches of skin cancer.

I ignore reasons two and three and focus my attention on number one. I mumble something about how nice the drive up to visit me on weekends will be, only she's onto her other favorite topic. Women.

She's convinced that a crucial part of every recruiting trip involves football groupies and whores.

"Were you a good boy?" she asks.

"Define good boy."

"Just tell me it wasn't like Boston," she says.

This is all my fault. Like an idiot I decided to tell her about my visit to Boston. She fixated on the strip bar episode, never mind the puking and push-up bit. I told her that the good man is an honest man and that I should get points for coming clean. "Like Confession," I said.

All she could say was, "A dirty stripper? How could you?"

I decide to change the subject and tell her more about Coach Roe and the way his wife looked all made up and bored. This calms her down a bit until I tell her I'm going to commit if Coach Roe offers.

She doesn't handle this too well and for a minute the line fills with the sound of muffled sobs.

"But it's so far," she manages. Something in me gives and I feel the distance over the phone line, listen to the slight hum and crackle. "You sound different," she says.

"It must be the phone," I say.

But I am and she'll never know.

In the morning Coach Roe offers me a full ride. I play it cool and say yes after thinking about it for ten minutes. He lets me phone up my parents from his office and tell them the good news. They are naturally disappointed because they had envisioned a little in-house signing ceremony with pictures of me, pen in hand, Dad shaking hands with the coach and so on. But they get over it when Coach Roe picks up the line to assure them they have a fine boy and that they have done one helluva job raising me and how I'm going to be taken care of by Michigan. Etc.

Afterward he says, "You've got four more months of Mom, Dad and apple pie, then I take over."

I swallow hard and look at my reflection in the trophy case, realizing that I've just made a decision that's going to affect the next four years of my life. That stupid "Be All You Can Be in the Army" song flutters through my head as Coach Roe goes on about reporting to camp for double session and how I should spend my summer. Then he gives me a brief stay-away-from-these-things speech. The highlights: No women (they make you weak and unfocused), basketball (I might sprain an ankle, ruin my scholarship and become a janitor; besides, basketball is for pussies). And then the usual suspects. No drugs. No drinking. Then the do's. Eat right, lift, run, read the Bible, and be good to my mother because she will be losing a son to "manhood and Michigan football."

I keep up my end of things by nodding to each of them as he ticks them off one by one.

I say yes sir and no sir until I'm practically humming out the sirs to the tune of "Be All You Can Be."

"And last but not least," he says. "We have a summer employment program. Put a little money in your pocket before you report to camp."

By July I've broken most of Coach Roe's rules. Once or twice a week Stork and I score a six-pack of Genny Cream Ales from old man Dugan's Beer Drive-Thru and drive up and down Lakeshore Boulevard looking for pretty black girls, because Stork has a thing for them. He says it's their names that get him: Showana, Diandra, Reanne, Sobande, Tumeka, and Violetta. That and the way they turn and walk away from you—and it's like follow me, this way to salvation.

I spend the days dinking with Heather, shopping malls, movies, ice cream, and sex. Telling her it's going to be okay when I leave, even though I've said it so many times I no longer believe it myself. Things change.

I can't stop shaking when we take off our clothes and she lets me enter her. For a few moments it's as if everything's going to end right there, until she says something stupid about checking the condom or how I'm going to leave her.

Lately, I've begun to get the sex and the clinginess mixed up. To remedy this I suppose I'm looking for faults so that when I get to Michigan I'll be able to put a damper on the missing bit and focus on football. For starters she reads too much Danielle Steele and has the annoying habit of recounting the plots to me before and after sex.

Heather, "Don't you think it would make a great movie?"

Me, unbuttoning her blouse, "Great."

"No, I'm serious, maybe even a miniseries."

"When is your mother getting back?"

"Don't worry about it. What about the part where the boyfriend tells her he missed her and how he was such an asshole for leaving her in the first place?"

I fumble with the bra hooks. "What book is this again?"

"The one on my dresser," she says, pointing to an embossed paperback with dog-eared pages.

"What about *Meditations,* have you read it yet?"

I don't know what I expected, anything, I figure, is better than Danielle Steele, so I gave her a copy of my favorite book—a piece of my heart. And she just set it next to the others I've given her, *Sometimes a Great Notion, The Painted Bird, Geronimo Rex, Fat City, Wiseblood* (I told her about the barbed wire and she said it sounded sick), *The Great Gatsby,* and *Executioner's Song.*

She crinkles her nose. "It's all that Greek and Roman stuff, it's soooo boring." She gets up from the bed and I want to tell her how she looks like Athena and talks like Olive Oyl. "It's all made-up myths. I need romance," she says. "Not icky old stuff."

I don't correct her. Instead I watch her walk to the window, shirt undone, bra dangling from her elbows as she looks out at the neighbor's house. I remind her that she's half-naked.

"Mr. Janosy's never seen boobies before?"

I nod my head pleasantly and motion for her to come back to the bed.

Why Heather?

Because I can.

And when we walk down the street together, hand in hand, people stare. She's that kind of girl. Stork says she's my trophy woman, big, blonde, and crazy for me. The kind of girl I can flick all my desires on, watch her smile, because all she wants is to be with me. Something about that blind devotion breaks my heart.

Heather, like my parents, has fallen into a maize and blue buying frenzy. Last week I noticed an official Michigan football bread knife in the kitchen. Her mom held it up in front of my face when I went out to get a glass of water and caught her pouring gin into a coffee mug.

"You like this?" she said, pointing the knife at my stomach and winking. I felt like telling her about her daughter's GO BLUE panties.

On Thursday after working out I come by to pick her up for a swim and she meets me at the door all smiles and hugs. Her mom's half-bagged and I can smell the Binaca on her breath.

I ask Heather what's up, my arms shaking from French curls and weighted dips.

"Come into the den," she says.

She leads me into the den and slides the door shut. It's an ordinary, East Cleveland den, drop ceiling, fake-leather couches, knotted paneling, and wrought-iron knickknacks that crowd the shelves along with family photos, dried starfish, and empty Chianti bottles with plastic flowers sticking out of their necks. Then there is the dead–father shrine, with candles and framed photographs.

"Look," she says.

On the coffee table sit two large packages wrapped in brown paper, topped with maize and blue ribbons. I try my best to look thrilled even though I hate presents of any sort because I hate pretending to be excited.

I do, however, manage to smile and finger the bows appreciatively.

"Open them," Heather says. Outside the door, I can hear her mother laughing loudly on the phone.

I peel back the brown wrapper on the first one and come to a box. Heather squeals and presses herself into me.

"You're going to love them," she says.

I open the box and I'm struck speechless. Heather takes my utter silence to mean that she's hit the surprise jackpot.

In the box there's a plaster figurine I take to be me dressed in a Michigan football uniform. The figure has this demented Hummel grin on its face and stands maybe eighteen inches tall.

I do my best to look thrilled; smile, kiss, and hug her. Heather opens the other box while I examine the ceramic me in uniform.

"Look," she says, holding another figurine. "You in your wrestling suit and . . ."

"And what?" I say.

"Look where I had my name painted."

She points to the figurine's bottom and waits until I read her name, smile.

Just when I'm wondering what the hell I'm supposed to do with them, Heather answers for me.

"For your room," she says pointing, north toward Michigan.

"Great," I say. What I'm really thinking is how much shit I'd take if I did indeed decide to decorate my dorm room with miniature versions of myself.

"Do you like them?"

At that very moment her mom comes rushing into the room all smiles. "They look just like you," she says "They even got the butt right." More laughs and I'm creeped out. It must be the gin, or at least I hope it's the gin. Because Heather's mom is no Mrs. Robinson, not even in a dark room.

I agree that they look like me and this makes both of them very happy. Heather starts on how good they're going to look in my dorm room. I just stand there for a few minutes listening to her prattle on and on about them: how hard they were to find, how much they cost and how I have to be careful because they could easily break (I should get so lucky). Right away I realize that I have to put a stop to this room-decorating frenzy.

"My mom will love them," I say.

Both Heather and her mom frown and I can tell that I've made a very large mistake, but I continue. "I'll put them in our basement until I go—for safekeeping."

They go for the safekeeping part, and for the rest of the summer I'm off the hook.

When I bring them home Dad takes one look at them and says, "You're so pussy-whipped Michigan's going to send you back."

Mom rolls her eyes at him, then looks at the statues.

"Cute but tacky," she says. "What are you supposed to do with them?"

"I don't know," I say.

"She shouldn't spend so much money," Mom says. "I mean what happens when you go?"

So I stick them in the basement next to all of the other trophies and plaques.

Jay comes flying down the wooden stairs and catches me with the statues.

"What do you think a pellet gun would do to them?" he asks.

I just smile and hope he takes it as some kind of encouragement.

"What about an M-80?" he says as I try looking at the one of me in a Michigan uniform without wanting to smash it. They don't look like me and I've yet to wear the uniform even though people are looking at me as if I'm already gone.

FOUR

I report to my summer job at Wanchek's Punch and Press. Several assistant coaches have set the whole thing up over the phone and tell me that all I have to do is show up and ask for Big Ed.

The parking lot reeks of old oil and gravel. The factory sits up on a small rise crowded with sumac trees and weeds. The building itself is this drab cinder-block square, with row after row of dirty windows.

Big Ed meets me in the front office. I can tell right away that he's one of those psycho booster/alumni because he's got on this ugly maize and blue tie and mentions football in nearly every sentence. I notice he's missing two fingers from his right hand.

"Are you ready to be a Wolverine?" he asks.

"I'm ready to work," I say.

He leans back his large meat-and-potato face and laughs.

"This is called getting set up," he says. "If you work, then Big Ed's not doing his job. You can pretend to work. How's that sound?"

"What do you mean?"

"Fuck around. You're not here to work—you're here to earn money."

"Sounds good to me," I say.

"Atta boy," Big Ed says. He's laughing so hard his gut rumbles beneath his shirt. When he calms down he points at the factory and asks me what I think of it.

"Looks like a factory," I say.

Big Ed laughs again and I start thinking how my old man's been trapped in one of these factories for most of his adult life and suddenly he isn't so funny anymore.

"You'll be paid fifteen dollars an hour," he says. "My man Luther's going to watch over you—give you piss-around jobs."

I tell him okay and he takes me in to meet Luther. We stop in front of a small office that says FOREMAN in peeling black paint.

Big Ed rattles the door with his fist.

"Hey, Luther, you in there fucking the dog?"

The door swings open and Luther bobs his swollen head and scowls at me before stepping out into the hallway.

"Call me Looother," he says.

"Luther's a loogie," Big Ed says. "Biggest goddamn Lithuanian in Cleveland."

Luther smiles. All of his teeth are pitted and stained.

"I hope he ain't like the last dumbshit we had in here," Luther says.

Big Ed laughs, his bald head reflecting the light as he tosses a few soft punches into my arm. "The last time I gave a recruit a job, Luther here told him to siphon gas out of one of the HiLos."

"The dumbshit drank it," Luther says, slapping me on the back. "You gonna do something stoopid?"

Before he leaves, Big Ed says, "Go easy on him, Luth—he's got to play football—know what I mean?"

Luther nods and flashes his fucked-up smile again and takes me on a tour of the factory. Rows and rows of two-story-high punch presses clang out product. After a while I get used to the noise of the presses until they feel like they're inside me. Several of the operators look up from their machines and nod, their eyes coming alive for a minute or two when they see me coming, thinking I'm fresh meat.

"You know how to paint?" Luther asks after the tour.

"I think I can handle it," I say.

"Good," he says. "Follow me."

He leads me to the lunchroom and points at this long stretch of cinder-block wall.

"You want this painted?"

"No, I vant a rainbow here," he says. "Make people happy vhen they eat lunch. Improve attitude, Big Ed says."

Then he shows me the paint and brushes and goes back to his office. I do my best with the stiff brushes and within an hour I'm high from the fumes.

Luther stumbles out of his office coffee mug in hand to examine my rainbow.

"Bossman," I say, dribbling paint on the tile floor.

"Your rainbow looks like shit," he says. He stirs his coffee with his finger, then licks it clean. "Do better—you making a fucking mess."

By lunchtime the fumes are so bad that everybody has to take their break outside. Several of the HiLo operators drag pallets out of the storeroom and set up makeshift tables for the workers to sit at.

Most everybody ignores me except for this big, bearded guy named Barry who works in the tool department.

He sits down next to me.

"Watch out for the hillbillies," he says, pointing at this group of haggard-looking men in blue work shirts and cracked-leather belts. "They'll thump you over the head with their Bibles and ask you to go fishing or to church."

I listen to them talk amongst themselves in hushed Kentucky twangs, *E-Z Read Scriptures* and *Amazing but True Bible Stories* propped up against their lunch pails.

"What about the rest?" I ask.

"Loser fucking central," Barry says. "You got your waste cases, bat-shit vets, and your average Cleveland shoprat trying to pay off his mortgage."

"Which one are you?"

"I'm the crazy Jew who knows better," he says, laughing as he pulls out the sports page of the *Cleveland Plain Dealer*. "And you must be one of Big Ed's big-shot football players."

I nod.

"I'm a baseball fan myself," Barry says.

"I've never understood that part," I admit.

"What part?"

"Fans."

"That's probably a good thing though because it's what you do when you've got nothing left. You watch, close your eyes and try to imagine what it must be like."

"It's not what you think," I tell him. "The playing."

"I've got a good imagination," Barry says, stroking his beard. "Have to, to work in a place like this."

I spend the rest of the week cleaning presses with degreaser and hiding in the storeroom, playing poker with Barry and this guy named Chris who says he's thinking about joining the navy even though he can't swim.

"Believe me," Barry says. "It doesn't fucking matter whether or not he can swim. He can take orders."

"I just want out of this town," Chris complains.

"What about college?" I ask.

Both Chris and Barry laugh.

"I'm not going to college," Chris says.

"Why not?"

"How many reasons you want?"

"But this?" I say, pointing at the factory.

"Tell him about your pussy pad," Barry says.

Chris' face reddens. "I need the money for my apartment."

"I keep telling him he should live in some shitbox, save his money and get the fuck off the job."

"I already told you guys—I'm going to the navy recruiter's office—that's how I'm going to get off the job."

Barry looks at me and winks before slapping down his full house.

I see Big Ed once a week at payday where he hands me a special envelope with my paycheck in it and some extra cash.

During our weekly poker game, Barry tells me that I make more than half the guys in the factory. I don't say a word about the extra cash.

"You're being bought," he says. "Just as long as you know that."

"Are we going to play cards or chitchat?" Chris asks.

"Straight, queen high," I say, slapping the cards onto the crate.

On Fridays, Heather picks me up for lunch in her faded red Sunbird. We drive over to the Daniel's Park dam and watch the old men fish the Chagrin's toffee-colored water for bullhead and rock bass. After we've eaten I roll over on my back and stare out over the river valley and think about how many days I have left.

"Seems weird I'm leaving," I say.

"Elwood," she says, eyes going moist. "I don't want to talk about it. Let's talk about something else—you pick."

"I pick?"

"No football either."

"Okay, books," I say. "Have you read any of them yet?"

"A little," she says.

"A little of which one?"

"*Great Gatsby* and I like Myrtle."

"You're not supposed to like Myrtle."

"Why not?" she says.

"Why not? Well, for starters she's a drunk and she gets her nose broken."

"You're mean and you don't give anybody a break," she says. She folds her arms across her breasts and tries to look away. "How many more days till you leave?"

"Twenty-one," I say.

"That makes me sad. Do you know what this is doing to me?"

I shake my head no and try to roll her up in a clumsy hug. But she pushes me away.

"Get out of here," she says. "I don't want you near me."

When I start to laugh I notice she's crying.

During my last few weeks of work Luther has me on the factory roof knocking hornets' nests off the copestone and cleaning the air vents. The roof is as long as a football field and snaked with gray ductwork and dome-shaped air vents that spin lazily in the breeze.

After lunch one day Luther comes up to check on me, his boots popping on the sun-softened roof tar.

He watches as I spray a large heart-shaped nest hanging from one of the old brick chimneys.

"You're not doing it right," Luther says as a clot of hornets buzz angrily out of the hive, darkening the air. "You up here fucking the dog all day and Big Ed he don't care."

"How then?" I say.

"Vatch this," he says, taking the broom and can of Raid wasp/ hornet spray out of my hands before wading into the swarm.

"You're going to get stung," I tell him.

He looks back over his shoulder and sneers at me.

"No fear," he says, attacking the nest. "The little buggers sense fear and that's how you get stung."

I watch as he douses the nest with spray and even manages to poke the broom soaked in degreaser into the mass of fleeing insects. The light gray nest darkens with the poison as white larvae drop out of its torn side and lie wriggling on the roof.

More hornets descend on him until he sets the spray can to fog and begins waving it around his head, causing hornets to drop out of the air in midflight, their bodies landing wing-down in the hot tar.

Afterward he hands me back the can, his forearms swollen and red. "Balls," he says. "Strap a pair on."

He steps back down the access hatch, leaving me to stare at the poison-soaked hive as sparrows glide across the roof, nabbing the remaining hornets. Underneath I can feel the machines rumbling and I go back to the air vents thinking about Heather, her breasts and the fact that she likes Myrtle.

After a good hour of work I get bored and walk the length of the roof looking for Chris by removing the air vents and peering down into the factory. I locate him and watch him work for a minute or two before I start throwing gobs of tar at him. He looks up and gives me the finger. Then he starts pointing at Donald, this whacked-out Bible thumper, working at the press next to him. I stick my head down into the vent to hear what he's trying to say. The heavy air fills my nostrils with the stink of old oil. Chris stops, scribbles something on a piece of cardboard and holds it up for me to read. It says, THROW SOME-THING AT DONALD.

I give Chris the thumbs-up sign and scan the roof for something to throw. I try a few small rocks, but Donald keeps on punching his red button, fishing product out of the press. On the workstand next to him, he has his Bible propped open and every so often he glances at it. Chris watches me, laughing with each toss, the snarl of machines drowning out all sound.

I remember the woman in the Cadillac and how she screamed, wondering if I hit Donald will the machines stop.

Chris scribbles again, SOMETHING BETTER!

I go back to the roof, poking around the edges until I find an old Blatz bottle under a mound of rotting oak leaves.

When I dangle it over the vent, Chris doubles up with laughter and points at Donald.

I lean over and take aim, hoping to drop the bottle next to Donald, hit his workstand maybe, and then put the vent cover over quickly.

Without much thought I let the bottle slip out of my hand and slap the vent cover back in place, laughing nervously to myself. I look up into the sun until my eyes burn and I no longer want to tear the vent cover off and see about the bottle.

After cleaning a few more vents I crawl back down the hatch and take the catwalk to the main floor. Chris catches me at the water fountain.

"Luther's onto us," he says. "He's asking questions."

"What happened?" I ask. My stomach flopping as I imagine Donald getting his hand mangled in the press. "Did he . . ."

"You didn't hit him, but you scared the shit out of him and he almost lost his fucking hand."

"Don't mess with me—this ain't funny," I say, hoping Chris will start laughing and tell me I missed by a mile.

"He got nicked is all."

"Nicked?"

"The guard caught his thumb and smashed it pretty fucking good. You should have seen that fucker praying, you'd of thought God was going to come down and start working the press."

"Is that it?"

"No, then all of the other hillbillies gathered around him and started laying hands on him, praying and shit. Creeped me out."

"Is he going to be all right?"

Chris nods. "Yeah, he's going to be all right. But Luther's going to be a problem."

"I don't know what you're talking about," I say.

Chris stands there a minute wiping oil into his pant legs, looking back over his shoulder for Luther or anybody else.

Then he smiles and says, "What fucking bottle?"

I want to tell him some bullshit from *Meditations* about living in the moment, shedding misdeeds and grief, instead I say, "That's right." And we leave it a secret between us.

Luther never says a word to me other than to give me more cake jobs. But Chris gets demoted to press number thirteen in the back of the factory with the other space cases and burnouts and Luther rides him about his quotas until it becomes harder and harder to get him to laugh about anything during our poker games. After a week or so he stops talking about the navy.

During one of our last card games he starts needling Barry about the pension.

"What do you want to know about the pension for?" Barry says.

"If I were to stick around, you know. Like if I decided I wanted to make a go of it here."

"What about the navy?" I ask.

"Fuck the navy—they told me I'd have to take a drug test. That's why I want to know about the pension."

"Pension," Barry says, then he makes like he's going to puke.

A week later I punch out for the last time and say good-bye to Barry and Chris. Barry slips me a joint and tells me to watch out for "them."

"Who's *them?*" I say.

"How the fuck should I know," he says. "There's always someone out to ass-fuck you. Watch out for yourself too."

Chris makes a big deal about shaking my hand and seeing me to the door.

"Maybe when you come back I won't be here," he says.

"That would be good," I tell him.

Donald catches me in the lunchroom. It's the first time since the bottle incident that I've even talked to him and his right hand is still bandaged from where it got caught in the guard.

"Me and the fellers wanted to give you something for good luck," he says. He hands me a small green Gideon Bible. "God bless."

He waits, as if I'm supposed to say something, and when I don't he smiles and walks away.

When I step out into the parking lot I toss the Bible into one of the old oil drums that line the building. It chongs against the side, sending yellow jackets buzzing out of the drum. I keep walking and smile when I catch sight of Heather waiting for me in her Sunbird.

"Hold on a minute there, Wolverine," this voice booms out. I turn and catch Big Ed stepping out of the front entrance. I wait and when he gets close enough I stick out my hand for him to shake. I can feel the stump of his two fingers when he grabs my hand.

"Do us proud," he says. "Wolverine."

I thank him for the work and I can see he wants to reach out and muss my hair or high-five me.

"Anytime," he says. "Think about us when you're out on the field."

"I will," I say.

And I will.

FIVE

Leaving's just like I thought it would be.

Heather bawls for three straight days and makes me a tape of "our" songs that I file away next to the boxes containing the ceramic figurines. Dad bitches and moans about how much crap I'm taking, but deep down, I think he's happy to have something to do.

Heather makes the usual scene and I can feel Mom staring daggers at her trying to remember if she ever cried over a boy leaving. Probably not, I decide. But in the end I get into the car with Dad and we pull out of the driveway and down the street.

As Dad turns the car through the streets, gripping the wheel, staring out clear-eyed and strong-jawed at the rows and rows of identical houses, I feel surprisingly calm about leaving Cleveland. Cicadas chirp and whir, sprinklers spit tiny rainbows into the air and I wonder what was so special about this street, or for that matter this town.

Three hours and twenty minutes later we pull into Ann Arbor. There are people everywhere, shirtless, flipping Frisbees, on the lawns with books open, bums poking in garbage cans and more women than I've ever seen. Oak trees line the sidewalks and there seems to be a gentle slope to everything.

Dad can't keep his eyes off the women and when he stares too long at this girl running in place at a stoplight she gives him the finger. I see it too and his face turns bright red.

"Must be summer session," he says, trying to ignore the girl.

I nod, noticing that I've never seen the old man this alive before, like there's this sparkle somewhere under his skin that the drag of work has kept hidden all these years. Then I start thinking about Chris and Stork and how in a few years they're going to be just like my old man.

When we find the football complex I'm given a map and told to report to the indoor facility. There's a line of parents and players standing just inside the door. Dad looks around the room, pointing out my possible competition: kids with bigger arms and chests.

Finally Coach Roe stomps into the room, his silver hair slicked back, long arms at his side as he paces, inspecting his new recuits. An audible gasp goes up from the parents when they see his stern face.

"Welcome," he says as he walks up and down the line, shaking hands and slapping shoulders. Several of the assistant coaches follow behind him with clipboards handing out room assignments, welcoming us to Michigan.

After meeting Coach Roe, Dad turns to me and says, "A real class act."

In the coach's wake a giddy bout of friendliness follows, as fathers introduce themselves and mothers make small comments to each other, which escalate into full chat. Dad gets it too and taps a stern-faced man in front of us on the shoulder.

"Joe Sullivan," the man says, shaking hands firmly. He introduces his wife and points at his son. After shaking hands, Dad quickly hides his stained palms behind his back.

The son turns to me and says, "Joe Jr. I'm a tight end."

I look him over: Docksiders, Republican cut, metal watchband, and pleated shorts. I know right off that Joe Jr.'s one of those rah-rah, do-gooder types that's watched a few too many John Wayne movies. That and the fact he introduces himself as a tight end, as if it's his occupation or religion. What would I say? Skeptic? Stoic? Asshole from Cleveland?

I go with the ever-trusty jock nod trying to look like every other guy in the room.

"You nervous?" he asks.

I nod again and he smiles while his old man and my old man jaw about Coach Roe. I hear the words great, opportunity, and legend.

"I've heard double sessions are a bitch," I tell him.

Joe Jr.'s smile drops. He checks his watch and stares at his shoes.

"It's supposed to be the hottest summer in years," he says. "That's what we're here for though. To improve and better ourselves."

I can see his lips quivering a bit and I realize his smile's gone because he's afraid, just like me. He signed a letter thinking it was going to be high school only bigger and now we're both in this room with the competition, wondering if when the pads are strapped on we'll be able to play with these guys and take the licks.

The line moves pretty quick and Joe Jr. doesn't say much else. Coaches, trainers, assistants, equipment managers, all file down the line shaking hands in a hurry, introducing themselves. Each of us sizes up the competition, trying to look big and mean until Kong, Michigan's returning All-American tackle, wanders by on his way to the weight room, humbling us with his muscle on top of muscle and dull anvil-shaped head.

Joe Jr. taps me on the shoulder. "Is that Denny Conger?" he asks.

"Kong," I say. "I wouldn't call him Denny."

"He looks even bigger than on television," Joe says.

I nod uneasily and watch as Kong stands, hands on crotch, his cold eyes scanning the room for anybody bigger or stronger than him. Then he ambles off toward the weight room.

Coach Roe moves up and down the line of parents and players, reading name tags until he comes to this thick-legged black kid who stands, parentless, listening to his Walkman and snapping his head.

Roe pulls one of the earphones off. "No head stereos, son," he says, loud enough for all of us to hear.

The kid looks at him a moment, his eyes wide with something, before smiling and pulling the headphones off.

Joe Jr. leans into me. "That's Purty."

"That's him?"

Joe nods. "Mr. Blue Chip, Everybody's All-American, 4.3 forty, supposed to be the next Walter Payton."

"Is he really that good?" I ask Joe Jr.

"His brother played for State, set every record there was until he blew out his knee in his last game. They say this one's better."

When Roe leaves, Purty slips the headphones back over his head, smiling to himself and moving to the music. I look at him and wonder if he knows how good he is or if he feels lucky or blessed in some way.

After we're signed in, a girl dressed in a yellow knit shirt and long blue shorts comes bouncing into the room, followed by several other similarly clad girls.

"My name is Jodi," she says. "And I'm a Lady Blue." She points behind her and introduces each of the other girls, who wave like cheerleaders and bounce around as if meeting us is the high point of their day.

"We help out with recruiting and social functions. Now, if all you proud parents will follow me. I'll show you where your sons are going to be eating for the next four years."

A red-haired woman in high heels and tight jeans standing next to her oversize son whispers, "Training table."

Parents love this shit and Lady Blue Jodi just smiles like she's taking them to see the wizard or something.

After the parents are gone this skinny trainer guy with scissors hanging from a string around his neck leads us to the training room. The air smells of rubbing alcohol, athletic tape, and sweat. Rows and rows of shiny steel whirlpools sit like empty coffins. Trainer man lifts his stick-thin arms and herds us into the testing room, pointing at this machine that looks equal parts torture rack and leg squat. I hear somebody mutter and groan when he sees the machine.

I look behind me and there's this massive guy with dark curly hair, a hatchet for a nose and horrible pimples. His name tag says Smith.

"Hey, Smitty," I say. "You acquainted with this fine piece of machinery?"

He lights up and looks me over. For a moment I'm Jack Nicholson to Smitty's Chief Bromden and we're about to get juiced.

"For the pegs," Smitty says, pointing at his legs. "They want to see what kind of mileage we got on them."

"Pegs?"

"Knees. They gonna ratchet that sucker up and you're gonna keep pumping until something gives—it's a fucking torture tool."

"Machine," I say. "There's a big fucking difference between a tool and a machine."

Smitty looks at me. "Huh?"

"Tools are something you use and machines . . ."

"I get you," he says.

I nod.

A big black kid with wide brown eyes and hands the size of dinner plates shoves his way up to the front of the crowd.

"It hurts, man," he says.

I read his name tag. Antuan Gale.

"Ant," I say. "Word is we're in for some pain?"

"Don't you know it."

Several others mention something about kicking the machine's ass.

Of course Joe Jr. volunteers to go first and everybody gathers around to watch him get strapped in.

The first minute or so, not much happens. Joe's just pumping away.

"Piece of cake," he says, smiling. "It's not so bad—" He stops mid-sentence as a grimace tears across his face and the machine sqeals. Joe Jr. leans into it, sweat popping out on his forehead.

"Fuck," he says, in between grunts.

"Stay with it," the trainer says, his face twisting itself into this Dr. Mengele grin, two parts smile, one part sneer, as he fiddles with the tension dial on the machine. Joe Jr. digs in and starts screaming.

Finally Joe Jr. gives and falls back on the cracked vinyl bench, his chest heaving. The trainer clicks the stopwatch off, scribbles something in his book, before helping Joe Jr. up to a sitting position. Joe's leg immediately goes into spasm, the muscles rolling and knotting as if someone's inserted ferrets under his skin.

"Complete muscle failure," Ant whispers to me. "Ain't that a bitch."

"Ready for the other knee?" the trainer asks Joe Jr.

In the end all of us take the test and something happens between us. By the time Purty lifts his piston-shaped black legs onto the bench we're all joking and giving each other nicknames. There's Bob Napalese a.k.a. Napalm, a big sullen s.o.b. from Pittsburgh; Jimmy from Jersey who's obsessed with Bruce Springsteen; Slope and Rope, matching black D-backs who come from the same high school and finish each other's sentences. Slope because he's got this fucked-up forehead that looks like an on-ramp and Rope because when we take the Whiz Quiz he's hung like a horse. The trainer holding the piss cup jumps back against the urinal wall.

"Motherfucker," the trainer says, staring at Rope's dick.

"It don't bite," Rope says. "I got a license for it and everything."

Vezio, this walk-on guard from Oklahoma, takes one look at Rope's dick and says, "Check it fucking out—you could knock down walls with that thing." Somebody calls him Sleazio and he nods like he's got dumbbells for brains and starts grinning.

Then there's Tim "Fuckhead" Wallace 'cause he stutters and blushes; Oly, a long-legged wideout with some unpronounceable name and an African accent; Vern "Bible Boy" Wheeler, because he starts speaking in tongues when they strap him into the machine. And Ant, who says he's going to play for the Dallas Cowboys someday; fuck himself one of those cowgirl cheerleaders till her tits fall off.

Some skinny white kid from southern Indiana who keeps trying to talk "black" gets tagged with Whigger by Slope.

"You guys gonna play me like that?" he says.

Rope laughs and says, "Shut the fuck up, Whigger."

And Whigger just shrugs his shoulders, accepts the nickname.

Smitty's name sticks and he says he likes it even though he's heard it before until somebody mentions Lurch.

"Fuck that," he says. "I'll take Smitty any goddamn fucking day."

Sleazio comes up to me and says to the crowd, "Big ugly white dude from Cleveland—anybody got any suggestions?"

"How about El Cid?" I say.

"You can't give yourself a nickname," Sleazio says. "What kind of shit is that? El Cid?"

"What about El Fuck?" Ant says. "But then again, Elwood's one messed-up name—looks like your mommy and daddy already done you some wrong."

I shrug and say whatever.

The name-calling's all right because we're all a little bit scared and lonely and the more we do it the better it makes us feel.

More names.

Joe Jr. is called Yo Joe and he doesn't say shit about it. Purty—Blue Chip when he does a full two minutes more than anybody else on the machine. There are others like Dean "Revlon" Bottin, who gets his name because we catch him combing his hair before and after the knee test and when asked he says, "Look sharp, be sharp." Everybody hates him.

Then I meet my competition, Frank Himes or just Himes. He

shakes my hand after I crawl off the machine and introduces himself. I look him in the eye and it's like this secret knowledge of enemies passes between us and we're both thinking about strapping on some pads and taking it out to the field. Instead we go funeral-quiet and let the feeling course through the handshake. Afterward Himes does a few pull-ups on the door frame until one of the trainers tells him to get down.

Napalm whispers to me, "I hope he takes an injury."

"Me too," I say.

We both laugh and watch as Himes makes an ass out of himself, grunting out the pull-ups.

"How did you get tagged with Napalm?" I ask.

He smiles, bows his head, pointing at this toilet-seat-shaped bald spot.

"De-fucking-foliated," I say.

"What can you do?"

All around the room guys are bullshitting about their hometowns, girlfriends, and favorite songs. The blacks pool off like oil into their own corner as do the rest of us big guys. The gold-chain crew hangs around the whirlpools, trading private-school stories and shaking hands like CEOs.

There are other tests. Doc A introduces himself and moves through us poking and prodding like he's at a cattle auction.

"Vitamin shot?" Doc A asks, his three chins gulping against his paisley tie, lips the color of raw bacon.

Several guys get vitamin shots while we wait to be questioned about our medical history, examined for hernia—balls cupped, hand up ass, cough. Even our teeth are examined briefly by this faggy-looking dentist who goes right on down the line sticking his fingers into our mouths without bothering to wash his hands.

Smitty comes out of the examination room and announces, "Doc says I got me some twisted testicles."

"That's a little more info than I needed," Bible Boy whines.

Smitty glares at him. "I got a corkscrew for a dick, Bible Boy. Know what that means?"

"It means," Sleazio says, "that you're going to need some of that threaded cunt."

Smitty looks confused, then smiles. "That's right," he says. "Where can I get me some?"

When I go back, Doc A sits in his swivel chair, folder propped open on his chest.

"Family history?" he asks.

I tell him.

"Mental illness?"

I tell him about Uncle Chester, suicide by way of train: head on tracks. Grandpa with Alzheimer's. Cousin Rick who once wrote a letter to the local television station claiming to be a drug-addicted vampire with knowledge of the whereabouts of Elvis, later committed to the nuthatch.

"I'll mark that down as a yes," Doc A says. "And you?"

"All-American," I say. "Apple pie, milk, and Mom."

Doc A gives me this wiseass smile before scribbling some more in his notepad.

"Sexual history?"

I start to tell him about Heather.

He nods. "Perfectly normal. Anything else?"

When I don't answer he pats me on the arms and says, "Good boy." I stand and head out the door and trot back out to wait with the others. Ten minutes later this bouncy-looking assistant coach hops into the training room and double-times us down the corridor and into the team meeting room.

We take seats in neat little rows of school chairs. An overhead projector with Xs and Os written all over it lights up one side of the room. To my right the wall is covered by chalkboards with the same Xs and Os and a depth chart with names under each position heading. There is another large blue eye covering most of the back wall and from the way I hear the others talking I can tell they were given the same song and dance about the Eye of Michigan watching over them.

I don't feel so special anymore.

Revlon and Yo Joe take seats up front and pull pens out of their pockets. Himes starts calling them eggheads, kiss-asses, brownnosers, and suck-ups until the door swings open and a flock of coaches enter and stand in front of the chalkboards.

There's one coach for every position along with grad assistants who run behind the coaches, taking notes and getting them coffee. Napalm calls them knob polishers. All of the coaches look the same in their double-knit golf shirts and polyester coaching shorts.

Napalm tells me that the fat guy on the left is Coach Unsworth—a real asshole.

"My old man says they called him Coach Unworthy when he coached at Central."

"What's he doing coaching here?"

"Couldn't hack the head job at Central, I guess," Napalm says.

I spot my position coach, Coach Peters, under the depth chart, scanning the fresh bunch of recruits with this jacked-up gleam in his eye, like he can't wait to get us out on the field.

Coach Unsworth steps forward and speaks first.

"Men," he says. "Coach Roe's been telling us all week how this recruiting class is the best Michigan's had in years."

"On paper," some other coach says. "All frosh are paper champions until proven on the field of battle."

"That's right," Coach Unsworth says. "Now, if you're all so hotshit good then we're out of a job." Motions to other coaches until they're nodding and clenching their jaws like some anal-retentive chorus of yes-men.

From somewhere in the back of the room somebody lets out a short laugh and the coaches stop nodding. The room falls silent and I'm praying it's Himes.

On cue Unsworth snaps—veins in the neck, fists pounding overhead projector, the whole nine yards.

"Something's funny, huh?" Unsworth growls. He gets in Revlon's face (his fault for sitting front and center) and growls, spit flying all over the desk while Revlon nods, sputtering, "Yes sir . . . No sir."

"Your mommies aren't here to wipe your asses and pick your noses anymore. You're Wolverines and Wolverines act like men and look out for each other. Do you understand me?"

Revlon, "Yes sir."

"We do things the Michigan way here and that's the right way." Etc. and etc. "The first thing you're going to learn is how to listen. Ears and brains open, mouth shut—that's the Michigan way. Because if any of you fucking comedians want to crack jokes when Coach Roe's talking, be my guest. Just know that I'll run you till your balls fall off and your lungs explode."

Revlon's still yessiring his neatly combed head off when I whisper to Napalm that he's going to be dead meat when Coach U gets ahold of him. Napalm nods glumly.

After Coach U yells himself out, Coach Direnzo introduces himself as Coach D.

"You guys fired up yet?" he says.

We manage some halfhearted yes sirs back at him and he seems pleased. Then he launches into this speech how nobody's better than anybody else and how we all start out equal. Then he asks us to introduce ourselves to the group. Everybody stands and sounds off about where they're from and what position they play. We're allowed to giggle when someone's voice catches or when Smitty drawls out his name and says he's from Texas.

After a few more rah-rah speeches we meet up with our parents, who look tired and wide-eyed from their tour of the facilities. A few of the mothers start crying when one of the assistants announces that we have two hours to move into the dorms and say our goodbyes.

The minute the last of the parents have left we report back down to the facility. I meet up with Napalm, who's still wiping his mother's lipstick off his neck.

"Seems sort of unreal, doesn't it?" he says.

"What?" I say as Himes yammers behind us.

Napalm shakes his head. "This."

"You mean summer double session?"

"Yeah," he says. "And how like it's all started now. High school's over and we're really here."

"I've thought about this day for months. You scared?"

"I don't have any illusions that any of this is going to be easy."

"Me neither."

Napalm smiles. "Try explaining that to Himes."

Bible Boy, Revlon, and Yo Joe make us all look bad by arriving ten minutes early and taking the front seats. Smitty saunters in three minutes late and Coach Roe eyes him silently for a full minute before snapping his yardstick across a desk.

Coach Roe, "You're late, son. You on Texas time?"

"I'm sorry," Smitty drawls.

A chubby assistant hands Coach Roe another yardstick and takes away the broken one.

"Sorry don't cut it, son. Sorry's for losers. Wolverines are never sorry—they're on time. And on time means early."

Smitty sits stone-faced as Roe screams about setting our watches ahead ten minutes to "Roe time." We haven't even played a down yet but every last one of us is looking around the room at the coaches, depth charts, the Eye of Michigan, and the chalkboard wondering what the hell we just got ourselves into. In two hours every minute of our lives is dictated to us. Coach Roe chalks out a schedule with angry, ham-fisted screeches on the blackboard.

"Write this down," Roe says, tapping the board with his new yard-stick. Then he reads it to us.

8 A.M.–12 Classes. We are to be polite, attend classes, say thank you and please, listen, ask questions, open doors for women, carry ourselves like "student/athletes."

12–2 P.M. Hit training table for a "light" lunch, before heading down to the facility for taping and game film.

2–6 P.M. Practice.

6–6:30 P.M. Postpractice workout with Harkens.

6:30–6:45 P.M. Shower.

7–8 P.M. Training table.

8–10 P.M. Study table. Schoolwork, playbook, or Bible.

"That's the good part," Roe says. "Right now we've got dog-ass double sessions where I intend to make myself a team full of ass-kicking, throat-ripping, helmet-sticking, God-fearing ballplayers who want to win the Rose Bowl this year."

Under the words DOUBLE SESSIONS ITINERARY Roe writes: PRACTICE. HIT! HIT! HIT!

An audible groan rises in the room. Several of the coaches start smiling and nodding like this tight-ass schedule's some good thing that's going to bring order, religion, and manhood to our candy asses.

Revlon and Yo Joe pepper Coach Roe with butt-kissing questions while the rest of us sit around feeling sorry for ourselves. Everybody gets yelled at at least once either for appearing to not be listening or for slouching. We are called twats, dumbshits, dumbasses, shitbirds, worthless, stupid, and finally frosh. Coach Roe mentions God every once in a while, looks up at the fluorescent lights and says we're on a mission to kick Big Ten ass and eat Rose Bowl for Christmas.

What can I say? Something gets to me and I feel reckless and full of great things. I look around the room and sure enough I can see this pride and sense of purpose welling up in everybody's face.

SIX

All any of us want is to be noticed by the coaches. So for eight hours a day we fly around the artificial turf spearing one another, popping forearm into facemasks, trying to hurt and maim between whistles. Life happens in ten-second bursts: wind sprints, sled drills, and spear-the-dummy. The sun beats down on us like hot cement and there isn't enough water in the world for us to drink.

Roe spends the mornings prowling the field, yardstick in hand, thwacking us on the legs when we line up wrong or jump offsides. Dogging it is forbidden, everything, even our trots to the water bucket have to be done on the hustle.

Coach Peters hovers behind us screaming, "Hit, hit, tackle, hit somebody."

But Unsworth outscreams everybody on the field and when one of the linemen fails to execute he crawls up inside the lineman's facemask and starts spitting out how worthless he is. He kicks players when they miss calls, drags Napalm out of a pile yelling, "Goddamn shitbird, Napalese."

And when Smitty fucks up a scrape block on Himes he kicks Smitty in the ass until he's rolling around the turf with his hands between his legs.

Bible Boy takes a knee injury after Himes spears him and now everybody's gunning for Himes. Purty runs like a gazelle and there are times when he streaks down the sidelines that even the coaches stop their nervous pacing to look on with admiration. There is grace in his efficient stride, arms pumping air, as he shucks and jives tacklers with small, lightning-quick moves.

"What's he got?" Jimmy says to me after watching Purty break one for twenty yards.

"Zen, man. Total fucking Zen," Napalm says.

"What the fuck's that supposed to mean?" Jimmy says. "Sounds like some kind of drug."

"It means he's one with the moment. He is what he is," I say. "Just like you."

"I don't know about that Zen shit. The sonofabitch, as the Boss says is Born to Run."

Jimmy stares at me a moment before bopping down the line of hands-on-hips scrubs, running his mouth and smacking helmets.

"Total fucking rockhead," I say.

Napalm shifts, nods his helmet, feigning interest on the field, says, "He'll go far."

"What do you mean?"

Out on the field the coaches swarm around a pileup, blasting their whistles as Fuckhead squares off with Ant. They throw punches at each other's facemask until Ant catches Fuckhead in the throat with a roundhouse and they hit the carpet wrestling.

Himes circles them yelling, "Kill. Kill. Kill." And the coaches eat it up, start smiling at one another.

"I mean," Napalm says, watching the fight, "it pays to be numb."

"Dumb?"

"That too, but I meant numb," he says.

"Out here?"

"No, man, of course I mean here, this is it—everything else in our lives is just breathing and waiting. Come on, Riley, don't bullshit me—you know what the fuck I'm talking about."

"You still want it, don't you?"

"Want what?"

"To play," I say.

"I thought that was what we were doing."

He stares, fiddling with his chin strap, sweat running down his nose.

"Do you?" he says. "Because I'm beginning to have my doubts."

"I must be fucked, because I still do," I say.

"Think about it for a moment, because from what I've seen so far there are some dumb, rockhead motherfuckers who live for this shit. And I already know I don't. Look around, Riley."

I scan the herd of helmeted, head-down bodies, as they take plays from screaming coaches, who stand behind the huddle, squinting, waiting for something to happen, and I feel as if I'm bumping up against some knowledge. Perhaps an understanding of some brute order on a team like this and my place in it for the next four years.

"You see?" Napalm says. I start to say something when Assistant Coach Hart, who everybody calls Hard-on Hart because he's always running around trying to geek us up, steps between us.

"Napalese," Hart screams. "You smiling because you're happy or because you want to go for a run in this gorgeous heat?"

Napalm stares at his feet, plays dumb until Hard-on Hart starts on me.

"Riley," he screams. "I hope and pray you two were discussing this fine sport of football."

"Yes sir," I say.

"Good, then. Tell me what formation that last play was."

"I'm on defense."

"That's no excuse, son. Matter of fact that's one piss-poor answer. That's a nonanswer," he says. "I'll pretend I didn't hear that. So I'm going to ask you again. What formation?"

I toss my hands up in the air.

"Are you fucking with me, Riley?"

"No sir."

"Then what the fuck kind of formation is this?" He imitates me throwing my hands in the air.

"I don't know," I say.

"We don't have an I-don't-know formation," he says. Then he points at the track. "Start running, Riley, maybe some blood'll decide it wants to take a detour to your brain."

He gives me this disgusted look and watches as I lumber off toward the oak tree and the track. I hear more yelling and as I round the first corner I catch sight of Napalm behind me, head down, running around the tree.

Over the next week Coach Peters rides me about my lack of foot speed and points to Himes when he wants to show me how it's done. I make up for my clubfeet by hitting like a sonofabitch, anybody and anything. We play Bull in the Ring and the guys are afraid to take their shots with me, same with the Pits where I hunker down into my wrestling stance and jack them up with my fists and forearms.

Everybody's black-and-blue.

At lunch Smitty shows us his bruised right forearm.

"Watch," he says, pushing down on the bruise. Tiny dots of blood ooze out of the pores. "It's like a fucking sponge."

"Fuck that," Himes says, pulling up his shirtsleeve. "Watch this."

We watch as he pushes on this ugly purple bruise until it starts moving up and down his arm.

Somebody asks Himes if it's his second brain and Himes goes after him.

Other guys start showing off their aches and pains. We talk about pissing blood and how much we hate our coaches. Nobody says a thing about Coach Roe, instead we all fear his attention.

We learn the rules only after somebody breaks one of them. When

Yo Joe sits on his helmet during a water break he gets read the riot act by every coach on the field.

Coach Peters, "Son, the helmet is why we play this game. It is your only weapon. Never place your ass on your weapon."

Coach U makes Yo Joe run a play without his helmet and when he comes off the field his nose is bloody and his ear hangs from his head at this crazy angle. Coach Treller twirls his finger and points Joe toward the track and tells him to run laps for the rest of practice carrying his helmet out in front of him.

We learn the "no women" rule when Slope gets caught talking to a girl in the parking lot. Rope says she looked like Chaka Khan and had an ass like a sterling pony. They make him run morning mile with an inflatable fuck doll duct-taped to his back and ankle weights.

Other rules:

No talking in meetings.

No sleeping during game film.

No steroids, crosstops or any other drug, including alcohol. Only Doc A's "vitamin" shots. Any player who pisses dirty is automatically stripped of his scholarship. It's rumored however that several of the seniors have been juicing over the summer.

No bars, fraternities or parties.

No fighting off the field. We are to behave like gentlemen.

No gambling.

No cheating.

Lights-out means lights-out.

No phone calls after lights-out.

And so on until our lives get pared down to one thing. Football.

The first week ends and the upperclassmen arrive. I see them walking through the parking lot, laughing, tossing around their duffel bags, punching each other on well-muscled arms and high-fiving.

After our last frosh practice Coach Roe assembles us in the meeting room and has us sing the Michigan fight song as the upperclassmen march in. The room fills up and we are told to take seats in the back. Revlon refuses until Kong grabs him by his neatly combed hair and shoves him to the back. Everybody laughs, even the coaches.

"Respect for your elders," Coach Roe says. "Lesson learned."

Revlon sulks, but accepts the abuse and takes a seat behind Fuckhead.

With the upperclassmen reported to camp, Coach Unsworth starts calling us two-legged tackling dummies. Everybody except for Purty gets put on the drill team where Coach Argent, a small potbellied man who chews cigars and rocks back on his heels when he talks, takes us under his wing and teaches us how to run the opposing team's offense or defense. For the rest of double sessions we pretend to be the Maryland Terrapins, our first opponent. We even get red jerseys and learn their fight song, so when the first-team O or D dogs it Coach Argent has us sing to enrage them.

On the first day of padded practice, fights break out all over the place. I get into it with Jerry Q, this tall, soft-shouldered backup tackle. The coaches watch as I pull Jerry's helmet off and start swinging.

"Kick his fucking ass," I hear somebody say.

We end up on the turf gouging at each other's eyes until somebody pulls us apart. After water break Jerry ambles over and introduces himself. We smack pads and smile.

"It's cool," he says. "They want us to fight. Shows we got heart."

"I get that feeling," I say.

"They figure the hate's a good thing, but it'll only last until the first game, then we'll hate them."

"Maryland?" I ask.

"Fuck no, the coaches."

"Everybody hates Coach U already."

"That's good, because he's a complete fucking asshole, but on the other hand we've got the best offensive line in the country."

"So then it works," I say. "Us hating them."

"Not for me. I'm just a backup and I'm sick of their bullshit. But the good ones do one of two things. Either they hate everything or else they get this kung-fu cool, overdrive sort of thing where nothing matters.

"You mean like Purty?"

Jerry nods, wincing, as Coach Roe whistles for a full-team scrimmage and the coaches start running around, marshaling their players and pulling laminated play folders out of their pockets.

Later Himes gets cocked by Bam Bam, the starting center, for going too hard. Bam Bam takes him to the ground with a headlock, ripping Himes' helmet off. The coaches let the fight go a little bit until Bam Bam, after several vicious punches to Himes' face, seems satisfied that he's cured him of his hero-for-a-day ways.

Other fights break out without warning like storms. I go at it in the Pits with this fat-assed second-year guard named Childers who tells me to chill out. I don't want to chill out. Instead I go full blast and embarrass him in front of Unsworth, leaving him with only one option if he's to save face.

He swings at me, letting out a torrent of fuck yous. Then Unsworth steps between us and grabs Childers by the facemask and drags him away.

"Son," he says, jerking Childers around. "You just got your ass kicked by a freshman. You want to show me something, show it to me in a three-point stance."

Unsworth lines us up again and Childers starts huffing and puffing at me. Ray Wolff or Wolfie, the starting defensive tackle, leans over and tells me to get him. Then Unsworth blows the whistle and Childers rushes me with everything he's got. When our helmets collide I look over Childers' shoulder and catch the snarl on Unsworth's face, pain shooting down my neck and into my arm as Childers grunts and his knees buckle. I pump and pump my feet until I feel him give and fall to the ground. I look up just in time to see the snarl drop from Unsworth's face and the faintest of smiles creeps across it before he looks at his fallen player with disgust.

"I hit my fucking son harder than that, Childers," Unsworth says softly. And it's the softly that kills Childers and makes him feel like a pussy.

I walk out of the Pits adjusting my shoulder pads, head down, feeling a little bad for Childers. Wolfie gets geeked and starts calling me El Crusher. I look over on the other side of the Pits and wink at Napalm, who gives me the finger, because Unsworth has been riding him like a dog from the first day of padded practice to toughen himself up. Napalm takes the abuse, careful not to react even when Unsworth proclaims him to be the most worthless piece of shit to have ever stepped into a jockstrap.

After Childers slinks to the back of the line Napalm takes his three-point and fires out on Tilman, a walk-on from Kansas. Napalm plants and drives for a few seconds before sliding off the block and falling on his face in front of Unsworth.

When he pulls himself off the turf Unsworth says, "Napalese, you're fat."

Napalm nods his head. "Yes sir. Thank you."

"Not only are you fat but you have no heart and you hit like a fucking thirteen-year-old girl."

Napalm eyes the ground as Coach U continues his tirade.

"Son, I am making it my mission in life to make you a ballplayer. I'll wake in the morning and say to myself, 'Coach U, you will make Napalese a card-carrying stud football player if it's the last thing you do in life.' "

Napalm gives the expected yes sir and Unsworth moves on to his next victim, Banchic, whose only sin seems to be that he can't ever remember his assignment on the tailback sweep.

The rest of practice happens, drill, hit, tackle, small yelling break by the coaches, more Pits, sack attack, Bull in the Ring (where I get slaughtered by the nose guard, Jeter) and another full-team scrimmage where I stumble around in the mix getting blocked and punched from every direction.

I get my payback from Childers in the locker room when he singles me out for frosh hazing. He waits until I've stripped off my pads and started on the ankle tape before attacking. Within minutes the entire team has gathered around to watch as Childers and Pete "the Shed" Shedowski grab me.

"You need to take a shit, don't you, Riley?" they say, hauling me toward the bathroom and the row of blue-doored shitters.

I struggle a bit and then finally put on the Jesus-turns-the-other-cheek stare. It rattles Childers, who can't seem to look me in the eyes as he tapes me to the shitter door, first my wrists, then long strips around my waist and legs until I can barely move. The Shed laughs and then starts wrapping tape around my head.

I let them have their fun, reminding myself that others have gotten it worse. On the first night, Kong and Chernak snatched Revlon out of his bed and shaved his balls with a Lady Bic. Now Revlon showers last and covers himself in the corner with a towel. Jimmy from Jersey had Icy Hot slathered in his hip pads and spent the entire morning practice dousing himself at the hose until his shoes were full of water and Coach Treller started calling him a water pussy.

Somebody pissed in Smitty's helmet and told him about it right before the morning lap. Smitty kicked ass that morning, hitting and blocking with newfound rage.

During training table Jeter gave Fuckhead a cup of spit and told him to drink deeply.

Rope was forced to walk through training table with his pants down. All twelve inches swinging at the salad bar as several of the salad bar attendants, shy girls with unfortunate faces and Pan-Cake makeup over pimples, dropped their bowls of lettuce and onions and just stared at Rope.

Crawdaddy, a farm-faced QB from Kentucky, had his room tossed and his playbook confiscated which put him in some deep shit with the coaches.

The Shed finishes his last roll of tape and then says, "Sing the fight song, little birdie." Laughs some more and stands back to admire his handiwork.

I oblige and sing "Hail to the Victors" horribly off-key and flat, the tape across my lower jaw not helping any. For some reason, singing in public is supposed to be the ultimate in shame. It's heaped on top of every form of abuse. Even Revlon, after having his balls shaved at three in the morning, was forced to sing "The Star-Spangled Banner" in falsetto.

"You sing for shit," the Shed says, walking away to finish undressing.

By the time I manage to free myself I'm ten minutes late to my postpractice workout with Harkens, our strength and conditioning coach, whose theory of weight training is what he calls "complete muscle failure." Muscle failure occurs after you have maxxed out at one weight, only to have a few pounds dropped off the bar or machine and the whole process repeated. So something as simple as bench press may take five sets of descending weight until you're unable to lift even your bare arms into the air. And like any sort of failure it hurts. Harkens likes to hiss in your ear about how good and pure the pain feels. How it's like drugs or good sex.

Instead, it's like having ground glass and Drano pumped into your bloodstream. Your head explodes and pounds. When you close your eyes the walls of your brain are paneled in lightning-bolt white. Oddly enough the muscle being worked goes numb while the surrounding muscle groups go into a sort of sympathetic burn. Some guys get off on the whole thing, screaming and yelling at Harkens for more. Most of us, I suppose, are like me and enter the weight room hating the clock on the wall, wishing for the next thirty minutes to just disappear.

Harkens makes me pay double on the squat machine for being late even after I try explaining to him how I was taped to a stall door.

"Then we'll do death dips," he says, leading me over to the dip station which is at the top of a ladder. When you fail at weighted dips you have two choices: fall the ten feet and get called a bald pussy by Harkens or else crawl back down the ladder with numb arms and hands and risk chipping your teeth on the rungs when your grip fails.

I puke after the extra set of dips.

"That's what I like to see, son," he says. "Pain."

Then he makes me crab-walk to the bench station while he rambles on about how in Vietnam he used to do pull-ups off the choppers as they swept through the valleys taking potshots at water buffalo and villagers.

"It was sickdog," he says. "This is chickenshit stuff. Mind over matter, thy will be done and all that crap—so I don't want to hear any of your bellyaching, Riley."

The empty bar collapses on my chest and I ask, "Am I done?"

"Riley, you don't know what hard's all about—ten more for Big Blue and I want to hear you count them out."

I count them out, thinking I have four more years of this moron yelling about pain, willpower, and Big Blue. My chest feels like it has barbed wire coiled around it.

"Candy-ass-country-club, baby jock crap. You hear me, Riley?" Harkens says, pointing at the weight room. I nod, remembering what Wolfie told me about how Harkens is medicated to the gills and a little whacked on pain, both the giving and receiving of it. So I tune out and let his words wash over me as I count out the reps.

SEVEN

My roommate's this creepy guy named Phil Langley from Center City, Michigan. He's a defensive end so that makes him a loner and unpredictable. He has no nickname, because he's one of those guys whose appearance and demeanor somehow defy humor. All you have to do is take one look at his tobacco-filled lip and dodgy eyes to know that this is one genetically deficient motherfucker. His one true talent that I have been able to identify is that he's adept at leaving Coke cans full of his tobacco spit on every available surface of our room. He also talks in his sleep, usually about food or some other crummy nonsense.

I don't tell him about Heather's figurines. The last thing I need is to have some food-obsessed defensive end making fun of me. So I hide them in the back of my closet and put beer posters on the wall like everybody else. While Phil hangs pictures of his girlfriend, Sally, over his bed and a rosary which I sometimes catch him stroking.

I don't consider him a friend or even someone I can talk to, but when there's nothing left of the day and we are both lying on our beds feeling for bruises I try.

"Phil," I say. "How are you holding up?"

"Pretty good," he says. "Pretty good, okay I guess. Do you think they'll have steak at training table?"

"I don't know, Phil, I guess you'll just have to wait and see."

"What if they don't have steak?"

"We had steak last night, Phil. If I was a betting man I'd say we're looking at pasta or maybe pork chops."

"Oh," he says, truly disappointed.

What can I say? He's one of those guys who live for training table. What can I possibly have in common with a guy who calls it a good day when there are deep-fried shrimp and Delmonico steaks for dinner?

At training table.

"Phil," I say. "You better go easy on those shrimp, we're getting timed in the mile and a half tomorrow."

"But I like them," he says, heaping them into a white Styrofoam takeout tray.

Then he waddles back to our room and calls his parents and lists everything he's eaten in the last twenty-four hours, how many tackles he made in scrimmage (zero, but he lies and tells them he made ten), how many guys are in front of him (four) and how much he misses them (Mom and Dad).

He gets all twitchy whenever I talk about women. He's worried I'm going to say something inappropriate about Sally, who I don't think he's ever fucked, because he's got this pure-love thing going with her. I tell him about how sweet Heather smells and the way her hair feels when it's wet.

"Do you love her?" he asks.

"What kind of love are we talking about?"

Phil shrugs his shoulders as if to say he wants a simple answer and not some deep rap on the nature of love.

"We'll talk about that later," I tell him. A lie.

He sighs, picks up his Bible, and starts mumble reading. After about ten minutes I want to claw my eyes out.

Finally, I give in and ask, "Do you believe in God?"

He stops, closes the Bible and stares at Sally's picture for a minute, his face fogging up as if I've just insulted him and he's not sure whether he should be angry or not.

"What kind of question is that?"

"It's a get-to-know-you sort of question," I say. "That and I'm going to go crazy if I have to sit here all night listening to you read."

"You want me to put it away, I will," he says, tamping a fresh dip of Copenhagen into his bottom lip.

"No—it's just you ought to try reading something else for a change."

He points at his playbook.

"No, not that," I say. "A book or something."

"I can't do that," he says, leaning back against the wall. "I don't have the time and besides the Bible's the greatest story ever told."

I shake my head at him.

"Shit, Phil—don't tell me you're one of those zombies who's going to thank his personal savior Jesus Christ when you make a game-saving sack."

He blinks at me.

"You're supposed to say, 'No, Riley. I'd never think of it,' " I say. I get up to go.

"You think you're so smart," Phil says. "So what if I read the Bible—what's it matter to you?"

I turn, "It matters because I've got to listen to it too. It's that or you're running your mouth about training table or Sally."

"It's important to me," he says. "I'm not like you, Riley. Things matter to me."

"What do you mean things?"

"God, I guess, and Sally," he says.

"You forgot food," I tell him.

He smiles for a minute as if I've just cracked some joke and I realize I'm not too far off the mark.

"Christ—you are one of those fucking zombies," I say.

"Your problem is that nothing matters to you," he says.

"If you mean God—well then yes, I'm an atheist," I say.

"What's that?" he asks.

I look the pointy-toothed motherfucker over, sitting on his bed, lip full of dip, glazed look in his eyes, and decide it's not worth my time.

"Forget about it, Phil," I say. "Read whatever you want—I'll put my earplugs in."

He smiles, picks up the Bible as if he's won some sort of debate and begins reading again, stumbling on every other word. I stuff cotton in my ears, but it doesn't do me any good because the bastard's got me thinking about what matters.

By the end of double sessions we are hard-hearted sonofabitches, full of ourselves for surviving the long hot days under the eye of Coach Roe in his tower. Even the screaming fits heaped on us by gung-ho coaches roll off our backs like water. In some sense we crave the attention because it gives us something to complain about—a reason to keep on keeping on out of spite.

After the third week Napalm's thinner and getting yelled at less and less by Coach U. Part of him, he says, fears that he will cease to exist without this attention and unlike Phil he knows there's something to this belief. Nobody yells at Revlon, instead they give him a blue blocking pad.

"Stand here," Coach Argent tells Revlon.

Revlon stands.

Whistle.

Kong and Shed plow him into the turf, followed by Thorpe. Nobody helps him up, no pat on the butt. Yo Joe and Bible Boy become lost souls too, food for the first team to gobble up and spit out. No matter how hard they try they've become nonentities. Yo Joe because he's slow, and Bible Boy 'cause he's got this do-good-Christian attitude, no heart, and a bum knee already.

Law of the jungle is that there are two types on the team, hitter and hittee. If you pop ass and stick like a fucking land shark you get respect. Fail to make a stick and not only do the coaches start on you with the pussy rap, but the other guys start whispering soft shit about you behind your back. Hittees get a life sentence to the scrub team, shower last, and eat only after the upperclassmen and junior mother-fuckers have eaten.

Coach Peters finally gives up on my slow feet, and hands me off to Coach U, who needs warm bodies. I imagine the whole deal going down in some meeting room, Peters and Unsworth trading bodies like playing cards.

But just like that I'm an offensive tackle. Himes gives me this stupid grin when I'm informed of the switch after practice.

"Looks like you and me just became enemies," Himes says. "Official fucking enemies."

I smile, acting as if it's the greatest thing to happen to me. I have no choice. As a ballplayer I'm allowed one emotion—enthusiasm—anything else the coaches mistake for lack of heart.

After training table Coach U pulls me aside and gives me a football-is-like-life speech before showing me the depth chart and how I fit into the backup slot behind Kong.

He says, "In a year Kong goes pro and if you work hard enough in spring ball . . ."

And I nod like crazy, trying to act all pumped up.

He calls me son and even pats me on the shoulder. I'll be damned if I don't feel a little loyalty for the man welling up inside me. And despite all the bullshit, the stuff about starting gets me thinking about contributing to the team someday and being a regular Joe.

"All of your deficits on defense will be assets when you move to offense," he says. "We score points, we protect, we know where the ball's going. Defense is stagnation and death, they *want* the game to be over. Offense on the other hand is about forward motion and time."

"I played some center in high school," I say.

"To be perfectly honest, Riley, I've had my eye on you from day one, you don't want to play defense. Offense is where it's at. It's more of a thinking man's game, leave defense to the nitwits."

"You mean to say offense is more cerebral?"

His eyes cross for a second and I worry that I've overstepped some invisible coach-player line.

"Son, all I'm saying is that you're too goddamn smart to be chasing after the ball on all fours. Start thinking of yourself as an offensive tackle. You like to hit and I like that. Know what I mean?"

I thank him and amble off to my room.

"It's a trap," Napalm says when I tell him about my chat with Coach U. We are sitting in my room just before lights-out listening to Jimmy blast Springsteen to the entire hallway. Every once in a while he bounds into our room demanding that we listen to the lyrics, most of which he's got wrong. Napalm ignores him and he stumbles out of the room mumbling "Born to Run."

"He's blowing smoke up your ass, so you go without a fight," Napalm says.

"He's right," I say.

"What do you mean *he's right?*"

"I'm off the charts on D. If I move to O, I back up Kong," I say.

"You're right, you don't have a choice. Even if it's a trap, you've got to go."

After making it this far, I know one thing. That despite all of the yelling and having our days scheduled down to the last minute, I am nothing without football.

I make the transition okay and Coach U keeps up with his nice-guy bit, showing me the techniques and encouraging me. Kong takes me under his wing and teaches me how to leg-chop rushing tackles and stop them with throat punches.

"All legal," he says.

I try them out in scrimmage against Himes, who's taken to lining up and whooping like an idiot, insulting people's mothers, challenging anybody who cares to take their best shot. Coach Peters goes nuts for this kind of shit and pretty soon the whole D-line's talking trash just like Himes.

"He's sort of a retarded, white-boy version of Muhammad Ali," Napalm says.

"Fuck him," Kong says. "I'm going to knock his ass out."

Kong hates any display of emotion. Offensive linemen are not emotional guys. Kong, all three hundred pounds of him, goes about his practices grim-faced and silent. Every play a new test to endure, each whistle a respite from the grind. There are no peaks and valleys in Kong's world, just punishing quality and simple physics.

"You rush," he says. "I block. You punch. I chop. Nothing personal."

Until Himes lines up in full-team scrimmage and starts calling Kong Roid-Boy and Juicehead, asking to see his track marks.

After that Kong makes it his personal mission to take any shot he can get at Himes and goes about this task with quiet zeal. And within a week Himes is spitting up blood after most practices, nursing three dislocated fingers, a carpet burn the shape of Florida on his shin that bleeds into his shoes, and a bruised Adam's apple from one of Kong's well-placed throat punches.

But that still doesn't stop him from talking trash whenever Coach Roe's in his tower or else out of earshot.

Just before Pits one day, Kong leans into me, points at Himes and says, "Look at the cockroach."

I look over on the other side and watch Himes bouncing up and down, mumbling to himself, trying to get the rest of the guys pumped up, leg bleeding, fingers taped together.

"He'd take that as a compliment," I say.

But then I look around at the sprawl of players moving in indistinguishable groups on the boiling turf. It's about ninety degrees in the shade, the plastic in our shoulder pads has softened. Waves of heat pour off the field, making the tape on our ankles feel like it's melting into our skin. Three dudes have already dropped during grass drill and there is Himes, jumping around like a jackass and I start thinking how maybe Kong's one insightful cat, how Himes *is* like a cockroach and that the only thing you can wish on him is bad, bad luck and hope that he'll eventually burn himself out. With that in mind I watch as Kong pulverizes Himes, pancaking him to the ground.

Unsworth practically cums in his pants, and starts pumping his fists into the air, screaming, "Kill, Kong—kill, kill, kill."

Then he lines me up against Big Money and I hold my own.

The next day during the warm-up lap Robeson, a backup defensive tackle, bumps me and gives me a thwack with his forearm. I fall back a few paces, listen to the rattle and crack of plastic and stiff joints, trying to decide what to do. Already, the fatties have lagged to the rear of the pack. Coach U is screaming, "Pick up the pace, pussies, pick up the pace."

If I back down from this small challenge, Robeson will own me. Another rule of the jungle is to never let someone get over on you. Do that and I risk becoming one of the permanently fucked: a scrub team bitch.

Robeson looks over his shoulder as we take the second lap and gives me this what-the-fuck-do-you-think-you're-looking-at glare. I run after him, jostling past the linebackers and D-backs until I'm right behind him. I wait until the third lap before I swing my knee into his thigh and at the same time chop him with a quick forearm. He crumples to the ground with a short scream. Nobody seems to notice and the pack keeps moving, bobbing its helmeted head to the finish line where we break out into formation for grass drills. Oddly enough, I don't feel a thing as trainers rush onto the field and hold Robeson on the turf as he rolls around clutching at his knee and howling. By the time we finish drills Robeson has been spirited off the field on a golf cart, ice bags tucked around his knee.

At the water cooler Wolfie sidles up to me and says, "I saw what you did. You're on offense now, Riley, not so smart."

I keep drinking.

"Shit happens. Maybe you and me meet in a pileup and you accidentally twist your knee," he says.

"I've got it coming. Don't I?"

Wolfie smacks me on the shoulder pads. "In spades, frosh, in motherfucking spades."

During full-team scrimmage I platoon with the drill team, running Maryland's offense against the first-string D. Nothing happens and the longer I wait for payback the worse it gets. I get timid, holding back on blocks and avoiding pileups where I might have my face gouged or my ankles twisted. Because I'm too careful, I get blindsided by Reems, the first-team linebacker, on a scrape block.

"Had to do it," he says. "C.O.D."

I pick myself off the turf, eyes buzzing. My head feels like it's full of blood and cotton. I know I've got one over on them, taken their best shot and walked away. Suddenly, I love the whole fucking game and I know why I'm doing this. Because I can. Because I am six foot six, weigh two hundred and seventy-five pounds and have muscle to burn.

By six o'clock bruise-colored clouds have shifted in from the east and all of us stop for a moment to stare at the sky as the rain starts. Small drops at first that ping off our helmets like gravel and cause the speed-sters to start grinding their black shoes into the artificial turf, checking their footing. Sweat becomes indistinguishable from rain and the coaches seem to get angrier the wetter they get. Finally Roe calls for the special teams and we end practice with several kick returns fol-lowed by wind sprints, which are made even more difficult because of our waterlogged pads.

I rumble off the field, my lungs full of hurt from the sprints, calves quivering, and look up at the sky. There is no lightning, only dark wispy clouds that move like a woman's hair in water. I find myself becoming accustomed to the small things, like the smell of sweat and the shine of wet plastic helmets. Or the rumble of sore joints and muscles as I become more aware of my body. I have more muscle and there is a certain hardness to my forearms and legs. The high school softness has been replaced by a road map of veins and cords. I look around and see the others, Kong, the Shed, Chernak, and Bam Bam, all of them, looking at their bodies with pride, thankful for having made it through another practice. Then I think about how it felt when Robeson crumpled under my chop—how I'm a motherfucker. His howl. And taking the shot from Reems, pushing myself off the turf because I had to.

Before I can get my pads off, Harkens steers me off to the weight room.

"Coach Roe tells me I'm to take some of the piss out of your rope. Says there was a little incident during warm-up laps, something about you playing kung fu on Robeson's knee joint."

"I don't hear it from him?" I ask.

"Chain of command. Shit rolls downhill, Riley, so open up and say ahh," Harkens says. "Take off your pads and tell me what happened."

I tell him about the bump and the glare and how I ambushed Robeson on lap three.

"You fucked up, Riley. You've got to pick your spots. Know what I mean?"

I nod.

"Can't say I wouldn't have done the same, but if you want to be a sniper then you have to learn to live with the consequences. Eat it or beat it. Now, it's my job to make you eat it—you want to start on legs or chest first?"

"Is it going to hurt?" I ask, dropping my helmet in the corner.

"Like you wouldn't believe."

By the time I get to the squat machine my forearms look like balloons and my chest feels like it's been plugged into a wall socket. Harkens doesn't even bother to count off, instead every exercise is done to failure, the weight dropped by ten pounds and then to failure again, until I can barely breathe or hold my arms straight and the pain feels like somebody's mainlining ice water into my veins.

Afterward, while I'm sitting in the ice bath, Robeson hobbles over to me on crutches, his knee in an air cast. The air smelling of rubbing alcohol and Icy Hot.

He stands there, breathing through his nose like he wants to say something or hit me, his black face smooth and calm.

I tell him I'm sorry.

"I had it coming," he says. "Besides, looks like you paid plenty and the knee's nothing. Sprain is all. I'll be back in two or three weeks."

"It was a shitty thing to do," I say, rubbing my blown lat muscles.

Robeson's mouth splits into a toothy smile as he leans his face into mine. I still half expect him to lean back and smack me with a crutch.

"Forget about it—I'm the one that went and played Billy Joe Bad-Ass," he says. "Got my black ass put in a sling because of it and by a frosh, no less."

"You mean the knee?"

Robeson shakes his head, easing himself onto one of the cracked vinyl benches next to me.

"Fuck yeah, the knee," he says, pointing at the cast. "I'll get two weeks, three if I'm lucky. Then it's back to the grind."

"You mean you're happy about it?"

"Elated. As far as injuries go, it's a good one. I'll walk again, no knives or weeks of physical therapy. It looks bad enough so the coaches won't ride me about being soft and best of all it didn't hurt all that bad. I mean not now, except for these fucking crutches."

"I still don't get you," I say. "You're happy I fucked your knee up?"

"Look, man. You're only a frosh and you probably think this is the greatest thing since eating pussy. Three meals a day, get your mug on television, make the parents proud and all that crap. But let me tell you that for some of us this sucks, especially if you're like me and there's no way you're ever going to start."

"What do you mean like you? You don't know shit about me," I say, looking him over.

"You're right, I don't—but as for me? It just ain't in the cards. Besides, I don't really want it bad enough and after you've made up your mind about something like that, well it's just not going to hap- pen. The coaches know when you've quit. You think Roe spends all that time up in the tower staring at the fucking sky? No, man, he's waiting for someone to distinguish themselves, become a Man of Con- sequence. A player. Same way he can spot somebody like me."

"You're second-string, maybe next year you start," I say, stepping out of the ice bath.

"Second-string my ass. I'm an endangered fucking species—a brother who don't really want to play ball. And I'm sticking around for the education?—fucks with their heads—know what I mean?"

I nod and he laughs. "Right now, Riley, you are what is known as an unknown quantity—they're waiting on your ass to do something."

"What do you mean?"

"Do the math. There are ninety of us, more than a hundred if you count the walk-ons. Only about thirty of us can ever play. That leaves practice and the sidelines for the rest of us. So they try to get rid of a few—cut some scholarships if they decide we're fucking up in school and we aren't ever going to contribute to the team."

"I thought they couldn't do that."

"Scholarship's one year renewable—that's why you've got to be looking down the road a piece," Robeson says. "Start looking at your options, decide what team you're on, whether or not you're going to be the fucker or fuckee."

"What options?"

"Look, my friend, if you don't six and you aren't a starter you've got to make it through."

"You mean deep-six?"

"Yeah, like fuck yourself up, get injured, quit—whatever the fuck you want to call it. If you don't six you've got four years of wobbling around out there on the field. What are you gonna do? You can't dog it—you've got to make it look good. Show them you don't suck one hundred percent or haven't sprouted a fucking pussy. But it gets old, man, real old and your body starts to go. Little things like lumps or bruises that won't go away, your back hurts all the time. What do you do?"

I shrug, "I don't know."

"If you quit—you lose your scholarship."

"Well, why not just suck it up and play?"

"Riley, I'm going to let you in on a little secret. Some of us aren't ever going to play. Take Jack Lousma for example. Heavily recruited: hits like a motherfucker, good feet, smart, and all that crap. Only thing is he'll never play a down because he smarted off to Roe his freshman year and then had the misfortune of dislocating his shoulder. Now he's third on the depth chart. No matter how good a spring ball the poor bastard has or how many tackles he makes in practice, he'll never have his number called in the big show—it's called the High School Hotshot to College Zero Shuffle."

"That's Jack Lousma," I say.

"Could be you, could be me. If you ain't going to be a star you've got to do it with style and watch you don't fuck up."

"How many guys that happen to?"

"Look, man—you're white—you've got that going for you. You think they gonna yank some white dude's scholarship and piss off his family and high school coach?"

"It doesn't matter," I say.

Robeson leans into me until I can smell his breath.

"Fuck it don't matter. Some nigger busts his knee for good—you think they're going to carry his black ass for four years when they can cut him and get the scholarship back? Fuck no, man—they ship him back to the hood. No harm, no foul and when they go back next year, waving around scholarships, ain't nobody going to think twice about grabbing one."

"I'm from Cleveland," I say.

"Full of white boys," he says, laughing.

I shake my head no.

He smiles, "Then we're cool—you understand my situation."

"What did you mean about not starting?"

"It's like this, Riley—there are twenty other guys just like Lousma that for some reason or another will never play, no matter what happens. Shit, half the fucking team could get wiped out in a bus crash or something and I'd still be riding the pine. Everybody here's good. That's the facts of life, man. Not everybody can be a star. Throw in the ass-kissing factor and things are fucked. It pays to go with the flow. Just take a look at the guys who're starting. Look for similarities— what they do on and off the field—and you'll see what I mean. The whole thing's a game, who plays and when, it's not really about talent, dig?"

"Why did you bump me if you don't give a shit?" I ask.

"Coach Treller was watching and I suppose it was a meager attempt on my part to make some frosh think I was a Man of Consequence."

"What about when I clipped you?"

"Like I said, I had it coming and now I take a little vacation, hang with my girlfriend, live a little. Look, man, I should thank you."

"Don't," I tell him. I look at the clock on the wall. Two and a half hours after Harkens let me flop on the weight room floor and I'm just now getting the use of my legs back.

"I don't want to be the one to pop your cherry, but all I'm saying is that you have to keep your eyes open. Jerry Q says you're a sharp guy. It don't pay to be smart. If you want to play for the coach and all that crap, your best bet's to play stupid like your boy Himes, do what you're told and become one of the 'fellas.' Coaches eat that shit up."

"I've been acting dumb all my life," I tell him in my best Jethro voice.

"Keep it up and you'll go far, just don't let it become you."

"We cool?" I say.

"Man, Riley, what the fuck do you think?"

"We just had one of those Lifesaver moments."

Robeson laughing, "Yeah, man. We cool."

I nod and watch him crutch out of the room and into the dark hallway. On the way out one of the towel boys slides me a sandwich and Coke and tells me I'd better hustle back to the dorms.

I feel strange walking up to the dorm alone, Robeson's advice going through my head. I'm wondering what team I'm on—what side I'd choose—and suddenly all that crazy love I had for the game after Reems creamed me is gone. It's just football. A game.

EIGHT

When the students begin showing up at the dorms, the streets swell with vans, station wagons, and beat-up family sedans, packed tight with cardboard boxes and suitcases. Students step out of their cars, high-fiving and catching up on the summer spent apart while tired-looking parents stretch and yawn, eyeing the boxes of clothes, stereos, futons, blankets, computer boxes, and desks. Fathers stand next to their daughters, hands trembling, as we hang out the windows of the dormitory, watching.

"Size," Napalm says, his face drinking in the activity from the window. "All those students looking at us like we're zoo animals or overgrown freaks."

"I wonder what it feels like," I say, pointing at the line of students.

"Like what feels like?"

"You know, normal, Napalm. Go to school to go to school."

"They're thinking the same thing," Napalm says. "Everybody wants what they don't have."

Nick, Napalm's roommate, a wideout from Connecticut, comes bursting into the room.

"We got pussy at twelve o'clock," he says.

Both Napalm and I look at Nick, his face a smooth plate of white skin, blue eyes and thin lips that seem free of original thought or introspection.

"Oh, really, Nick," Napalm says.

"Hot Chinese chicks, redheads, twins, and tons of blondes," Nick says, adjusting his collar and running a hand through his hair. "Shit, I even saw a black chick I'd fuck silly."

"You're a real humanitarian, Nick," I tell him, winking at Napalm. "Nobel Prize material, don't you think?"

Napalm grins, "Go slap your moves on them, Nick."

Nick's smooth face wrinkles for a minute. "Better than sitting in here with you two homos talking bullshit," he says, stomping out of the room.

Napalm turns to me and shakes his head. "You know what I hate about Nick?"

"That he gets away with it?"

He nods and we sit for a while, watching the courtyard, listening to the snatches of conversation that float up the wall like static while I tell Napalm about Robeson's advice.

"How come I don't know who he is?" Napalm asks.

I shrug. "You think he's full of shit?"

"Maybe, maybe not. He's right about not being a star. You tell some of these motherfuckers they're never going to start they'd have a fucking nervous breakdown."

"Himes would cease to exist," I say.

"And that's precisely our problem—we don't live and die for football. Sign me up with Robeson," Napalm sighs. "I'm beginning to wonder what the hell I've gotten myself into."

"You serious?" I say.

"What the fuck do you think? Coach U's convinced I'm a sack of shit."

"But this is the big time," I say.

"Big time what?"

"Football," I say. "Where I come from this is it—I mean I've made it."

Napalm sighs. "You start getting rah-rah on me and I'm going to have to kick your Cleveland ass. You're too smart to swallow their crap without tasting it first."

I smack my lips. "I'd like to thank my personal savior Jesus Christ for allowing me to play this great game of football and my parents—for, well—being my parents . . ."

Napalm laughs and then stops. "I'm fucked, but you're fucked worse," he says.

I can only nod.

After practice Coach Roe calls a full-team meeting and lectures us about assimilation and how we're to begin classes, etc. Several hands shoot up to ask what assimilation means.

"Into the student body," Coach Roe says.

Everybody starts cracking jokes, even the assistant coaches get into it. We are a week away from our opening game and we've survived double sessions which entitles us to a little looseness here and there.

Coach Roe lets it go for a few minutes before raising his hand for silence and blasting us with another lecture on the evils of women. Kong nudges me.

"Here we go again," he grumbles, grabbing his crotch.

"Women are fine and wonderful creatures," Coach Roe says. "However, there are some women who look at you and see stars. They will do *anything* to be with you and in the end they'll drag you down, put weak thoughts in your head, and before you know it you're out sniffing daisies with the rest of the longhaired Romeos. Now, I'm not saying you should avoid the opposite sex, just be on the watch is all. Women take and as Michigan ball-playing studs we got nothing to give except pain and misery to our opponents."

I look over at Kong, watching as he mouths every word of Coach Roe's speech.

"The same goes for what I like to call instant friends," Coach Roe says, scanning the room a minute, pacing. "Childers, stand up and tell us about instant friends."

Childers stands and blankly recites that an instant friend is anybody who befriends you because you are a football player: handicappers, gamblers, drug dealers, blackmailers, reporters looking to tarnish Michigan's reputation, etc.

Coach Roe interrupts him, "Can women be instant friends?"

"Yes sir," Childers says.

Roe smiles and tells him to sit down.

"Any questions?" Roe asks, fixing his rock-jawed gaze on the room.

After a minute Whigger raises his hand and asks, "What if, like, we're engaged to be married?"

The room falls silent as everybody takes stock of Whigger, who after being made fun of and tortured for his "black" talk, snappy clothes, and horrible unrhythmic attempts at rap has been exiled into a racial no-man's-land. He has become, for lack of a better offer, his own best friend. After hearing Whigger butcher Run D.M.C., Monte James, a.k.a. Big Money, told him he'd better start acting like a white boy or else he was going to put a large black hurt on Whigger's ass and make him white as dice.

After that, Whigger did straighten up his act. He let his fade grow out and started hanging around Jimmy from Jersey's room trying to groove on Springsteen.

I think about this as I check out Big Money shaking his pumpkin-shaped head at Whigger's question.

Coach Roe makes his way to the back of the room to get a closer look at Whigger, whose real name is Donald Marvin.

"Son," Roe screams. "What in San Hell are you talking about?"

Roe snaps a yardstick across Whigger's desk.

"My girlfriend," Whigger says, his voice cracking.

"Girlfriend? Frosh aren't allowed to have *girlfriends.* Hell, when I was

your age all I thought about was football. Women were a distraction. I didn't have time for a girlfriend." He stops to shake his head in disbelief. "I must be failing in my coaching duties if you've got time and energy for women. I mean, son, we're here to go to the Rose Bowl, anything less and I have failed—we have *failed.*"

Whigger just sort of slumps there with this goofy look on his face, listening as Roe sentences him to a week of extra workouts with Harkens.

Roe catches me smiling.

"Riley," he says. "You find any of this funny?"

I tell him no and Kong nudges me again.

"Are you in love like Donald?"

"Yes sir," I say, then pause. "I am in love with football."

Roe calms down a bit. "Good answer, Riley. Maybe you ought to tutor Donald on his priorities."

I nod and Roe moves on, letting the room quiet down before launching into his game plan for our home opener and announcing the travel squad. Purty's the only frosh to make the traveling team.

Afterward, Jimmy taps me on the shoulder as a whole group of us wander out into the parking lot, ready to begin the walk up to the dorm.

"Travel team? I don't get it. The game's at home," he says.

"They stay in a hotel the night before the game and get special meals, watch movies, like *Rambo, Rio Bravo, Patton,* or *Rocky,*" Napalm says.

Jimmy from Jersey's face drops slightly. "We're like being left behind?"

"Depends on how you look at it," I say.

"What do you have in mind, Riley?" Smitty asks.

Napalm says, "What he means is that they'll be locked up in some hotel room and we're free to roam."

"Even the coaches?" Smitty asks.

"Even the coaches," I say.

"Party," Jimmy screams.

"Maybe if you scream a little louder we can invite the coaches," Napalm says. Jimmy flips him off.

"Let's call it a get-together and keep it to ourselves," I say. We shake on it and walk silently up the hill.

Later on Napalm and I are sitting around my room, playbooks propped open on our laps in case an assistant coach should stick his nose into the room and ask what the hell Napalm's doing out of his assigned room. Phil sits behind us, sprawled on his bed, dip in mouth, staring at Sally vacantly, listening to us talk.

"Hard to believe we've got four more years of this shit," Napalm says.

"What do you mean?" I ask.

"I mean, I hate it already. I feel like I'm being watched all the time."

"You are," I say. "The Eye of Michigan is upon you."

"Laugh all you want. I bet you half the fucking team buys into that crap. Not me, not for one minute. You know what Coach U told me the other day when I missed that block on an off-tackle slant?"

"Soar like an eagle and shake like a dog?"

Napalm laughs. "No, man. I heard that one though. He tells me that I have to want the block, that I should be able to *see* the block in my head."

"How the hell do you *see* a block in your head?"

"He's into that visualization shit. You think that's bad, I heard Coach Terrazzo telling the receivers to close their eyes and imagine the ball was a big juicy tit," Napalm says.

"Somebody should be taking notes on this," I say.

"I'm beginning to think that it pays to act like some stupid fucking animal," he says.

Phil lets out a grunt from the bed, like he's got something to say.

"Does that mean you don't ever want to start?" I say.

"It means I want to get through this. My old man would have a fit if I quit. What about you?"

"Undecided," I say, trying to imagine what my parents would say or if it would throw the old man into an even deeper funk.

"The coaches like you—you've got that going for you. Me—I'm a whipping boy. I'm the fat kid."

"Coach U swears he's going to make a man out of you," I say.

"I hope not. Let me guess, he's smacked his wife a time or two. His son, let's call him Junior, is one of those jarhead freaks out to prove something to his old man, by joining the Rangers or Navy SEALs. And the three most important men in Coach U's life?"

"John Wayne," I offer.

"Of course and . . ."

"Patton?"

Napalm thinks a minute, then nods. "Seems obvious, but don't forget his daddy, who probably taught him everything there is to know about how a real man should act."

"You forgot God," I say.

"That too," Napalm says, nodding in agreement. "But I bet you he refers to him as the Big Man."

"You guys," Phil says, unable to hold himself any longer.

"Can it, Phil," I say.

Phil gives me his version of a bad-ass stare before returning to his playbook.

"Sounds like you've got Coach U figured out," I say.

"And I'm supposed to let him make me a man? Mold my fucking life?"

"What about me?"

Napalm looks at me. "All you've got to do is keep your mouth shut and step up to the plate when the time comes."

"What if it's not that easy?"

He considers this a moment. "Well then, you're fucked."

———

What passes for bonding happens in Jimmy's room after practice. Eight of us huddled around the Trinitron watching *Monday Night Football,* waiting for one of the coaches to roust us and tell us to hit the sack. After the Broncos run the score to 21 to zip, Fuckhead switches the channel to a rerun of *Three's Company.* I'm on the floor with Napalm and Smitty, a two-liter bottle of Coke between us that Smitty picks up every minute or so and slurps out of loudly. Whigger's up on one of the beds trying to talk white with Yo Joe and Vezio. Sleazio saying, "Rock or country fucking music. Just pick one and—I'll even loan you some tapes, 'cause you can't go around listening to Michael Jackson. Even the brothers hate that vinyl-pants-wearing motherfucker."

"I'd definitely do the blonde," Smitty says, pointing at Chrissy on *Three's Company.*

"No shit," I say. "Who wouldn't?"

"Question is," Napalm says, "do you give Janet, or whatever the hell her name is, the old steel pole?"

"Fuck yeah," Whigger says. "Matter of fact she'd be a tiger. See, nobody pays attention to her, but I tell you what, you get her out of them nappy-looking slacks and she'd put a dick-lock on you so bad."

Jimmy stares at Whigger until he stops talking and sits, hands on his crotch, hustling his balls back and forth.

Yo Joe starts complaining, "Put the game back on."

"What are you, gay or something? We're having ourselves a little philosophical discussion. Fuck Elway, fuck the Broncos and fuck *Monday Night Football,*" Fuckhead says.

Vezio gets up, grabbing his can of Copenhagen off the desk. "I'd bang Mrs. Roper," he says.

"Sleazio, you are one brain-damaged, short-bus-riding retard," Napalm says. "If you're handing out charity fucks, why stop there, I mean, Jack's got a nice ass and while you're at it Mr. Roper could use a little lubrication vacation."

Unfazed, Vezio continues, "I'll tell you why, first off you know she's horny. I mean you never see those two other chicks acting horny. What do they do? They march around in bikinis and pajamas all day, I mean you'd think you might see some high-beam action once in a while, right? Instead it's like they got Frigidaires in their pants or something."

"Janet's always got a camel toe going," Smitty says. "Even in slacks."

Vezio raising his hands. "Fuck the camel toe, I'm talking about getting laid."

Napalm makes as if he's going to puke. "Vez, you're making me sick to my stomach."

"Okay, then you got the experience factor," Vezio says.

Smitty gives him the thumbs-up. "There you go, Vez, a chick's got to know dick to fuck it properly."

"And that's where you come in?" Yo Joe asks.

Vezio nods, "I'd take my chances."

"That's still some faulty fucked-up reasoning, Vez," I say.

"Listen to Riley," Jimmy says. "Coming from a motherfucker who takes a chick's IQ before he fucks her. I mean you got your priorities all whacked the fuck around. I'm not saying Vezio's right, but at least he's talking tits and ass."

"You've seen pictures of Heather," I say. "She look like Mrs. Fucking Roper?"

"Yeah, Riley. She's got a set of tits on her. I'll give you that, but you can play speed bag with those until they fall off—the question is are you getting any?"

"I'm getting it."

"How come I haven't seen a picture?" Fuckhead asks.

"No shit you're getting it?" Jimmy says.

"It's good," I say.

Smitty asks, "How good?"

"Good enough, that's all you need to know, Smitty."

"Come on, Riley. You can't get us all worked up and just say it's good. Does she swallow?" Vezio asks. "Because five gets you ten Mrs. Roper sucks, fucks, and cooks a damn good omelet."

"She swallows," I say.

Fuckhead high-fives me before I can say anything else.

Smitty sits up, pointing at the television. "We've got camel toe."

Fuckhead says, "I bet half you motherfuckers haven't even seen a pussy let alone smelled one."

"Whatcha you talking about, white boy?" Whigger says.

Jimmy cracks him on the head with his palm and Whigger blushes.

"What did I tell you?" Jimmy says. "White—think, white mother-fucker."

"Leave him alone," I say.

"Fuck you, Riley," Jimmy says. "I'm trying to help him."

On the television Mrs. Roper's trying to grab Jack's ass. Vezio starts grunting and has to spit out his chew. "Look, man, you guys need any more proof?" Vezio says.

"She's all yours," Napalm says. "Report back."

"Vez," Yo Joe says. "I think you'd have the market cornered if you were to start bagging old ladies. Like a service, man, you could set yourself up as a charity."

"Shit," Vezio says. "Let me tell you a story."

Everybody groans.

"Back in Oklahoma," he says, "I was dating this chick for like two months . . ."

Smitty interrupts, "What did she look like?"

Vezio shrugs his shoulders.

"Come on," Napalm says. "We need visuals. If you're going to tell a story you've got to give us something to visualize."

"Big tits?" Fuckhead asks.

"Oranges, man," Vezio says. "You know, just enough. But her ass . . ." Vezio pauses to spit.

"Yeah?" Smitty shouts.

"It was nice."

"Nice? Come on, Vez, you can do better than that," Fuckhead says. "What was it like?"

"It's not the point," Vezio says. "Let's just say she had a nice one, okay?"

"What's this got to do with fucking Mrs. Roper?" Fuckhead asks, pointing at the television. Shot of Chrissy in red string bikini watering the plants and Jack falling over the couch.

"You guys are confusing me," he says. "I'm trying to tell a goddamn story."

"Come on, we don't got all night," Smitty says.

"Okay," Vezio says. "So I'm dating this chick, right. Two months and I'm racking up a big zero in the bare tit department. I mean we're talking nothing. I'm the big stud football player and she's captain of the cheerleading squad, you'd think it would be a regular fucking cack fest. But no. I'm the only guy not getting laid. Fuck, even the glue eaters and burnouts are getting some."

Smitty flaps his hands at Vezio, impatient, ready for the good parts.

"So she's got this hot mom. A few wrinkles, but still pretty fucking hot. I start thinking about her—how she's got this real bitchy voice, that kind of turns me on, and how her daughter's giving me the stiff-arm every time I go for a little b.t.—I mean I'm so horny I'd eat her underpants."

"Yeah?" Smitty says.

"I'm getting to it," Vezio says. "So one day I'm waiting for Jeanie, that was her name, to pick me up after practice. Instead her mom shows up and tells me Jeanie's sick with a stomach flu and wants to drive me home. I get in the car and what happens? The minute I get in the car I get wood."

Jimmy gets up from his chair, punching the air. "Did you fuck her?"

"I set my duffel on my lap, which as you know only makes things worse," Vezio says.

"I hear you there," Fuckhead hoots.

From the floor Smitty says, "I'm getting kind of horny."

We all scoot away from Smitty a few inches.

Jimmy screams at Vezio, "Come on, did you fuck her?"

"Okay, so then she starts in on me with that voice, asking me if I mind she runs an errand first. I tell her no problem. I'm ready to cum right there. So we ride around a little bit before stopping at the fucking grocery store, but get this, she parks back by a Dumpster and puts her hand on my knee and says, 'Craig, you ever wonder about older women?' "

Vezio pauses, looks around the room, nobody's watching television, all eyes are on him and he lets go this little smile.

Finally Smitty's drawl breaks the silence. "You gonna leave us hanging?"

"Did you fuck her?" Whigger asks.

Vezio keeps grinning.

"He's full of shit," Fuckhead says. "You guys believe this crap?"

"Swear to God," Vezio says, raising his hands.

"How was it?" Jimmy asks.

"The thing about older women is they got like this greasy skin, you know, sort of like sweat, but better. You kind of slide around on them," he says. "But the fucking . . ."

"Come on, Sleazio," Jimmy says, nearly out of his mind.

"Oh, it was good, because there's none of that messing around foreplay crap. I mean she knew what she liked and how she liked it. It was like being the fuckee and not the fucker."

I take another long pull of Coke, look around at the door, then check my watch, wondering when some coach will bang on the door and tell us to break up the party.

"Okay," Napalm says. "Now, I'm not saying I wouldn't have done it, providing you're telling the truth. But I still don't get how you arrive at fucking Mrs. Roper."

"He already told you," Whigger says, licking his lips.

"You catch a disease?" Fuckhead asks.

"She was married, asshole," Vezio says.

"Yeah and you were her first. Come on, Vez," I say.

"You guys are just jealous," he says.

Smitty passes around some potato chips, grumbling about our lack of beer. Then Napalm launches into the story about how his first fuck sat on his dick and nearly broke it in two. I've already heard the story so I sit back and let him tell it.

Coach Peters interrupts with two swift knocks before swinging the door wide open.

"Aw-right," he says. "Get your asses to bed before I start kicking them. You guys need your beauty rest."

We all get up and exit past Coach Peters as he biffs each of us on the back of the neck and says something smart and hard-ass about how it's no wonder we're always dogging it. I walk down the hallway feeling slightly stupid about boasting of Heather. When what I wanted to tell them was that beyond all the sex she's just a trophy, that she likes Myrtle, uses hair spray, and won't read the books I get her and she loves me the way you feel when the sun hits your face, blind and happy. And I think I'm better than her. That's the fucked-up part.

NINE

"You see any you like?" Jimmy asks.

We are sitting on the front steps of the dorm watching the students. It's our first day without morning practice and I'm beginning to feel like a human being. The aches and pains are now at a manageable level and the presence of other people on campus has lightened everybody's mood.

"Any what?" I ask.

"Riley, you blind? The women. I mean I haven't even thought about women. Just football."

"Well, now that you mention it." In fact there are hundreds and I'm getting this sick feeling down in my gut, just looking at them.

Rope ambles down the steps and sits, stretching his long dark legs out into the strip of sun coming through the cottonwood tree that shades the front of the dormitory.

"You white boys really think you got a chance with these women?" he asks.

Jimmy from Jersey gets this sour look on his face as if he wants to say something to Rope, but doesn't.

"A multitude of women," I say.

Rope clicks his tongue. "You know what, Riley, you say some

fucked-up shit. I mean, nobody understands what the fuck you're saying half the time. Why don't you talk like the rest of the guys?"

"I suppose I should assimilate with the fellas. Is that it?" I say.

"Rope's right," Jimmy says.

"Talking like Joe Bookworm ain't going to score you none of this
coed pussy."

"More for you, then," I say.

Rope just smiles, smacking his lips. "Ain't that right as rain."

This gangly-looking kid with glasses and pleated pants shuffles up to
us on the steps, holding a bright yellow orientation folder under one
arm, asking, "You guys ballplayers?"

"No, man. We in the premed program," Rope says.

"Come on, guys," he says, blushing.

"Sure, we're on the team," I say.

"The field hockey team," Jimmy says. "Want to see our sticks?"

Both he and Rope start laughing.

"You guys going to kick State's ass this year?" the kid asks.

Jimmy says, "Before or after we kick your ass?"

One of the kid's buddies yells something at him from across the
courtyard and using this as an excuse he stumbles away from us, face
red, folder dangling from one hand.

"You didn't have to say that to him," I say.

Rope high-fives Jimmy.

"We didn't, but it was fun," Jimmy says.

"It was fun," I repeat.

"Don't even start on me, Riley. Like you're some kind of Boy
Scout or something. That's how they expect us to behave."

"I just find it interesting," I say. "You always do what's expected of
you?"

They let it drop and we all watch as two girls walk across the street
in tie-dyed sundresses, light catching their hair as the taller one looks
over her shoulder at us and waves. They disappear behind a row of
minivans and for a few seconds all three of us stare, waiting for them to

emerge back into view. I look up into the sun and follow a jet trail that cuts the sky in half, trying not to think about Heather.

"Did you see that? It's like they know something," Jimmy says.

"They do know something," I say.

"What?"

Rope breaks in, "It's the black thing."

"Get the fuck out of here," Jimmy says. "She's white."

Rope just gives Jimmy this Zen monk look, eyes half-lidded. "If I wasn't so sore from Harkens, I'd come over there and kick your racist, hillbilly ass."

"All right," I say. "Everybody just calm down."

"Hillbilly? I'm from Jersey, you stupid fuck."

"No hillbilly, Klan motherfuckers in Jersey?" Rope asks.

Jimmy starts to push himself up.

"What Rope's saying is that there's a little fear and desire syndrome," I say, looking at Rope for some sort of nod.

"Fear and desire," Rope says, rolling the words like cigar smoke. "I like that, Riley, it's got a ring to it."

Jimmy looks at me as if I've just betrayed the white race.

"What the fuck does that mean?" Jimmy asks.

Rope leans up the step. "It's a black thing."

"I've never heard of that," Jimmy says. "But I got a white thing says you're full of shit and jive."

"Watch," Rope says, picking himself up off the steps and walking over to the nearest group of girls. We watch as Rope says something slick and they giggle amongst themselves, flipping their long hair.

Jimmy stares at Rope, then whispers to me, "What's wrong with you, man?"

I look at him like I don't know what the hell he's talking about.

Snatches of Rope's rap float across the cement to us as he focuses his attention on the tallest girl in the group, a long-faced blonde with delicate wrists and a crooked smile that sticks to her teeth. She shifts about nervously from foot to foot like a volleyball player getting ready to serve. Rope says something that makes her smile and she stares at his well-muscled arms before punching him lightly on the shoulder.

"I don't fucking believe this. So what if he gets some nigger lover's phone number? What does that prove?"

My enjoyment of watching Rope work his charm on the girl disappears when I look over at Jimmy, sitting in all of his ignorant glory, hands on crotch, squinting his stupid little pig eyes at Rope.

"Jersey boy, you're one ignorant fuck," I say, getting off the steps and walking back into the dorm. I look back over my shoulder before disappearing into the fluorescent haze and food smells of the dormitory to see Rope writing what I imagine is his phone number on her pale white palm.

When I knock, Napalm's just rolling out of bed. Nick lets me in and then goes back to standing in front of the mirror flipping his shirt collar up and down.

"Up or down?" Nick asks, pointing at his collar.

Napalm looks at me and groans. "Hey, Riley."

Nick demonstrates the look with the collar up and then down. I notice he's got a gold chain with a football helmet and his number hanging from it.

"I already told you, Nick, up means you're a fag. Ask Riley," Napalm says. "It's like this high sign or secret handshake."

"How come I never heard of it?" Nick says.

"I'm afraid he's right, Nick. It's like the earring thing," I say.

Nick flips his collar down. "It just doesn't look right."

"Go ahead, then, wear it up, see what happens," Napalm says, pulling on a pair of sweatpants.

"What the fuck am I doing taking advice from you two slobs?" Nick says, flipping the collar back up and pointing at his reflection in the mirror.

"You look kind of cute," I say.

"Cut it out, Riley," Nick says.

"No really, there's something about you I can't quite—"

"He's got a nice ass," Napalm says in his best lisp. "So fuckable."

Nick flips us off and stomps out of the room, his cologne dragging behind him like a ball and chain.

Napalm thanks me for scaring Nick away and pulls out a two-liter bottle of Faygo and some cold pizza.

"You pick out your classes yet?" I ask.

He shakes his head and pulls out a grease-stained class schedule.

"Nick says we've got to run everything by Roe. Says Roe told him what to take and who to take it with."

"They don't leave much to chance, do they?"

"It's all bullshit and lies. They want to know what you're taking, not because they give a shit, but because they don't want you to flag out."

I nod, "Seems kind of stupid."

"Jeter can't even fucking spell and I heard Bates trying to read the sports page yesterday and the motherfucker was mouthing the words."

"Then what about us?"

"It doesn't matter. It's one of those blanket things like study table. If one guy's a dumbshit, then we're all dumbshits."

"Phil says that Roe pulled out this big folder on him with all these test scores and shit and just dictated his class schedule to him."

"When do you see him?"

"At noon and I don't think he's going to like the classes I'm taking," I say.

"Let me see."

I show him my schedule: English 125, Classic Civilizations, Intro to Film and Video, and History of the Vietnam Conflict.

"You're right," he says. "I'd say you're in for a little corrective surgery." Then in his best Roe voice, John Wayne with a little George C. Scott as Patton, "That's just not how we do things around here, son."

A half an hour later I'm ushered into Roe's office and seated at a large table. Coach Roe sits to my right, pen in hand, ready to look at my class selections. To my left Len Raimy, the team's academic advisor, who according to Wolfie was a tailback on Roe's first Rose Bowl team, and no rocket scientist sits fumbling with a pile of folders.

Roe slaps me on the shoulder.

"You made it through double sessions, Riley. I didn't think you had it in you," Roe says.

Len snickers and chews on his salt-and-pepper mustache as Roe flips through a stack of manila folders, finds mine and slaps it on the desk. Len opens it and begins going through the contents clucking to himself and shaking his head while Roe gives me his student/athlete spiel.

"Let's see what classes you've chosen," Roe demands.

I slide my schedule across the table to him.

There's a good minute or two of dead silence before he pulls out a pen and shakes his head. I look up at the wall of pictures. Roe with the Lady's Club, Roe with the local Boy Scout troop, the Masons, Alumni Club, Press Club, etc. Grin plastered on his face, shoulders back and hand outstretched for a nice firm shake.

"There," Roe says, handing me back my schedule. All but one of my classes, English 125, have been red-inked out and replaced with others, Intro to Sports Management and Communications, Geology 101 (known as Rocks for Jocks, because the instructor's a die-hard football fan and gives any athlete an automatic B+), and Theories of Sports Refereeing. "You overshot yourself there, Riley. What you want to do is ease yourself into college life. Prove yourself, then I see no reason why you can't take one or two of these classes—off-season, of course."

Len glances down at the tangle of red cross-outs and class numbers and says what I imagine he says at every one of these meetings, "My job's to see to it that you stay eligible."

I feel my face redden as I look down at the classes Roe's chosen for me. I know it's useless to say anything or do anything except smile.

"Anything else, Riley? Coach U tells me you're a real comer, that offense suits you," Roe says, checking his watch. He taps Len on the shoulder.

Len pulls out a tablet, signs his name, says, "When you go to buy textbooks, give them this form and have them bill it to the football department."

Roe smiles proudly as if Len's just said something insightful. I get up to go, wadding the schedule in my pocket. When I'm at the door Roe reminds me about study table.

"No problem," I say.

Himes, who's been waiting outside the door, leaps up from his chair saying, "Do I smell an O-lineman?" Laughing at his own stupid joke and winking at the secretary, who lets out this trilling giggle.

"No, Himes, that would be the shit between your ears," I say.

His face goes suddenly blank. "Hey, man," he says. "Why did you have to jump all over me? I was just fooling."

Len pokes his face out the door and points at Himes. "It's Hime Time," he says.

"I'll see you in the Pits," Himes mumbles before high-fiving Len and barking like a dog. For some reason no one else in the office, the secretary, Len, even Coach Roe, finds Himes' behavior the least bit strange.

I don't know what's worse, watching a grown man call somebody Hime Time and high-five him like a nineteen-year-old kid or the fact that Himes'll probably take Roe's academic advice as if it were the word of God.

The secretary gives me one of those boys-will-be-boys smiles and goes back to her half-eaten jelly donut. The heavy oak door clicks shut and I can hear Coach Roe's laugh and Himes barking.

On my way out I drop Roe's revised class schedule in a trash can.

I go back to my room and call Stork in Cleveland. His mother says he's at work and that I should call in the evening but not too late because he's very tired. Her broken English reminds me of home and when I close my eyes I can almost see the gray skyline of Cleveland, taste the air (aluminum and car exhaust) and hear the lap of Lake Erie. I wonder how the time's passing for Stork. His last letter to me ended with "Job sucks. Cleveland one, good guys nothing." No word on where he's working or how long or if he ever got up the nerve to talk to one of the black chicks with the crazy, love-me names.

"You're going to get fried," Napalm says after I've told him about my plans to ignore Roe's "academic" advice and take the classes I want. We are walking down State Street on our way to practice. One week before the big game and already there are GO BLUE banners hanging off the overpass, dangling from office windows. Cars slow down, honk and wave at us, upperclassmen taunting us with the promise of a ride down to the practice facility.

"Fuck 'em," I say, shrugging my shoulders. "What can they do?"

Napalm crosses his eyes at me, "Gee, Riley, probably nothing. Take your fucking pick. Harkens? Morning mile until Christmas? Study table until you graduate?"

"Bring it on," I say.

"They're going to break you or else wait until you flunk a class, then they're going to fist-fuck you real good."

Deep down, I know that Napalm's rooting for me to take some sort of stand, even if it's with what classes I can or cannot take.

When we hit the parking lot and catch sight of the yellow doors leading to the locker room, Napalm looks at me and says, "I feel like this is all we ever do. Walk and practice."

I nod, trying to muster what little enthusiasm I can for the six hours we're about to spend, getting our ankles and wrists taped, watching game film, meetings, more meetings, practice, and finally into the loving arms of Harkens and his meathead henchmen where we'll be reduced to twitching biceps and blown pectorals. But the day happens and the week creeps by.

I begin to settle into routine, most of it football. But I manage to call Heather twice a week. And after Phil goes to sleep, I read until the book drops from my sore hands and my eyes close.

When I go to class people point at me and whisper, because I am usually the only jock in the class.

After lecture I wait in line to ask my Vietnam history professor questions and listen as he talks to slim-shouldered, soft-handed students. Girls with morning ponytails and no makeup, guys in hats. His words trail out long convoluted sentences as he cites recent readings chapter and verse until both his point and the question are a fuzzy mush of words. His long potato-shaped face bobbing and nodding to each simple question. When it's my turn I ask what he meant by "mutual assured destruction." He looks me over, noticing my thick neck and black turf shoes with my number written on them.

"MAD you mean?"

I nod and he fingers his beard a bit more.

"Perhaps your experience with sports can shed some light on the theory, hmm?"

"I know what it means," I say. "I just don't know how it makes any sense."

"Have you completed this week's reading?" he asks.

I nod and he goes on speaking slowly, mouthing the words, exaggerating the vowels, dropping sports metaphors before patting me on the shoulder and telling me that if I do the reading I'll understand the lecture.

"I already said that I've done the reading," I say.

"Right," he says, smiling. "I forgot. But perhaps you could apply the model of MAD to some mutually absurd aspect of your life, that no matter what you do—by that I mean any decisive action on your part—results in your destruction, yet there may come the day where action is your only choice, metaphorically speaking. Am I being unclear?"

"I get it," I say, and walk away.

This happens two more times. After that I stop waiting in line and act my part, by arriving late, sleeping and leaving early. I ace the first quiz, entertaining the fantasy that I've somehow confused him, put a mindfuck on him.

The other guys on the team tell me that it's a good idea to let the professor know that I'm a football player.

"They go easier on you that way," the Shed says. "If that don't work tell them you can get tickets and if you don't get any satisfaction go to office hours and stand over their desk and breathe real hard like you're going to kick their ass if they don't give you the grade you want."

Most of the guys follow the upperclassmen's lead and go to class when they feel like it, get groupies to write papers for them. Not me. I am on a mission to walk into Roe's office, toss my grades on his desk and let him tell me I should be taking Rocks for Jocks.

All of our talk centers around the team. Most of the other frosh sit around for hours analyzing every word and move of the coaching staff, trying to get a read on where they stand on the almighty depth chart and how many years it'll be before they start, if ever. Napalm and I sit up some nights talking about the crazy people on the team and all the sick and twisted shit that now seems normal. How Fred Freeman, who's been suspended once for pissing dirty, holds clinics in his apartment on beating the Whiz Quiz—Visine bottle of your girlfriend's urine stuffed in jock, two flecks of Drano under your fingernail (place finger in stream of piss), drink one bottle of apple cider vinegar, two gallons of cranberry juice to flush the system. Eat a bottle of aspirin.

How Bam Bam's back muscles are so big he gets kidney-sized boils where his shoulder blades meet. Before practice the trainers heat the boils with warm compresses until they explode like flesh-filled land mines.

Or the Shed, who can drink forty-two beers in one sitting and still make it back to his room.

How Wolfie hasn't showered since the first week of double sessions. His hair looks wet and he has pimples up and down his arms. How, once when he was pissed at his roommate for drinking the last beer, he took a shit in his bed and proceeded to wipe his ass on every article of the guy's clothing. He has a pit bull named Einstein who's trained to bite blacks and gays.

"They smell funny," Wolfie says when asked how the dog knows.

Bates has begun keeping a hit list in his locker and last week he erased his number three man, Jelton, with a spear to the back that sent Jelton twitching to the training room on a maple back board. I'm number ten on his list. His reason: I cut in front of him at training table one night and scooped up the last of the rigatoni, an event I have no recollection of. On the field I avoid him, hoping he will drop me from the list in favor of a new entry. Surprisingly enough Himes is absent from the list.

Brad Calvert, last year's All–Big Ten safety, is in a complete body cast. He says he'll be back next year and every once in a while he wheels himself out onto the practice field when one of the coaches is trying to dredge up some inspirational speech about playing hurt.

Then there's Ackley, who has to be shot up with a nail-thick cortisone needle in all of his toes before he can practice or play. Trainers pin his legs still by sitting on them as Doc A works the needle in and out of the joint. You can hear him moaning from the taping room.

And Kong, the best pro prospect Coach U has produced in years, who can push his dick and balls back into his stomach. Then parade around the locker room like some giant, blockheaded woman called Kongarella. He bench-presses 425 pounds, has a girlfriend/groupie named Sue who he swears he's never fucked. "Only blow jobs," he says, pointing to his bad back.

We spend seven hours a day with football, staring at game film, going over plays on chalkboards, and having team meetings where Coach Roe brings in people to lecture us about our lifestyle. We get the safe-sex lecture from Doc A. And a woman named Gladys, from the School of Social Work, lectures us on gender sensitivity and racism while the coaches sit behind her smirking at the way she lifts up on her toes to reach the top of the blackboard.

"Erase stereotypes," she says, tapping the chalk against the board.

Jim Waters jaws at us about academic success and tips for more effective study habits. Afterward we are given a reading comprehension test and told that we need more study table.

Hard-on Hart spews his time management spiel at us—how we should block out our days, set aside hours and minutes. Then Roe has him hold up his daily planner.

"Every minute's accounted for," Hart says proudly.

The assistant coaches seem to know everything we do with our free time. There are spies, who report back to the coaches when ballplayers are spotted at a bar, strip club, or hanging out in front of the liquor store. When we jump class and spend the day watching soap operas in our room, ordering takeout pizza and burritos, Hart or Treller gives us hell about it at practice and threatens to tell Roe.

When Coach Roe wants to see you they send a trainer to your room or an assistant coach to knock on your door at sunrise. If you don't answer, they key the door.

During the first week of classes, Ant awoke to a pounding at his door, decided to stay in bed and ignore it. Two minutes later he heard a key rattling in the lock and before he knew it Hart was standing front and center staring at Ant and a groupie named Sleepy Sarah.

TEN

Classes break up the monotony. Nobody says anything to me about my schedule. The rest of the guys go off to class together, lugging empty knapsacks, their pockets full of Power Bars, bananas, and Tylenol Threes. At training table everybody jokes about their cake classes and I play right along.

Jimmy from Jersey, who I now despise almost as much as Himes, thinks I'm one of his best buddies and can't stop talking about the party we're going to have when the traveling team goes to the hotel. Smitty's already bought a bottle of whiskey and Napalm thinks we should invite anybody who wants to come.

"What do you mean anybody?" Jimmy says.

"Students," Napalm says. "We don't wanna have a dick farm."

Jimmy smiles. "Good fucking idea."

By the end of the week everybody in the dormitory knows who we are. For most of us it's our size that makes us stick out. The smaller players, kickers, backs, and walk-ons, who want to be noticed wear warm-ups with the words FOOTBALL or PROPERTY OF printed in large yellow letters across the front.

Then there are the shoes.

Everybody wears their black turf shoes to class. Our numbers scrawled on the white Nike swoosh by Rotten Bobby Alvarez, the equipment manager who sits behind his blue plywood counter reading *Chic* and *Hustler,* screaming about tits and ass. Rotten Bobby's thirty-five years old, has crooked coffee-stained teeth, beer gut, and just a few wisps of hair left on the back of his head that look like leeches clinging for dear life. His skin is a dull gray color. Sometimes I hear him complaining to the coaches how come they don't recruit more Mexicans. They laugh, pat him on the back and tell him to have one of his towel boys see about the locker room.

He says things like "We're gonna slide State ten fucking inches of premium, USDA, maize and blue cock—Johnny Holmes style."

Napalm's theory as to the existence of Rotten Bobby is that he's the necessary fuckup who, despite his appearance and profanity, does an A1 job. He makes the coaches feel good about themselves when they look at him drooling over his porn mag collection, talking about chicks who love dildos or how we are going to gang-bang State this year.

After practice Rotten Bobby comes into the locker room screaming at me for forgetting to turn in my laundry bag for the week.

"What do I have to do, Riley?" Rotten Bobby says.

"Hey, Bobby," Wolfie yells. "You a tit or thigh man?"

"Don't distract me. Can't you see I'm trying to teach the frosh something?"

But Bobby goes over to Wolfie anyways and leaves me standing in front of my locker with my neck hurting, grinding bone against bone.

"You're catching it today," Napalm says.

"Fuck it," I say. "He's just doing his job."

Napalm nods. "I'm not arguing with you there, it's just a little bit screwed up for the coaches to be preaching all this clean-living bullshit and to have someone like Rotten Bobby around."

"Paradox," I say.

Fuckhead looks at me. "Good fucking word. Man, Riley, some-times you say some primo shit—let me shake your hand."

I let Fuckhead dangle as Himes comes around the corner, slack-jawed, glaring like some pissed-off catatonic.

"You talking mumbo jumbo again?" he says.

Napalm starts laughing and sticks his head into his locker. Steam from the showers billows out around our feet and Dante Roicheau, this fast-as-fuck wideout from New Orleans, is singing "The Banana Boat Song" in the shower stalls, his voice echoing out into the room.

"Fuckhead and I here were just discussing paradox as it relates to Rotten Bobby—care to comment?"

Himes drops his towel, his eyes going cold even though he has no idea what the fuck I'm talking about.

"You think you're better than everybody else, don't you?" Himes growls.

"Not everybody," I say. "Just . . ."

Himes smacks a locker and by this time several others have gathered around us, sensing a fight.

I see Himes' arms twitch, as his hands curl into fists. His entire body dotted with lavender bruises as Rotten Bobby wheels his cart down our aisle yelling, "Fuck 'em. Fuck 'em all. Come on, you cunts, get fucked, get sucked, bend right over backwards and take it up the ass."

Kong pads by on his way to the shower. "Get him," he whispers.

Himes explodes first, but I'm ready for him and slip his clumsy lunge and put him in a headlock. We hit the floor wrestling and I manage to crawl up on his shoulders and swing a few short punches into his open mouth. A little chin music and my fist comes away red. I lean my head over his, coiling my arms through his arms and over his neck. Himes lashes his head back into my nose a few times with a series of short, effective head butts until I can smell his hair and taste my own blood. White and then bits of orange static float across my eyes and I know he's broken my nose. We roll around and I get back on top of him and manage to pry his shoulder up with a half nelson, ramming my knee into his exposed face three times until I feel something pop and then a wetness on my knee, his shoulders loosening. Blood and saliva form a pool on the tile floor, oozing as it follows the grout lines.

"Get the fuck off him," I hear somebody yell. Several sets of hands pull at my arms. I rest my head against his back, listening to the breath rasping in and out of his chest and for some reason it calms me.

I let the hands drag me away and Wolfie puts me in a bear hug while Bam Bam does the same with Himes. Both of us are bleeding and panting when Coach U comes roaring into the room and takes a look at our bent noses, Himes naked and bleeding, me with my face on fire, and starts shouting.

"Pa-fucking-thetic, Riley," he yells.

Paces, nostrils flaring.

"You dumbfucks are going to pay for this."

Etc. Etc.

Everybody else begins slinking back to their lockers and the showers. Himes mumbles something I can't hear and wipes the blood from his mouth.

"Looks like you two went and had your periods all over each other's faces," Coach U says. He looks between us a minute before speaking again. "Have we failed you as coaches?"

Nobody says a word.

"Answer me, goddammit."

"In what way?" I ask.

Coach U bites his lip and raises a hand toward my face, but pulls his slap at the last minute. "Too much goddamn energy. You got time to fight, then we must be doing something fundamentally wrong."

Wolfie lets go of me, giving me a shove. Coach U starts yelling for Harkens and before we know it both Himes and I are strapped into opposing Nautilus machines and told to start lifting. In between stations, Harkens makes us shake hands or help each other off of benches when we're taken past total failure on the squat machine or incline press.

Afterward Himes and I part ways at the door. Harkens stands on the fly machine with this satisfied look on his face, lecturing his two toadies on muscle groups and blood capacity.

"See the way Himes' forearm's covered with veins?" he says. "Engorged. Maximum blood flow. Right now his muscles are thanking me. All that acid burn will make the muscle come back twice as strong."

My head goes light at the door and I wobble a minute.

"And look at Riley's quads—"

Potts, toady number one, a square-headed ex-marine, grad assistant—a Harkens-to-be—squints at me. "Looks mighty painful."

"It's the ultimate high," Harkens says.

Himes turns to Harkens and says, "You can't hurt me." Sweat pouring down his face, wetting the dried blood around his nose.

"Oh yeah?" Harkens says.

Himes, mouth open, eyes dull as pennies. "No pain, Coach, no pain."

Harkens slides off the fly machine and motions for Himes to come back. I stumble off to the showers where I can hear Himes screaming like a burnt idiot child, the clink of weights, Harkens' cool nuclear countdown, "One—two—three—three—four—come on—four—good—what about five?"

Groans.

Afterward Robeson crutches over to me. He's got stim wires running down to his leg that cause the muscles around his kneecap to jerk involuntarily.

"Feel like a fella yet?"

On Friday, after a light helmet-and-shoulder-pads-only workout the traveling team boards a bus. Everybody is dressed in blue blazers, brown slacks, hair combed, necks tucked into knotted ties as they step up into the rumbling door of the bus. There are thirty of us who have been left behind, mostly freshmen, a few sophomores and walk-ons and other members of the drill team.

No training table, study table, lights-out or room check. Nothing. And we all know it.

The entire town's lit up with incoming carloads of fans, their headlights tipping and bouncing up State Street, fresh from the freeway. Frat boys load kegs of beer into beat-up sedans and stand around their purchase like proud hunters, watching for girls, checking themselves in the store windows. Scalpers work the corners with creased squares of cardboard that say NEED TWO TICKETS, their brushed-gold rings and watches glinting in the streetlight.

"Holy shit, we're free," Fuckhead yells at the dark parking lot.

Himes shuffles up to me and Napalm, both eyes black, his nose swollen.

"You look like I feel," he says to me.

I touch my black eyes, fingering the bump that used to be my nose. "Twins," I say.

Himes smiles. "Looks like we both got the shit end of the stick."

"It was stupid," I say. Napalm snickers and I know what he's thinking—conceding stupid to Himes seems pointless.

"I'd do it again," Himes says proudly, his blackened eyes giving him a sort of hollowed-out look, equal parts lonely and soulful.

Is that possible?

"You two better watch it," Napalm says. "Or before you know it you'll be buddies."

"Fuck that, man," Himes says. "I just hurt too bad to start again. Besides it's party time."

He jogs off, bouncing into Jimmy before dispensing a neck slap to Whigger, who smiles, happy for the attention. Then he spins in front of Slope, Rope, and Ant, who are working out a rap about Coach Roe which includes the words blow, toe tag, body bag, slow, and dough.

"It's the crazy white boy," Ant says, stopping midrap.

Himes grins, all of the loneliness and soul I thought I saw a few minutes ago gone, banished. Back to Himes the Cockroach, open-mouth, blank-eyed Hime Time from Pennsylvania.

"Who's room?" Napalm asks.

"Smitty said he was willing," I say.

Smitty nods. "Green grass and high tides, boys."

By the time we hit the dormitory courtyard, everybody's pushing and punching each other, trading insults, boasting about how much and how long they can drink, fuck, and fight. Jimmy from Jersey grabs this small-shouldered guy with bright red hair who happens to be passing in front of our group and screams, "Join the party, bro," before tossing him into the swarm where he's buffeted with forearms and neck slaps and expelled on the ground after being spun around by his backpack by Himes and Whigger.

"I've got a bad feeling about tonight," I tell Napalm as I watch the kid pick himself up from the ground.

"Oh really," Napalm says, "what gives you that impression?"

Within an hour the hallway's one big mass of bodies. Several parties joined together in loud beer-swilling unity. Everybody has their stereo or boom box cranked, all playing different music, the air heavy with cigarette smoke, sweat, and beer. Women and other nonplayers stand around looking at us like we're zoo animals, staring at our oversize arms and thick necks.

Smitty marches up and down the hallway with a half-empty keg on his shoulders, spraying the crowd with beer. Nick, collar up, walks through the tangle of arms and shoulders looking for women and when he spots one, saying, "Ladies." Smile, flash of gold chain. Napalm and I are forced to do several beer bongs, by the Slotsky twins, demented walk-ons from Garden City, Michigan, who eat lit matches and keep matching pythons as pets. I run down the hall toward the bathroom, my stomach rumbling.

The bathroom smells of vomit and lemon-scented cleaner. A couple of guys are crowded around the sinks talking about tits, beer, and the game tomorrow.

"It's simple," Whigger says. "Black dudes score more pussy than your average white boy."

I sneak out the door and creep up and down the hallway looking into rooms for an empty bed or chair to sit and soak in the buzz. Himes and Jimmy have Revlon pinned to a bed, feeding him shots of Dickel. He sputters, the whiskey running down his chin and staining the bed.

All over the place there are guys punching walls, head-butting doors. Ant has a beer poster taped to his back that says BUD ME. A little past the fray in one of the dead-end rooms, Bible Boy's playing Parcheesi with two engineer-type dudes in glasses and high-water pants. I stick my head in the door and hear the strain of violins coming from a small radio perched on the window. One beer can between the three of them and no women.

"Hello, Riley," Bible Boy says, smiling. "Come play."

I shake my head no, step into another room and see Robeson holding court from the bed. His wired and braced knee flexing involuntarily every other minute from the stim pack as his big black hands flutter in the air like crows.

"Riley," he says. "Come have a drink and tell us about size-ism."

"Hey, Robe," I say, beer bong in my head like a gas-soaked rag. I hold up a finger for them to wait, before tromping back out into the hallway and looking for Napalm.

I find Napalm in Smitty's room filling a wine bottle with piss, Hank Williams Jr. wailing on the stereo. Smitty hoots along to Bocephus, doing his best knee-slapping, Texas-boy routine.

"Pull out your pecker and piss for posterity," Smitty says. Napalm finishes, slamming the cork down into the neck. Smitty grabs the bottle from Napalm, holds it to the light.

"Goddamn you got some fucked-up piss. Hot as hell and you got these white bits of kidney cheese floating around."

Napalm saying, "What are you going to do with that?"

Smitty shrugs and whips the bottle out the window.

"Robeson's down in room 312," I tell Napalm. "You want to meet him?"

Smitty stomps over to me, whiskey bottle in hand.

"Show him the wart," Napalm says to Smitty.

"My pussy-eating wart?"

Napalm sways a bit, nods.

"This is one fucked-up wart," Napalm shouts. He's into the freak stuff and keeps a book called *Human Oddities* next to his bed. He says that looking at all those messed-up people makes him feel lucky.

I look around the room. Revlon is passed out under the sink, vomit in his hair. Somebody's taken his shirt off and scrawled LOOK SHARP BE SHARP on his back in Magic Marker.

Smitty sticks his tongue out and wiggles it at me until I can see a pale white finger of flesh in the middle of his tongue about the size of a raisin and full of little pink dots.

"What the fuck's that?" I ask.

"That's my secret sexual weapon," Smitty drawls.

"Tell him why you don't have it removed," Napalm says.

Smitty slaps an arm around my shoulder and leans all of his drunken three hundred and ten pounds into me.

"Where I come from, women love two things," he says. "Led Zeppelin and good old-fashioned muff diving. Led Zep IV to be exact."

"Must be a southern thing," I say.

"Side one, maybe," he says. "But side two, I don't give a shit if you live in China, Peru, or the fucking Congo. Side two's straight-up fucking music. Women hear those drums and their juices start flowing—know what I mean?"

Napalm laughs, beer foaming out of his nose.

"How does this relate to that thing in your mouth?" I ask.

"I work the wool, you know, fingers and all until they get to scratching like polecats, just begging me to take them higher. Then I give 'em this."

I look at Smitty's pie-shaped face.

"You do what?"

He sticks his tongue out, waggling the wart at me.

"Drives them crazy. They start grabbing my ears like I'm some kind of big dildo or something."

"It was disgusting the first time he told me," Napalm says.

"You put the wart in pussy?"

Smitty just grins and nods.

I tell Smitty that I think I'm going to be sick. His smile drops. Revlon rolls over in his own vomit and groans. Seven kinds of music fade and pump. Everybody seems to be talking at once and I feel pretty drunk. Women wander by the door, look in at us and smile wanly, before continuing on down into the heart of the party. Jersey boy and Himes come crashing down the hall, wrestling, spilling lesser bodies and half-empty beer cups in their wake. Somebody claps at the spectacle.

"Smitty," I say. "If I was you, I'd keep that wart to yourself. Northern women might look upon it as a birth defect."

I think about what Heather might say about Smitty's wart.

Then he says, "We'll see, Riley. Maybe you're right, maybe not. Maybe I pull this wart on some uptight Michigan chick, word gets around and pretty soon I'm knee-deep in Midwest pussy."

I pull Napalm out of the room, past the wrestling match and several chugalug contests down to the room where I spotted Robeson earlier.

"Riley," Robeson says, looking up from the bed.

A shy-looking black girl with straightened hair and gold hoop earrings sits next to Robeson holding a plastic cup between her knees. Across from her, against the wall, is this woman with jet-black hair, blunt bangs, and a bored look on her face. She stands.

"Kate," she says, blowing smoke in my face. She's wearing black work boots and a skirt made out of red and blue bandannas that flutters around her thighs when she sits back down. She has the whitest skin I've ever seen, the kind you want to touch and can't stop thinking about.

Sitting next to Kate is this actor-type dude, slouched against the wall, dressed all in black, smoking a cigarette with his middle fingers.

I introduce Napalm to Robeson.

"He a fella?" Robeson asks.

"Far from it," I say.

"How come we've never met?" Napalm asks.

"It's a big team and I keep a low profile," Robeson says, motioning for us to sit.

Napalm nods, shakes Robeson's hands and eyes actor dude suspiciously.

"This here's Rollie," Robeson says, pointing at the actor. "He isn't a fan and he's no drug dealer—what does Roe call them?"

"Instant friends," I say.

Robeson chuckles. "Yeah, instant friends. No, Rollie's no instant friend, he's a philosopher."

Rollie nods, waves his cigarette hand in the air loosely, squinting at us through the smoke. My first inclination is to beat him for wearing black and trying to look severe, but the philosopher bit throws me. I've never known anybody to describe themselves in those exact terms.

"Tell them what you're interested in," Robeson says to Rollie.

"Violence in sports," Rollie says, eyeing my swollen nose and black eyes.

"It's part of the game," Napalm says, plopping down on a stain-spangled futon that sits under the window.

"I'd like to hear more," Rollie says.

I sit next to Kate, who hands me a glass filled with something that smells like bourbon.

"Drink," she says.

"What is it?" I ask.

"That would take all of the fun out of it, wouldn't it?"

I drink and the bourbon rolls across my tongue like lighter fluid.

"All secrets are disappointing," she says, blowing more smoke in my face.

Robeson's girlfriend smiles at me and drops a hand into his lap.

"This is Millie," Robeson says. "My number one woman."

Everybody nods and Millie puts her hand across her mouth as if she doesn't want anybody to see her smile. Jazz moans out of a small radio that sits balanced on the window ledge next to a line of empty beer cans.

"We were talking about size-ism," Robeson says.

"I just saw a wart on a guy's tongue," I say.

Rollie makes a face as if I've just dropped the conversational ball and sucks on his cigarette.

"I didn't know that was possible," Robeson says, taking a sip from his glass. "I told these guys you'd elevate the conversation, Riley, and you come in here talking about warts."

"I'm drunk," I say.

Robeson eyes me. "Just don't be drunk and stupid, it's easy to catch around here."

I nod and Kate runs her small hands across my sore shoulders. Napalm notices and nudges me with his shoe, winking.

Robeson continues, "As I was saying, people equate size with stupidity."

Just then Himes pops into the room dragging this Asian girl by the hair.

"Fuck," he says when he sees who's in the room.

Rollie takes one look at Himes. "Funny how one comes to the conclusion that size goes hand in hand with Neanderthalic behavior."

The girl frees herself from Himes' grip, smiles drunkenly, pushing him playfully back out into the hallway where they continue wrestling.

"Himes is a fella," I say.

"And the coaches love him," Napalm says.

Robeson sips his drink. "He's just the sort of guy who makes the profs think we're all stupid. That's why they talk to us in that slow, I'm-not-sure-you-can-understand voice."

"What's that?" Kate asks.

Robeson, "It's—when—they—talk—to—you—real—slow—like—you—been—eating—retard—sandwiches—and—you've—got—bolts—in—your—neck."

In her best zombie voice Kate says, "I—think—I—get—it."

Everybody laughs and Rollie waves his cigarette around in the air until we stop. "Back to Himes," he says. "Is he any more violent than the next guy?"

"He accepts the game for what it is," I say.

Robeson looks at me. "Good point, Riley. At some level Himes is only satisfying his role in life, playing his part. Football's a violent sport, hence the pads and helmets which facilitate collisions and injury, so Himes is only playing the game as he understands it."

"Absolutely," I say. "Only it ain't that fucking complicated. He acts like he does because he can—because he's a big fucker and only another big fucker's going to tell him to stop."

Kate interrupts, "What the fuck are you guys talking about?"

Rollie glares at her. "Let them talk."

"My man Riley is beginning to see some things," Robeson says. I smile and listen as Robeson lectures Rollie about how everybody thinks ballplayers are stupid and violent and how they're pretty much right. Kate leans her head against my shoulders.

Later, after Millie and Robeson have gone home and the party's fanned out onto other hallways and rooms, Kate leads me into an abandoned room, its occupants too sloshed to find their way back. It is a typical jock room: fake maple furniture, beer posters, dirty jeans, damp towels, beer cans on windowsill, swimsuit calendar, GO BLUE flag on wall, photo of Jimi Hendrix (predictable guitar-on-fire shot), unopened textbooks, and boxes of cereal on top of the minifridge.

Kate regards the mess, shakes her head and leads me to the bed. Her hair falls down around her face and she stares at it for a while before looking at me. I tell myself I should be thinking about Heather, who, even in my current state, strikes me as twice as good-looking as Kate, but there is something about her dark hair and pale skin that I can't stop looking at.

"Robeson's full of shit. Same with Rollie," Kate says. "You know that, don't you?"

I tell her I don't think so.

"That means you're full of shit too," she says. "What if I told you that you guys still sound stupid to me?"

"I'd have to get mad."

She smiles and stares at my face awhile. After a few minutes she says, "I like scars." She leans into me. "Can I touch your nose and black eyes?"

I close my eyes and let her small hands flutter like minnows across my face.

"It's so hot," she says, kneading my swollen nose between her fingers.

"Your hands are cold," I say.

"Cold hands, warm heart," she says. "My mother has cold hands and my father still walked out on her. Then she started wearing tight red dresses to the bars in town. And it's such a small town, only three bars. People with tiny little brains and big hands."

"Strong back, weak mind, you mean."

"Exactly. It's our town motto—but then that's a little more information than you needed."

"I didn't ask," I say.

She frowns, goes over to the minifridge and sweeps the cereal boxes onto the floor before opening the small door and reaching in for two cans of beer. She crunches back through the spilled cereal.

"You would have," she says. "Besides I know where you're from."

"Where?" I say.

"Midwest. Boresville or something like that. Your favorite book besides your playbook is the Bible, because God has helped to make you a better player. You love your mom. Want more?" she says, smiling. "I'm right, aren't I? I used to be a cheerleader for guys like you. You're all alike."

"You're drunk and wrong."

"Maybe so, maybe so. But what if I said I wanted to kiss you?"

I don't say anything, instead I examine her face, trying to pin down some element of it, a crooked tooth, blemish, or dimple. She comes across the room to me, her lips swollen and wet. When we kiss I taste beer and cigarettes as her tongue brushes across my lips.

"There," she says, pushing herself away from me. "Feel better? I just kissed a jock and I swore to myself no more dumb jocks. No more 'Ride shotgun with me in my daddy's pickup, rub my back, come to my games and see me hurt somebody' guys."

"I have a girlfriend," I say, wincing, half expecting her to slap me or bite my neck.

Instead she turns and tears a beer poster off the wall. Two blondes in bikinis on sand, red lips, beer bottles, sunglasses, and matching mail-order cleavage.

"Figures," she says, ripping the poster in two, separating the women, the beach, the sky. "Where did you say you're from?"

"Cleveland."

"And the girlfriend?"

I nod.

"How horribly cute. Now she'll hate me."

I stand up and pull the pieces of beer poster out of her hands. My neck tenses and I feel that nervous lightness in my stomach as she leans up to touch my face again.

"Is it broken?"

I nod, leaning to kiss her, and she turns, offering me her neck instead. I brush my lips down her hairline, into the dip of her shoulder, wanting to smell something other than beer.

"Enough," she says, pushing my face away. Her thumb bumps my nose, sending a dagger of pain down my face. "I'm too drunk. I've got to go."

I watch her walk to the door, kicking dirty towels out from under her feet, an empty pizza box. At the door she turns and flips me off, runs her tongue around her lips and laughs.

"You're lucky I'm drunk, Elwood Riley, because I've got a secret."

I follow her into the hallway, watching her float through the remains of the party. When she gets to the stairwell door, she turns and waves at me, mouthing something I can't hear over the music. Before I can yell out to her, she dips her shoulder into the large door and slips out of sight. I want to run after her, ask her about the secret, but Napalm materializes from a smoke-filled room and slaps an arm around me.

"Did you fuck her?"

I shake my head no.

"What the fuck did you do, then? That Rollie dude said she's crazy."

"I think I just fell in love," I tell him, feeling slightly corny.

"Well, then there's something you should know, Riley."

"What?"

"Rollie also said she was Coach Treller's daughter."

"Get the fuck out of here," I say.

"You still in love?" he asks.

"I don't know what I am," I say.

When I hit the lights in my room, Phil does this creepy Dracula rise out of the bed, dip in mouth, pointy teeth sticking to his lower lip.

"Heather called," he says. "Three times."

I groan, lowering myself into bed, thinking about Kate and the way her hands felt on my nose, the taste of her kiss. Then I force myself to picture Heather until I can recall her long legs, bottle-blond hair, and tanning-bed brown skin. Everything but her face.

ELEVEN

Game day rolls around and there are fans tailgating all over the place, dressed head-to-toe in maize and blue, burning sausages, swilling beer, and singing "Hail to the Victors." On the way down to the practice facility two shirtless guys with maize and blue body paint covering their matching potbellies and hairy backs run through the traffic-clogged street playing catch with a Nerf ball. Mr. Blue makes a tossing motion at Fuckhead in front of the liquor store. "Go out and hook left at the telephone pole," he shouts. "I'll hit you."

He pumps the ball at us until Fuckhead trots out to the telephone pole and catches Mr. Blue's pass.

"Hey, all right," Maize says, high-fiving his buddy and smacking bellies.

"These people are apeshit nuts," Napalm says, bleary-eyed as he watches Fuckhead dodge through the traffic, ball under his arm, striking Heisman poses in front of windshields.

We meet up in the taping room and wait for the travel team to arrive via bus and police escort. Most of us sprawl out on the vinyl taping benches groaning about our hangovers except Himes, who jumps on the first available door frame and begins doing pull-ups, roaring about how he's ready to kick some Maryland ass.

"Himes, you're riding the pine, just like the rest of us frosh," Ant reminds him. "Shitcan the rah-rah stuff and chill."

Himes ignores him and assumes the push-up position, until Smitty staggers over and kicks his arms out from underneath him.

"You're gonna make me puke," Smitty says. "One more push-up and I'm gonna heave lunch."

Himes takes one look at all six feet nine inches of Smitty, nods and gets off the floor. Then Revlon pukes into an empty whirlpool tub, his face pale, hands shaking, hair perfect, teeth white and straight.

"Sorry," he mumbles.

Nobody says anything until one of the assistant trainers/bootlicks tromps into the room and hits the fluorescent lights. "Christ," he says. "Smells like you guys had a party." The air is heavy with Revlon's vomit. Poisoned, sour-smelling sweat leaks out of my armpits, staining my shirt, until I can't smell Kate anymore.

An hour later, after we've had our ankles taped, we jog over to the stadium and meet up with the traveling team, who step off the bus in their solemn navy blazers, game faces, shiny shoes and cheddar-yellow duffel bags slung over their shoulders.

We take lockers. Showers drip and the coaches pace and check game plans, hustling chewing gum and tobacco around their cheeks. Coach U slaps Kong on the ass, "Pancakes, son. I want you blocking like a goddamn bulldozer flipping those fuckers on their backs, hell-bent for election. Pancakes, big man. Pancakes."

Kong locks his jaw, nods, pounding his fists.

"I am," he says. "I am."

I notice Hard-on Hart creeping up behind me just as I'm clipping my shoulder pads into place.

"Coach U knows about the party, Riley," Hart says.

I let my face go flat. "Yeah?"

Hard-on Hart steps up under my chin, until I can smell his cologne and game-day sweat fighting it out. "Yeah, well, somebody saw you at a party in the dorms last night. Alcohol and women, is that any way to behave before the home opener? All that hard work and you just piss it away with a party."

"But . . ."

"I don't want to hear any excuses. Believe me, you weren't the only one. Someday this is going to be you," he says, pointing at the starters pulling on their pads.

He walks away, leaving me to consider the implications of being seen at the party. I slip my game jersey over my shoulder pads, thinking of Kate, then Heather, sitting in front of the television back in Cleveland, waiting for the game to start, hoping to spot me on the sideline. I think about my parents too, Mom smoking, stubbing out butts in her American Eagle ashtray, Dad stroking his beer can with flat, stained thumbs. A bowl of potato chips on the coffee table, next to a tub of sour-cream dip. Jay on the floor, hands under his head staring up into the screen. And I think of Stork on the factory floor, the air heavy with machine oil, cigarettes, and the reek of overtime bodies, trying to make it through another Saturday away from family.

Hart works the room, creeping up to any frosh he sees, mumbling something to them and then backing away.

I scan the room for Treller and catch sight of him next to the water jug, his Adam's apple working up and down as he stares at his clipboard. I try to place his face with Kate's and can't. Her black hair, soft white skin, and his swollen nose, strong jaw, wind-tanned skin, and crazy coach's eyes.

Then Harkens claps his hands and tells us to file out for pregame warm-up. We trot down the tunnel and out onto the field in complete silence. Offense and defense divide and run through light calisthenics, scissor steps, peanut rolls, up-downs until our arms glisten with a thin sweat and the stands begin filling with people.

We return to the locker room and sit down on several long yellow benches, starters up front, frosh and scrubs in the back. Smitty sits down next to me, groaning.

"Riley, I'm not going to make it through the next warm-up," he whispers.

"You've got to, Smitty. Just suck it up and then we chill on the sideline for the rest of the game."

"If I get hit I'm going to puke, my daddy's watching me."

"You can't puke in front of a hundred thousand people."

"Watch me."

Coach U shoots us a look, putting a finger to his lips, the room damp with silence, only the sound of equipment being adjusted, tape loosened.

Then Coach Roe enters the room from a side door. I expect one of his patented rip-roaring speeches to send us out on the field with sand in our guts and blood in our eyes. Instead he just stares at us, head poking the air like a hot coal as the whole room falls completely silent like we're waiting for some sign to lunge out of our seats and go running down the tunnel and into the crowd.

But we wait for permission from Coach Roe.

Up front, Wolfie takes up a rhythmic grunting followed by Ackley, who starts slapping his pads until the air seems charged.

My hangover disappears.

Coach Roe raises a hand and the grunting stops, his lips drawing into a sneer.

"Execute," he says. *"Execute."*

And it seems to be the perfect word, menacing, double-edged.

A voice answers back, "Execute."

Coach Roe nods, bares his teeth and points to the door. All ninety of us leap up and crowd the doorway waiting to slap the GO BLUE board before trotting out into the tunnel.

Inside the tunnel Chernak screams, *"Execute."*

Several guys repeat the word back to one another. Still others answer back with private sounds, grunts, growls, throat rasps, and fist pounds. Bam Bam grabs me, taps his right shoulder pad until I ram my forearm into him three times. He turns the other shoulder.

I hit and hit. Others do the same, following some predetermined pecking order—underclassmen hitting upperclassmen, as pads settle over nervous shoulders and warm bodies for impact and collision.

Coach U jogs down the tunnel behind us screaming, *"Hit, hit, hit, hit, hit, hit."*

Coach Peters, *"Come on now, Big Blue, come on now, Big Blue."*

As we inch closer to the opening the roar of the crowd drowns out every noise we can make. The brass of the band glints back at us as they strut off the field, instruments held high, majorettes unfurling a large GO BLUE banner at the fifty-yard line. Roe works his way up to the front of the line, yelling, "Let's go, Big Blue." He takes the field and the team follows his lean figure into the roar.

I reach the mouth of the tunnel. All around me guys seem to be floating, the noise of the crowd making us forget we're attached to bodies as we swirl and mass at the fifty-yard line after touching the banner. Everything drops away and for a few precious moments I feel like I've got high-test gas in my veins.

Maryland clumps in front of us, rows of shiny red helmets. Then we split the field in half and jog down to our end zone for hitting drills, Coach Argent calling for all frosh to line up in three-point stances.

"Come on, newbies," he says. "Move it. Hunker down, hunker down. Game day, goddamn game day. Fine day to be sucking air through a facemask."

Argent stabs a crooked finger at the turf, his face a checkerboard of skin sags and wrinkles, dull gray eyes and weathered coach's throat.

"Even receivers?" Nick asks.

Argent rolls his head and points at the ground again.

"Get down, get down. Knock the shit out of your ears and assume the position," he says, this time more gravel in his voice, hooded eyes sharp for a moment.

Nick tries his best three-point stance imitation, fingers touching the turf in fear.

Smitty leans into me again. "You've got to help me, Riley. I don't feel so good."

I wave Napalm over, just as Argent starts yelling at us for taking too long.

Napalm takes one look at Smitty and says, "I don't know what the fuck we're supposed to do, but if you have to hit somebody just fall down."

Smitty nods, the smell of whiskey whistling out of his facemask as Argent works his way down the line, chucking us on the ass or helmet, saying, "Get down or get killed."

We hunker down, upperclassmen forming rows in front of us. Big guys take big guys, small with small, six to a line.

"Aw right, newbies, we got to warm up the starting team. Take a hit, roll back up and wait for the whistle," Argent says.

I look up at Kong's melon head, his face grim and wet with sweat as he clomps his fists together. Next to me Smitty wobbles down, groaning in front of Bates, who seems to be having some sort of seizure under his helmet.

"Hup," Argent yells.

Whistle.

Kong plows into me and I can hear Coach U screaming, "Drive, drive, drive, now finish—pancake."

Kong's legs pump as he drives me skidding across the turf before pancaking me by the goalpost. When I pick myself up I can hear the crowd again.

Smitty looks like roadkill after Bates rolls off him, muttering obscenities under his helmet.

"Aw right, double-time it back," Argent yells.

I help Smitty off the turf and crouch at the goal line. Fingers to turf, waiting for the whistle. This time I get the Shed, who heaves himself into a three-point, panting and walleyed. We go three-quarter speed and I let him finish up his block by tipping me to the turf.

Smitty, however, isn't so lucky. I smell the vomit first and look up to see Smitty lolling on the turf like a heart-shot deer as he fumbles with his helmet.

Then a blur of maize and blue to my left as Bates jumps out of line, running full blast at Smitty's prone figure, spearing him, pumping fists into Smitty's curled body.

Hart sprints over and begins yelling while Argent just flaps his hands, shaking his head and whistling for us to line up again. Before they can drag Bates off Smitty he manages a few kicks to the stomach which only make matters worse. Trainers rush out onto the field, rolls of tape jangling on their belts, plastic training boxes slung under their arms. Several body-painted fans lean over the railing to hurl taunts, cheers, and balled hot-dog wrappers at Smitty.

After a few more whistles, I look down the line and realize that others might follow Smitty to the sideline, swarmed by trainers for what is essentially a hangover. The starters and reserves take their shots and Revlon, to his credit, manages to survive several nasty hits from Childers and Reems.

Finally Coach Roe blasts his whistle and assembles the team on the thirty-yard line for a word or two. Napalm and I hang toward the back. The swarm breaks with a single grunt and we head to the sideline to watch the coin toss.

Most of us frosh stand hands on hips as the game happens, the coaches scurrying up and down the sideline wrapped in phone cords and headsets. In between series somebody like Kong or Bam Bam stumbles to the bench, grunting at me to get him a towel or water bottle.

We score and stuff them on D.

The band plays, cheerleaders ram stiff arms into the air, vault, lift and yell as the drone chants to the first few rows.

Taylor, the team's golden boy, connects with Lawson on flag route and the crowd comes to its feet, cheering the gain. All manner of trash rains out of the student section, a *Norton Anthology of American Literature,* half-eaten chicken, hats, ice cubes, and paper airplanes made out of programs.

Coach Treller turns toward the sideline, yelling for Purty. Purty runs and huddles with him for a minute before trotting out to the hash.

Purty's name and number crackle across the PA system and all of us frosh come alive on the sideline, to watch Purty pop his cherry.

"That's one of us," Yo Joe shouts.

The zebra places the ball, blows the whistle as both teams break huddle. Purty stands alone in the backfield while Taylor checks off at the line, settling his wideouts before taking the snap.

Purty takes the first handoff right up the gut, shimmies outside a few yards before getting stuffed by number 75, a large shovel-headed defensive end.

Short pass for a first down. Taylor to Higgs at our own forty-five.

I scan the crowd again, trying to wrap my brain around the fact that one hundred thousand people are watching the game as beach balls float up and down the student section, held aloft by finger jabs and palm slaps. Guys with beer-can hats and M sweaters sway drunkenly to "Hail to the Victors."

Maryland stuffs our fullback.

The PA announcer crackles out the yardage, second and long.

Huddle breaks.

This time Purty takes the handoff, fakes left, before stutter-stepping it outside again, juking a blitzing safety, gliding to the sideline, eating up the yardage. The crowd comes to its feet, not because we need the score, but to watch the run. There is something magical about a long run—the way the ball carrier defies each tackle as his feet race ahead of his body, cutting on a dime whenever a defender blocks his path. Purty knows how it should look. He pumps his arms, long black fingers slicing the air like fan blades, feet eating up the green.

Purty makes it to the eight-yard line before he's hauled down by a D-back who has the angle on him.

A small silence falls on the stadium. Purty picks himself up and trots back to the huddle, just as the crowd roars back to life.

We hit end zone on a little out number by Higgs, who stabs the pigskin into the air, basking in the glow of one hundred thousand plus score-happy fans. Hats and gloves tumble out onto the field. The band starts a cheer and the crowd answers. Inflated condoms swirl in lazy latex arcs and everybody on the sideline starts talking trash.

We kick the extra point, putting Maryland down by two TDs.

At halftime the coaches break us into groups. Us frosh drift to our groups and stand in back, listening as the coaches make adjustments and yell encouragement to sweaty faces. Coach U, red-faced, neck cabled with veins, "Trap the fuckers. On that 32 Belly Dive, I want to see *blood*. Shed, you pull and trap that fucking near-side tackle—Kong scrapes and we should have the fucking Grand Canyon to run through."

Other coaches go on the same way while Roe paces silently around the room, playsheet rolled tightly in his fist, jaw working on gum.

Just before we head back out to the field Roe gathers us for a team prayer and tells us to take what is rightfully ours, that we can only lose the game now.

In the second half we take what is ours. Purty breaks another long one and Taylor goes ten for ten with a string of short-out passes. When he comes to the sideline, photographers call out his name.

By the fourth quarter I can see the fight go out of the Maryland players as they go about the loss, heads down, arms at sides, tackling with a grim, clock-sputtering determination.

Napalm bops into me.

"You see it?" he says, pointing out at the field of blurred uniforms.

"Yeah."

"They've given up."

"Can you blame them?"

Napalm shakes his head.

"I've been watching my parents up in the stands and they look bored," he says.

"I'm bored."

He laughs and shakes his head.

"How un-Michigan of you, Riley."

"I can't help it. Something about me not being involved. To tell you the truth, part of me wants to see Maryland score one."

He nods and we watch as time drains off the game clock. The crowd utters this collective moan as the game ends and they're faced with the prospects of leaving their seats and dragging their victory-warmed hearts back to tailgate parties and hotel rooms.

Napalm and I run off the field behind the starters and into a locker room full of television lights and well-wishers. I watch Kong, the Shed, and Bam Bam as they settle into their locker spaces, pulling pads and cleats off, their faces lined with fatigue, happy to have the whole thing over. They smile and accept congratulations from timid-looking reporters, assistant coaches and other players. And for a moment I get this feeling that I know what the whole game's about, why we play, but it fades the minute I catch sight of Hart glaring at me.

After the game, word gets around about a party at Taylor's house. The coaches send us off with a speech about next week's game as Rotten Bobby traipses through the locker room collecting our game jerseys, screaming, "You fucked 'em up, Big Blue."

Napalm and I meet up after he's had dinner with his parents and seen them to their hotel room. He's quiet at first, as I explain that the reason my parents didn't make the drive was that my father had thrown his back out at work and had to spend the weekend lying in bed, eating aspirin and drinking beer for the pain.

I don't tell him about the way Dad's voice sounds dead or the way he sighs and sucks air through his teeth 'cause he's too fucking tired from work.

Before we head out Napalm checks himself in the mirror and I turn to look out the window at the town as the sun fades into streetlights and neon signs.

In the elevator Napalm turns to me. "Parents," he says.

"Everybody's got them."

"Yeah, well I've got them worse."

"Driving you crazy?"

"Right away my mom's putting her hand through my hair, telling me I look *puffy*."

"Puffy?"

"What kind of shit is that?"

I laugh.

"And my old man doing the heart-attack jaw grind, staring into his fettucine Alfredo, mumbling something about taking a bath on some stock. And suddenly I'm sixteen again."

He rubs his eyes, sighs and shakes his shoulders as we descend. "But Nick's parents . . ."

"Let me guess. Nick didn't fall far from the tree?"

Napalm nods, "His old man looks like a used-car salesman, cologne, pointy shoes, tight suit, and this bulletproof hair."

"And mom?"

"Miss Piggy with a little streetwalker thrown in. My mother was horrified. It was all she could talk about at dinner. Now, Nick's sister's another story."

"She look like Nick?"

"Hot as balls, Riley, and only a senior in high school. Real cool too, I caught her looking at my Stones tapes so I asked her if she's a Keith or Mick fan."

"Mick, right?"

"Wrong. Most chicks go for Mick, but she says Keith, and I'm in love for like a minute or two."

"This is Nick's sister?" I say.

"And she was bored with the whole football thing, kept lying back on my bed and complaining about how hungry she was and how she wanted to go home. She gets this faraway look, starts pouting and bam—I'm getting wood right there in front of my parents."

The elevator dings and we exit into the bright, quarry-tiled foyer.

"And your parents?" I ask.

"I don't want to talk about it," he says, kicking open the glass door. "I got enough grief to last me the rest of the season."

"Taylor's party?"

He nods and we walk south on State Street.

"We're breaking training rules," he says.

"Wouldn't be fun without them," I say.

Then, after a minute or so of silence, I tell him about Hart's warning before the game.

"He's just trying to scare you, see if you'll shit your pants."

"What if I have to see Roe?"

"Smitty's the one in the stewpot. I mean the motherfucker tossed his cookies during warm-ups."

"What about Bates?"

"Totally fucked up. I'm making it my goal in life to steer clear of that crazy motherfucker. Plus, you notice how he and Himes are all buddy-buddy?"

"Yeah, but Hart said something to me," I say.

"We were all there. Why would he single you out?"

"I don't know—that's the fucked-up thing. I get the feeling that they're watching me, waiting for me to screw up."

"Fuck that Kate chick and I know one coach who's going to be all over you like a cheap suit," he says.

We turn on State, hooking a left on Packard. Cars zip by trailing exhaust, their headlights bouncing off the white clapboard houses, blinding us for a minute. We duck under an elm tree with low branches that sweep the sidewalk and I pull off a branch and begin stripping the leaves.

"I can't help it, Hart rattles me," I say. "What if they yank my scholarship?"

"They can't and stop worrying about it," he says. "I'm telling you, Hart just wants to see which way you're hanging."

"I just like to know the rules before I break them, like Freeman with his Whiz Quizzes. I lose my scholarship, I go back to Cleveland and probably end up working in some factory for the rest of my life. What about you?"

"If it happened to me?"

"Yeah, say you lose your scholarship, what then?"

"I go back to Pittsburgh."

"That's it?"

"It's only football," Napalm says. "That's where they've got us. I mean it's just a game."

"Then what do your parents say if Boy Wonder comes home from the big time?"

"That's another story. I spent my freshman year of high school in Valley Forge Military Academy, because they thought I needed structure."

"What happened?"

"I hated it. Wouldn't you? I mean it was like the junior jarhead convention twenty-four fucking hours a day. Clean this. Drop and give me some push-ups. Run. March through this swamp. Clean toilets with a toothbrush. After six months I figured a way out—I became the best cadet I could be, marched until I thought my feet would fall off, kept my room square and tight, studied all night and pulled straight As. I even volunteered for weekend watch duty. If there was dull metal, I polished it. Christ, I even polished the fucking doorknobs."

"I don't get it."

He nods, holds up a finger. "That was just the beginning. I waited until I was sure word had gotten back to my parents at midsemester, that I had, quote, 'exceeded all expectations' and that I was being considered for one of the plebe junior command positions. Then I set about making myself sick."

"How do you make yourself sick?"

"First I tried going outside with wet hair and when that didn't work, I stayed up for days and took walks without my coat."

"It didn't work?"

He shakes his head. "So then I ate this kid's Kleenex and got real fucking sick."

"You ate a Kleenex?"

"I'm not proud of it, but hell yes. Desperate times call for desperate measures. But it worked. After a week of not taking care of myself I was sure I'd parlayed the cold into full-blown bronchitis—but I wanted pneumonia."

"Pneumonia? What's this have to do with losing your scholarship?"

"I'm getting to that. So break rolled around and I said my good-byes before taking the bus home. At this point every joint in my body ached, my sweat was ice-cold and smelled like hard-boiled eggs. My lungs were so clogged with shit that it hurt to breathe and I'd developed this shake.

"At any rate I survived the bus ride and took a cab home. I remember because the driver thought I was on drugs or something and kept talking about the fare, wanting to know if I had enough money for the miles. When he let me off I was shaking so hard my teeth were rattling. It took everything I had just to make it to the door. It was snowing and the flakes felt like somebody was putting matches out on my face. I can still see the look on my mother's face when I opened the door and said, 'Merry Christmas,' right before I hit the deck."

"You never told anybody this?"

"Nope, but I think my dad had it figured out though. At any rate, I got what I wanted and after spending two weeks in the hospital, they withdrew me from the academy and let me go to school with my friends."

"I don't know if I could do that to myself."

"That's what Robeson's talking about with that bullshit about not sixing and finding a way out."

"What do you mean?"

"I didn't quite quit the academy, you see it was a matter of getting out with my dignity and having it quit me."

"Yeah, but you knew what you were doing," I say. "That took foresight and cunning."

"That's not what matters. What matters is what other people think. Sometimes I wonder what it'd be like if I'd stuck it out. Would I be neater? More polite? Organized? And now I'm here—after all that bullshit I end up with a football scholarship?"

"Our problem is that we don't care enough, Napalm. Half the time I keep wanting this to be like high school."

"Riley, shut the fuck up—you're depressing me."

"All I'm saying is what if an opportunity to get out were to present itself to you?"

"You mean like an injury?"

"I don't know."

"Depends," he says. "All I know is that you'd better be careful what you wish for."

TWELVE

Taylor's house is a shabby-looking, two-story box with peeling paint, cracked windows, and a sagging front porch shaded by several small sumac trees. We follow the music and enter the front room. Upperclassmen with girlfriends and groupies file by and nod at us ever so slightly. Rickety-looking card tables are scattered throughout the room, a different drinking game at each. In the living room the couches have been pulled back to make room for an impromptu wrestling match between Banchic and Billy Joe Burke. Childers, Fuckhead, and Reems sit spraddle-legged on a crooked couch while women wearing loose Michigan football sweatshirts sit on their laps, cheering the match on. Smashed beer cups litter the floor and skitter across the room whenever Burke breaks free from the bear hug and charges Banchic as he tries catching his breath and drinking a beer at the same time. I watch Nick wander around the party calling every girl he talks to Michelle. Most of them giggle into their drinks, while others walk away.

"Nick, what the fuck are you doing?" I ask.

"I'm going to marry a woman named Michelle. Why waste time?"

From the couch Fuckhead says, "He's been doing that all night."

The woman on Fuckhead's lap cocks her head, sniffing the air like an antelope. I see the way Fuckhead looks at her, locking his arms around her waist, afraid she'll spot one of the starters, dart off his lap and be gone.

We skirt the wrestling match and stand back out of the way in the dining room. Purty appears with two giggling blondes, one under each arm. Both of them have dark roots, thick lips, too tight jeans, and large oversize sweatshirts. The taller one I recognize as one of the Lady Blues, but she stares straight through me while the other one inspects her chipped nails and shakes her head.

I lean into Purty. "Nice run today. I wish you could've seen the people in the stands."

We run through an awkward series of handshakes that ends in a finger snap.

He looks at me. "You Riley, right?"

One of the girls giggles, patting his flank like a horse.

I nod, knowing he's looking at me as a bench-riding frosh, something he's above.

"I heard the crowd," Purty says.

"He was awesome," the taller girl says.

Both squeal and shake Purty, who looks a little far off, his heavily lidded eyes staring at something else across the room.

When I don't fill up the space with words, he tips his head at me, wading through the crush of people, the girls trailing behind him.

Napalm rolls his eyes. "You sounded like a fucking fan, Riley. Were you gonna offer to suck his dick next?"

"You saw it."

"Everybody did. The trick is to act like it's no big deal. That's what we're all doing here. You see anybody else drooling over him?"

"Well . . ."

"Besides the women?"

I look around at the people, just a bunch of guys with beer cans in their hands, laughing, punching each other on the arm every minute or so. Girls snake through the crowd looking up into faces trying to figure out who's who, while guys in gold chains and silk jackets make friendly with the players, hanging on their every grunt.

I shrug my shoulders. "No."

"My point exactly. We're all stars here. Get it? Everybody looks up to us. I know it's fucked, but it's the truth, so let's get drunk and have some fun."

"But we didn't do shit today except sit the bench."

"We're on the *team,* Riley, it doesn't matter what we did or didn't do today."

We wade through the living room, sipping our beers and trying to blend in. Every so often a drunk upperclassman slops an arm around us and offers his hard-won wisdom. Most of it along the lines of "Someday, when you're a starter . . ." or "Drink up, you dumbfucks . . . Take a look at all the pussy."

At about eleven we're asked to sit in on a poker game. Bam Bam looks up at us, his massive arms rippling under his sleeveless T-shirt.

"Twenty apiece," he says, pointing at a pile of chips. "You pay me."

Both of us nod and take seats. On the counter behind me Himes pounds the buckled Formica, challenging Bates to an arm-wrestling match. Bates, who's been lurking in what passes for a den (three lawn chairs, a milk carton crate, two *Playboy* centerfolds taped to the wall and a broken television, no picture, sound only), leaps out of his seat and rushes Himes, saying, "You wanna piece? You wanna piece?"

Bam Bam rolls his eyes and calls Follow the Queen. Then he shuffles and offers a cut to this nervous-looking guy who sits twisting a thin gold ring, staring at Himes and Bates, who, as they lock wrists, begin grunting.

Bam Bam watches the guy twist his ring a minute, before pounding the table impatiently. "Hey, Cheswick, you gonna cut or stare at the fucking cards?"

Cheswick runs his fingers through a spotty mustache and makes a show of knocking the cards, pushing the deck back to Bam Bam for the deal. Behind us, Himes grunts and groans as Bates slams his wrist to the counter sending a Mason jar full of tobacco spit sailing to the floor where it spills on a pile of coats. Neither of them moves to do anything about the coats and after a minute the room fills with the warm, sweet aroma of tobacco.

Ackley leans into me, his face scraped clean and pink like an old man, and offers me and Napalm some whiskey out of a silver flask.

Napalm nods and Ackley pours into plastic cups.

We take our cards.

"I've got a fiver says you jock sniffers got shit," Cheswick says, tossing a blue chip onto the table where it clatters and spins for a moment.

I fold. Himes is standing behind me, licking his bloody knuckles from where Bates has slammed him. I can hear his open mouth panting and for a minute I consider telling him to fuck off.

"Hey, Himes," the Shed says. "You a housefly or something?"

Himes gapes, "Huh?"

"Back the fuck off the table."

"Sure, man," Himes says, backing off.

The Shed looks behind him. "Hey, Bates, come get your boy," he says.

Bates grabs Himes by the neck and grunts at the countertop, motioning for Himes to stick out his arm again, this time for a beer. "If not, you make my hit list," Bates says. "And then I have to kill you, put you out of commission like these other brain-dead fuckers."

Himes holds out his hands to show Bates how scared he isn't.

"Okay, Rambo, strap a pair on and let's have another go," Bates says.

We pause the game and watch as Bates, who has the team record for weighted dips, slams Himes to the countertop again. Himes mutters something about steroids and getting lucky before ducking into the other room.

"Anybody else?" Bates shouts at us.

"Better living through chemistry," Bam Bam says after Bates has disappeared out the back door.

"I'm telling you, the guy's going to blow a gasket one of these days. Be one of them burnout head cases," Shed says.

"That would be a real loss to humanity," Cheswick says. "You fags want to play cards or talk shop? Or maybe we should watch some more arm wrestling."

The Shed smacks Cheswick on the arms, nearly tipping him out of his chair. "Listen to Tony fucking Vegas."

"Let's just play," Cheswick says, straightening his shirt collar.

We play and drink, Cheswick taking almost every other pot. The Shed starts challenging us to drink and when we don't he threatens to sic Bates on us.

After an hour or so I can't even focus on the cards with Cheswick's idiotic chatter buzzing in my ear.

"Man," Cheswick says. "This is too fucking easy. I feel sorry for you guys. Every time we play cards this happens and now we got new guys. Must be the helmets. That or the steroids you guys are pumping into your asses. But if you want to piss your money away then I guess I have to—flush."

He snaps a royal flush down on the table to collective groans. The Shed mumbles something about cheating, but Cheswick keeps up his banter, rattling his chips, stroking his puny mustache. I deal Low Card in the Hole, fold after the last card and watch as Cheswick jacks the pot up to eighty dollars until it's just him and Bam Bam staring over their hands at each other.

Cheswick calls and flips four of a kind under Bam Bam's nose. Bam Bam tosses his cards away and grabs him by the collar and lifts him out of his seat.

"Take your fucking pot," he growls.

"Come on, Bam Bam," Cheswick whimpers. "It's not my fault you don't know how to bet. You guys are lucky I didn't bring Go-Go with me, he'd have cleaned you out hours ago."

Bam Bam shakes him once more before dropping him back to his seat. "Yeah, but Go-Go knows how to keep his pie hole shut," Bam Bam says.

"I can't help it if I'm good," Cheswick says, raking his chips in.

After losing the last of his chips, hanging around on a small boat, Napalm quits the game, pushing back his chair, inhaling, relieved.

"Hey, dummy, want some charity?" Cheswick asks.

Ackley starts laughing and looks at Napalm, waiting for him to say something.

"What did you say?" Napalm asks.

The Shed leans his bucket-shaped head forward. "You're going to get killed, Cheese Whiz. Especially if you think we're gonna protect you from a frosh."

Cheswick clinks his chips around nervously. "I get killed, you can forget about those extra tickets for the State game."

Napalm gets up and stands over Cheswick.

Before he can say or do anything Bam Bam says, "Here." And lashes a swift backhand to Cheswick's nose. There is a soft crunching sound, like boots on snow, and Cheswick's face lights up in red. "I warned you. Napalm here would have done you worse, so consider yourself lucky."

Cheswick's eyes tear up as he tries to keep the blood pooled in his palm. Ackley goes to the sink and gets him a tea towel dotted with tiny blue football helmets and hands it to Cheswick, who buries his face in the cloth.

"Fuck you," he sputters.

The Shed starts laughing beer foam all over himself.

Ackley steps between Bam Bam and Cheswick, trying to prevent any further violence. "That was stupid, Bam Bam," he says.

Bam Bam shrugs his shoulders and begins gathering the cards. "Fuck him. I'm sick of his big-shot mouth."

From under the blood-soaked tea towel Cheswick squeaks, "Cash me out and give me my fucking money—I'm done playing with you retards."

Bam Bam paws through Cheswick's chips, stacking them by color, while Cheswick sits there muttering into the bloody towel. Napalm taps me under the table and lets out this little grin.

When we cash out I've lost sixty dollars, half of my money I have for the month. Napalm and I go back out into the living room to watch more wrestling, more women pressed into corners by hulking bodies, wide hands crushing them.

Ackley comes up behind us.

"You boys ain't properly medicated just yet," he says, passing us another bottle. "And take some of these."

He holds out a handful of pills.

"What are they?" I ask.

"A little bit of everything, fruit salad, mix and match."

I pick two blue capsules and Napalm takes a pair of yellow and black pills.

Ackley smiles and passes the bottle again. "That's my boys."

We drink and swallow the pills. The rest of the party happens in this whiskey/pill blur of bodies and voices. The pain in my neck increases somehow and Ackley's there whispering in my ear how this chick's looking at me, how she wants me. So I go over to her, pick her up and pin her to the ceiling. Somebody cranks the music and I shake her, smiling up at her drunkenly until I notice she's screaming and put her down only to have her slap me and run off.

Wolfie comes up to me. "Riley, you're supposed to fuck pussy, not lift it."

I nod and he passes me another bottle and motions for me to drink. The last thing I remember is Ackley snubbing out cigarettes on the back of my palm and me laughing.

"You're one of us," he says.

And me saying, "No."

———————

I spend Sunday in bed trying to sort out the last few days: Hart's threat, Kate's hands on my broken nose and the fact that her dad's a coach, Cheswick bleeding into a towel, the groupies at the party and the fucked-up shit I remember doing but not feeling.

Then I think about Heather waiting by the phone.

I wait until Phil pads off to the library, hair raked straight down over his skull, dip in, cheap cologne, and backpack slung across his shoulder, before calling.

On the third ring I get her mom. "Long time no hear," she says before bellowing out Heather's name. Heather picks up and I play it cool, ask her about school and if she watched the game.

"Where were you?" she asks.

For a minute I think she wants me to account for the missed phone calls and all of the other crap in between.

When I don't answer she says, "I looked and didn't see you once on the sideline. What a boring game."

I agree.

"Did Phil tell you I called?"

I wince, glancing over at Phil's neatly made bed (a sure sign of mental illness), the rosary and calendar with days marked out in thick black lines (days left until he sees Sally? The Apocalypse?).

"No," I say flatly.

"Well, I called three times on Friday and he said you were out. Are you going to talk to him about giving you messages? I mean what if it were some kind of emergency and I had to get hold of you? Or your parents."

I tell her to leave my parents out of this and she gets quiet.

"I just get nervous is all. Can you understand that?"

I tell her I can, that I'll try.

Then she says, "Sometimes I'm sitting here thinking of you so far away and it's like I can't breathe. It's not a good feeling, Elwood."

"Okay," I say. "Okay, I'll say something to him."

Then she brings up her Homecoming dance and how I promised to come home for it.

"I can't wait."

She sighs, sensing my lack of hoorah. "If you don't want to . . ."

"I didn't say that—it's just things have been kind of crazy up here," I say, trying hard not to let my guilt seep over the phone line.

"What's the matter with you? You sound different. It's like you're not even listening to anything I say."

I tell her several times I'm listening, before steering the conversation back to Homecoming. Then she asks me about practice and about the other guys on the team, if they're really as big as they look on television.

"Bigger," I say, happy to be talking about something besides Homecoming.

She keeps up with the questions until I give a full (false) accounting of my time spent since our last phone conversation.

Satisfied that I've been a good boy she says, "I love you. You know that, don't you, Elwood?"

"I love you too," I say. Something flops in my gut as I picture her mooing into the phone, doing her shoulders up the way she does, all alone in her chintz-smothered room: pink bedspread, plastic sparkle lamp with lace trim, Polaroids of us taped all over the mirror, and marble softball trophies topped with gold-painted plastic figurines. I hang up, roll back onto the bed and stare at the ceiling. The pit in my stomach won't go away, equal parts dread of Hard-on Hart making good on his threats and the Heather problem. Then Kate.

I go to my desk and find this flimsy calendar with pictures of trees and sun-dappled rocks, a waterfall or two and advertisements for a bank with different savings plans scripted across the bottom. I flip it open, find the weekend of the Homecoming and circle it with a black marker.

With the sun creeping out of my window and the calendar still smelling of get-high marker fumes, I pull a beat-up copy of Marcus Aurelius' *Meditations* from a bottom drawer where I've stashed all of my other books. I stare at the cover painting of Marcus Aurelius, sword in hand, noble look on his face, before opening the book and reading quote after quote, looking for something to make me feel better about Homecoming and having to face Heather with all that I've done in the last few months.

I find what I'm looking for in Book VIII, number twenty-two, "Attend to the matter which is before thee, whether it is opinion or act or word."

I read the quote again, only half of it makes sense, but I try and memorize it anyways. Anything worth knowing takes time, especially if it comes from books and I don't have to learn it the hard way by fucking something up.

Then I pull out some mail I've been saving. A letter from my mother and two cards from Heather, perfume and all. Corny, I think. Nothing like Whigger's woman, who sends him her pubic hair in little waxed-paper envelopes scented with musk.

I open the letter from my mother.

Hope all is well, the letter says. We didn't see you on television. Heather stops by once a week and gives us updates. We understand about not calling, with rates so high. Your father's not doing so well. Trouble at work. He won't say what, but I worry. We are so proud of you. Your father is proud of you, he'd never tell you, but he is. I know.

(More crap about the weather, food, neighbors, work.)

We'll try to call you sometime this week. Still planning on making it up for a game. (She lists possible dates, asks about tickets and how far in advance I need to know.) Have you made friends? How are your classes? The coaches? Hope to see you soon.

The letter ends with all that love stuff, a few P.S.'s asking about the food and how my money's holding out and a hello from Jay, who she says misses me, although he won't say so.

I sit in the half-dark room and stare at the letter, wondering what trouble there could be with my father. Drinking? Foreman? Enough, I decide, for Mother to mention. And why the P.S. about money?

After a short nap I prowl around the women's side of the dorm, half looking for Kate, half killing time. The thick scent of tampons, hair spray, and baby oil carpeting the air as I creep down three floors of long L-shaped corridors, peeking into rooms, staring at flyers on the wall, trying my best to look inconspicuous (six foot six, broken nose, black eyes).

On the third floor I surprise and scare this round-shouldered girl stepping out of the bathroom, towel wrapped across her chest, hair wet and dark.

"Oh, my God," she says, leaping back against the cinder-block wall. "You scared me."

I can see the moist white clumping of deodorant under her smooth armpits and for some reason this excites me a little, and I think about sticking my tongue under there and tasting.

I look down at my feet. "Sorry."

She recovers, pushing a sheet of thick wet hair out of her face. "You looking for somebody?"

"No . . . I mean yes," I stutter.

"Well, which is it?"

"Yes," I say. She catches me staring at her armpits and pulls the towel up higher. "A friend of mine."

"She have a name?"

Two athletic-looking girls step out of their rooms, one in soccer shorts, the other in jeans and a tattered flannel shirt.

Shower girl pins me to the wall with her gaze.

"What's the problem, Jill?" the one in flannel asks. Jill flips her hand at the girl, tells her it's nothing, before smearing her wet hair back again. "A name—you have a name for this mystery girl?"

"Kate."

She shakes her head as the two other girls disappear back into their rooms, slamming the thick wooden door behind them.

"Wrong hall. No one named Kate here," she says, jabbing her thumb over her shoulder at the doorway. I slink away and creep halls five through seven and get accosted by this hulking dorm attendant who has a face like a brick wall and comes off as one part lesbian, two parts John Wayne.

She brushes by me, turning to watch as I lope uneasily down the hall, looking into open rooms: televisions, braided loop rugs, lace bedspreads, and Diet Coke cans. My will begins to dissolve, and I run the Marcus Aurelius quote around my head as John Wayne lesbian follows me to the door, her breath rattling out of her big chest. I slam my arms into the large metal door and she sucks in her breath, as if she's waited for this moment to defend her hall of women from evil black-eyed men all her life.

I turn to her and scream, "What—what do you want?"

I realize she is scared and I stomp down the hall thinking of deodorant creases in armpits, wet hair, and Kate.

Over on the men's side of the dormitory I slide into Jimmy from Jersey's room because he's got the Boss blasting and an open door. He's on the bed, mouthing the words, tears in his eyes. When he sees me he sucks it up and smiles, high-fives me.

"I'm bored out of my fucking mind," he screams.

The music's so loud I can feel my hair trembling and the bruise around my nose suddenly starts hurting.

"Oooh," he says, getting up to close the door, dialing Bruce down a few notches to normal. "You slaughtered for money?"

I nod, thinking of the sixty bucks I donated to the poker game and the two-week wait before our first scholarship check. Even then peanuts, which makes me wonder how some of the guys drive Jeeps and Trans Ams, wear thick gold chains and designer sweaters.

"Check it out," Jimmy says, reaching under the bed. He pulls out a dark blue duffel and lays it on the floor between us. "Open it."

I lean and zip the cover back, revealing three pairs of brand-new turf shoes.

I look at him and he smiles, stops to hum to the music for a second, then smiles again, obviously proud of himself.

"Shoes? What's this got to do with me being broke?"

He rolls his eyes at me, drags the bag toward him, plucks a shoe out, holding it aloft.

"How much you think this is worth?"

I shrug, wondering how he managed to come by three pairs of official team shoes and why he's showing them to me.

"Some Jew boy offered me fifty bucks for my shoes after geology class. His parents are loaded and his old man's one of those eat, drink, and die Michigan fans. Said he wanted some black shoes so he could look like one of us."

I wince. "How did you get them?"

"Simple," he says. "I took them. Then there are these."

He drops the shoe next to its mate, grunts and fishes under the bed again. This time it's a garbage bag, which he carefully spreads open for me, revealing ten official sweatshirts with large maize Ms printed on them.

"What's the matter, Riley?"

I pick up one of the sweatshirts. "Holy fuck, Jersey boy, you've been a busy man. Here I thought you were just thumbing your ass waiting to crack the starting lineup like all of these other sad sacks."

"The team owes me."

"You've got a point there," I say.

Jimmy's eyes go blank. "All right, Riley, don't go getting all deep on me—you want in on this?"

"Want in on what?"

"Do I got to spell it out for you? I sell this shit. You need money—all you've got to do is help me out."

Without thinking I nod my head and watch as he puts everything back, smiling and humming to the Boss.

Then Jimmy starts telling me this story about his father. How the old man left when he and his sister weren't even out of diapers. Just walked out the door one day and disappeared. And how right before he's about to sign with Michigan and his face is all over the local papers the old man shows up again and starts begging for money. Then there's a fight.

"Fucked him up good," Jimmy says.

He sighs, gets up and goes to Fuckhead his roommate's desk and starts fingering a silver-framed photo of Fuckhead and his woman at some beach. Fuckhead's woman is something to look at even in Polaroid and I notice there are scratch marks on the desk where the frame has been moved so many times. I sit quietly for a minute and watch Jimmy's face droop into a sort of smile.

"If things go right, in four years I'll be able to buy Mom a house," he says.

"What do you mean?"

"I get drafted," he says.

Poor bastard, I think, he *has* bought into the rah-rah dream of a pro career. Part of me wants to run the numbers on how few of us actually make it to the pros and manage to avoid injuries long enough to make real money.

"What about you?" he says. "You ever think about it?"

"I'm just trying to get through this," I say.

We sit for another ten minutes before I get up to go.

"These are all mine," he says, stabbing a finger under the bed. "All you've got to do is shove a pair of shoes into your bag after practice. Piece of fucking cake. Then you give it to me and I convert it to cash."

"That's it?"

"I'll let you know about the something bigger I'm working on, but for now, all you've got to do is walk out of there with a pair of shoes or jersey and presto fucking chango—I get you cash. You still want in?"

"Why not?" I say.

Jimmy high-fives me.

"Just keep your mouth shut—don't go blabbing about this."

When I get back, the room smells of tobacco and Phil's after-shave. I fumble with the lights. Phil's on the bed, arms folded across his chest, dip in, thousand-mile stare pasted on his face. I notice a strip of white athletic tape running down the middle of the room.

He rises, arms still folded. "Heather called."

"What's with the tape?" I ask, noticing that even the television and minifridge have tape on them.

"I've divided the room equally," Phil says, pointing to the tape.

I take a minute to admire his precision, contemplate the possibilities. "I don't get it."

Phil squints at me as I step along the line and into my bed.

"My parents said I should look after my stuff," he says. "I don't want to be taken advantage of so I divided the room."

I take another look at the tape, too tired to fuck with him or even argue.

"The television poses a problem," I say. "After all it's yours and the tape suggests that I'm now half owner. Which would mean that I'm therefore responsible if something were to go wrong."

"Huh?"

"I'm half responsible, according to the tape."

After a minute, in which I imagine I can hear the gears clacking away in his brain, he grunts, "You're right."

"And what about the fridge?"

"We'll make it the floor," he says. "Guess I got carried away, after I heard what Smitty did to his roommate's stuff."

I shake my head. "What's that?"

"Tossed Crawdaddy's television out the window."

"Maybe he didn't like what was on," I say.

Phil crunches his face up, does one of those fist clenches like he's Charles Bronson. "If someone ever did that to my television."

"I get the picture, Phil," I say, trying hard not to laugh in his face.

He calms down and goes back into his Count Dracula pose, squinting at his playbook.

I kill my light and listen to the playbook's pages turn, the mumbling of numbers and words as he drills the contents of the book into his brain. Bingo, 5–3 Blitz, Falcon, Double Eagle Shift, and End Crush 69.

THIRTEEN

Monday morning I roll out of bed to a kick and a bang on our door. I look out the window at the purple predawn dark and hope the knocking will go away. I listen for a minute or two and the only sound is the rattle of delivery trucks backing up against the dorm.

But then another bang shakes the door.

Phil mumbles something as I fumble with the lock. When I pull the door open this pimple-faced backup water boy and dirty-laundry sorter who Rotten Bobby calls Jockface steps into the room.

"Elwood Riley?" he askes, his narrow eyes full of early morning sleep crusties.

I nod and remember that I'm naked.

"Coach U wants to see you first thing this morning," he says, slipping me this crooked, shit-eating grin as if he's somehow busting my stones.

"Now?"

"First thing," he says before skipping out of the room. "You got any questions?"

I shut the door on him and dress.

On the way down to the offices I realize I'm not the only one. Up ahead in the gloom I see the familiar shuffle of Smitty and behind me,

Ant and Fuckhead walk, hands in pockets, their words trailing white from their mouths in the chill air. The first rays of sunlight tip over the trees and buildings and I'm temporarily blinded as I breathe into my collar and focus on the sound of my feet hitting pavement, careful to keep a steady rhythm.

We meet up in the waiting room. There are nine of us, not everybody at the party, but a good cross section and all of us freshmen, as if Taylor's after-game party is exempt.

Secretaries begin showing up, pulling covers off typewriters, pouring water through coffee machines. I catch great wafts of middle-aged-lady perfume, one part sex, two parts prim and proper. Smitty catches it too. I can see his nose snuffle and go up in the air like a hound as he works his tongue around in his mouth, flashing me the wart.

The grad assistants filter in, walking stiff-legged to their group office with bags of donuts clenched in hand, baseball hats shoved over bed head hair, their ex-player bodies puffy and swollen from too much food and not enough exercise.

"We're doomed," Fuckhead says. "It's about the party."

"No shit," I say. "You think they were going to serve us breakfast?"

Fuckhead says, "Come on, Riley."

Then one of the grad assistants walks by and shakes his head at us. When his back's to us I flip him off and everybody snickers.

"What the fuck are you doing here?" Smitty asks me.

"Same thing you're doing here. Selective punishment," I tell him.

Ant shakes his fist. "How come we the only ones down here?"

"We're the unlucky few," I say.

Ant does the thousand-yard stare. "I feel a fist-fucking coming on."

"I don't get it," Fuckhead says. "Where's everybody else?"

"Spies, motherfucker—you better wise up to the fact," Ant says. "Ask Riley."

I tell them what Robeson told me about there being spies all over the town who report back to the coaching staff whenever they spot a football player standing in front of a liquor store or with a woman.

Just then Coach U sticks his head out of the door, curls a fat finger at me and growls, "Riley."

Fuckhead hums "Taps" under his breath as other position coaches enter and call out names. Ant gets up to go as does Rope and finally Fuckhead. Before the door closes behind me I look back at Ant, who raises his fist to his chest and salutes me.

I step into the office and Coach U points for me to sit, grabs his coffee mug and starts blowing on it.

"How are classes going?"

"Great," I say, trying my best to sound chitchatty.

He nods a few times past normal, purses his lips, squints and blows on his coffee some more before running a chubby hand across his smooth skull and leaning back in his chair.

"You know why you're here?"

I don't move. Instead I stare at his face, his skin the color of raw bacon from the wind, rain, and yelling. I look closer at the broken capillaries webbing his cheeks and nose. A drinker, I think.

"Don't play stupid with me, Riley."

"Okay," I say. "I won't play stupid. What do you want me to say?"

He grins. "For starters tell me about this party."

"I wasn't the only one there."

"That's not the point," he says. "Was it the right thing to do?"

For a moment I consider telling him that the whole frosh squad was at the party, but I don't.

I shake my head no.

He grins again, sucks coffee through horse teeth and plays like he's just squeezed a murder confession out of me. "I don't suppose you want to tell me what happened," he says. "Who all was there? It's too early for me to yell. Coach Roe doesn't know about this yet. So you get one fuckup, Riley. One do-over and this one's it. But I've got to be honest with you. For a guy who's not contributing to the team, you've got some mighty big balls to be running around having a good time while the rest of us are preparing for the game. Not to mention Taylor's party."

I freeze at the mention of Taylor.

"But how . . ."

He puts a hand in the air.

"Never mind, Riley. What Taylor does is his own business, after all he's a starter. Had himself a pretty good game, don't you think?"

"But . . ."

"The fact of the matter is that we know what goes on. Now, for an upperclassman to go to a party is one thing, but a frosh?"

"It was stupid," I say, half hoping it's what he wants to hear. My stomach flutters as I try my best to look serious and large, flexing my arms.

"Then I got Smitty puking during pregame which gets Bates all excited. It was one big fucking distraction, Riley—you ever think about that?"

"I'm not Smitty," I say.

"Goddamn right, son. But you're supposed to be your brother's keeper and all that. I thought you were smarter than this—I mean quite frankly, Riley, we expect a little more out of you. Some of these guys get confused tying their fucking shoes, but shit, son, you're sup- posed to be sharp and we expect guys like you to prevail in situations like this."

"I'm supposed to tell Smitty maybe he better not drink so much?"

He slams his fist against the desk.

"Don't get smart with me, Riley, you stupid fucking cunt. I'm putting you on morning mile for the rest of the year, so you and Coach Hart can get acquainted."

I swallow hard, trying to come up with something to say. "Thank you."

"Don't mention it," he says. "Now get out of here. Next time all you have to do is invite me."

He smiles and winks and I give him the old fake chuckle and slink out the door.

Smitty gets the finger next and before the door even closes I hear the screaming.

Outside, Fuckhead asks me what happened and I tell him about morning mile and Coach going psycho.

"Coach Harris was real cool about it," Fuckhead says. "He's not like the others."

I roll my eyes at him.

"No, man, I mean it, he's a pretty cool guy."

"That's it?" I ask incredulously. "Fuckhead, rule number one: No coach is a nice guy, cool or any of that other shit. So you must have told him something."

Fuckhead's face begins to shake and I see that he wants to tell me something.

"I told him everybody else was there. Then he asked who and I told him."

"You named names?"

"He said I was very helpful."

"You're going to be a popular man, Fuckhead."

"What do you mean?"

"Did you tell him who was at Taylor's party?"

Fuckhead nods.

"Smart, Fuckhead, real smart. Does the term FUBAR mean anything to you?"

I watch him mouth the words, "fucked up beyond all recognition."

"It's going to be ugly," I tell him.

Before practice a few of the fellas get called into weight room for a little postparty penance with Harkens, who lets them know that they can thank Fuckhead for the workout. He becomes a marked man.

Kong tries to rip Fuckhead's helmet off and bite his ear, but Bates pushes him out of the way and starts strangling him. Guys go out of their way to run him over, step on his hands, spit on him, gouge his face and eyes.

When I bump into him at the water cooler, his face looks like a circular saw's had its way with him, his breath whistling through his split lips and swollen nose.

"I'm dying here, Riley," he splutters.

Napalm cruises up, spots Fuckhead. "Ah, Benedict Arnold," he says. "Getting it while the getting's good?"

"Fuck you, Napalm," Fuckhead manages.

Roe goes hard-ass on us, doubling up on the hitting and sled drills. Then we have this killer long scrimmage where Argent makes Fuckhead play fullback for a couple of plays until he can't get up from the turf.

After showering I scoot over to Reems' locker and scoop one of his extra pair of shoes into my duffel bag. Nobody catches me and I exit the locker room into the dark of the parking lot, sweat pricking my armpits, the slight pulse of blood in my ears, and walk three blocks before reaching into the bag to touch them.

I go straight back to the dorm, open the closet and dig out the long cardboard boxes that contain Heather's plaster figurines. I unwrap the wrestler first and it looks nothing like me, soft lip, eyelashes painted brown, chubby legs, oversize head. Stupid, I think. Stupid. Stupid. Stupid.

I take it over to the window ledge and rap it lightly on the cold stone until a crack runs up the leg.

No voodoo here.

Then I open the window and toss the figurine out. It spins, catching the reflection of the streetlamps. For a moment, I catch sight of the pale face, brown dots for eyes and pink mouth, as it whistles in the air before descending into the dark. I wait until I hear the oriental tinkle of smashing plaster. Somebody yells something from down below, I ignore them and do the same with the football figurine.

Then I stop by Jimmy's room and toss the shoes in front of him.

"Riley," he says. "Welcome to the club."

I tell him it was easy.

"It's the scam of the fucking century," he says, shoving the shoes under his bed. "You have to wait for the money though—a day or two."

"No problem," I say.

"Goddamn right it's no problem," he says, laughing and slapping his knee.

Phil's still sleeping, arms folded, mossy teeth bared, when I get up for morning mile. I step on the white tape that divides our room to see if he flinches in his sleep. He doesn't. Then I leer at the picture of Sally and smack my lips before tossing on some clothes, as every joint in my body cracks and crunches in protest.

Outside, fog hides the trash-filled lawns and rusted-out bicycles abandoned on parking meters and street sign poles. There's the faint aroma of fresh-baked bread in the air and the clank of cafeteria workers gathering chafing dishes, as I check the back of the dormitory, looking for plaster splatter on the street. No trace of the figurines and I wonder where they've gone to. My hands feel cold and there's nobody on the street, just piles of newspapers ready for delivery. No neon signs or bums picking through the trash and I think what a perfect freeze-dried world it is for a couple of hours every day and how for some messed-up reason I feel like running. Then I try to remember the Marcus Aurelius quote and I can't.

There are others at the track, Smitty, Ant, Fuckhead (who looks like old produce, his body a map of bruises and cuts), Slope and then a couple of upperclassmen who have designated weight problems, which means they can't run a mile in under fifteen minutes, which if you know anything, is about as fast as walking.

We wait silently watching the pigeons fight over an old donut.

"This is gonna suck," Smitty drawls. Several of the upperclassmen lie down on the rubberized track like beached whales, patting their bellies, staring up into the cold blue sky.

Hart pulls up in a shiny new Trans Am, radio blaring, tires squealing, vanity plate that reads NUMBER1. He exits the car smacking his hands and crowing about what a great morning it is and how he just loves the morning-mile detail. He plays buddy-buddy with us, even leaps up and musses Smitty's already sleep-tangled hair until one of the upperclassmen tells him to fuck off and stop being so cheery.

"I love this job," Hart yells. "You're lucky I'm in a good mood, fatboy."

He has us stretch a little bit before blasting the whistle and telling us to hit the track.

I take off running and try to keep up with Slope, who glides elegantly at the head of the pack, his long fingers slicing the air out in front of him like fan blades. The fatties take off walking and go about their four laps while Hart runs around the inside of the track calling them names.

"Next time I'm going to bring a little piece of pussy and dangle it in front of you guys," Hart says. "Motivate your fat asses."

The Shed walks past him on lap number three, smiles and makes a show of wiping the sweat from his forehead. Hart throws up his hands and goes back to the bleachers to wait for the last of the fatties to finish up.

After the other guys have drifted back to their cars Hart sidles up to me and says, "I knew you'd fuck up, Riley."

I stare and nod, give him the motherfucker look while inside my guts are churning, wondering if anybody could have possibly seen me take the shoes or drop the girl at the party.

Then Hart stomps off and leaves me standing there.

Back in the room, Phil's still sleeping so I pad off to the showers and get my ear talked raw by this pointy-faced premed major who washes himself no less than eight times, from head to toe.

"Got a thing about germs," he says, dumping Phisoderm over his head. "They live in your underpants, you know, and sneak out at night."

He keeps hopping showerheads, complaining that the last one didn't have enough pressure.

"Germs hate pressure," he says. "I'm from Grosse Pointe. It's a terrible name, don't you think?"

"Never heard of it," I tell him.

When he doesn't do the hand thing to point out exactly where he lives, just like every other dumb cluck from this state, I know he's not right in the head. I try my best to ignore him and lean into the stream of water rubbing my sore neck.

"What's the matter?" he asks.

I point to my neck. "Football."

He stops soaping himself. "Do you have any idea what you're doing to your body?"

"I'm a little banged up is all."

"Listen," he says. "They show us pictures in class of spinal cord injuries, and half of them are football players."

"I'm sore," I say. "You learn to live with it."

"C-5 and C-6, that's where it happens."

"Where what happens?"

"That's where your body absorbs the blows."

"What does C-5 and C-6 have to do with it?"

"Cervical vertebrae," he says. "They've got numbers."

"I don't know anything about that."

"You will—you think our necks were made for playing football?"

"I never thought of it."

He shakes his head at me, continues scrubbing his scalp, saying, "Think about it, think about it."

I take the opportunity to leave the clean bastard standing there and go back to the room.

I towel off and throw some clothes on. Then I sit there thinking not about my neck, but about the team and football and how Napalm seems to be the only other frosh who understands what it's like. How there's no fun to be had anywhere and even the big-dog starters seem grumpy and constantly pissed off. They don't show the bumps and bruises on television, or the long practices, cortisone needles as big as tenpenny nails, the yelling, and hours of boring film meetings where you watch the same play a dozen times until the coach feels that when you go home and close your eyeballs the play's going to be running on the back of your eyelids.

Even the hotshots like Taylor and Higgs walk around sick to their stomachs all day on account of the pressure. Then there's all the other crap, like spies and Whiz Quizzes, extra workout with Harkens—it's enough to get a person thinking of his options and how most of us don't have any. It's NFL or bust. And bust as far as I can figure is selling used cars or loading trucks with HiLos in Chicago or Detroit or sitting in a bar screaming at some game on the television, letting on that you "used to play," that you "could have went big time." But, in the end, bust means hanging around town, getting fat and drunk, tailgating, and settling for the third most pretty girl you ever kissed that still sees stars when you tell her stories about your playing days. Only no one seems to know this.

Then there's my neck that's been keeping me up nights with its tiny needles of pain, which only seem worse the more I worry. And how maybe I should have asked about C-5 and C-6, should have said, "Yeah, it worries me."

Phil wakes up, groans spitting out his overnight chew.

"Riley," he says.

"Mmm," I say.

"What are you doing?"

"Thinking," I say. "Recording my thoughts—you got a problem with that?"

He gives me this sour look and gets up and goes to the sink where he scrapes his hair across his head with this dandruff-encrusted brush of his before sitting back down on the bed and reaching for his tin of Copenhagen.

"How was your run?" he asks.

"A1," I tell him. Then he gives me this sly little smile, as if to say he's somehow happy he didn't get singled out. He stares at my running shoes, which, at this moment, are on his side of the room.

"I got lucky," he says. "I was at the party."

"You'll get yours. Luck's luck, you know?"

And I leave it at that, even though I know the bastard's thinking about how many cheeseburgers he's going to wolf down for breakfast and that he's heard enough of my philosophical crap about good luck, bad luck, and in-between-shit-happens luck, best to focus on what fills you up in life, things you can wrap two hands around and strangle to death, not some slippery, not-for-sale crap like luck.

The week thumps by and all eyes are on the games. Several guys pull up lame or take knee twists, sit on the sideline swaddled in ice bags and Ace bandages. A couple of the walk-ons sprout pussies and quit, go back to their studies and rush some rich-boy fraternity.

The days are marked by who gets injured and how.

Revlon gets his dick stepped on in a pileup. The trainers tape it to his leg, pack it in ice and shove him into one of the dark blue vans used for hospital runs and recruiting visits when we want to keep the southern boys out of the snow and ice.

At this point in the season everybody hates everybody for a few minutes. What makes matters worse is that we're all too worn-out and bruised to do much of anything about it. So if a fight does break out, it's usually a pretty sorry thing to watch—all talk and no heart.

After a witnessing a fight between Kong and Lousma, I mention to Bam Bam that we're getting a bit misanthropic.

"Riley, I have no fucking idea what you're talking about, but it sounds good," Bam Bam says.

Then there's all the other fucked-up shit like Alvin Garner, one of the starting cornerbacks, who starts preaching separation of the races in the locker room.

"We going to send all you dirty motherfucking white boys back to Sweden or some other cold-ass place," he says.

Wolfie steps out of the shower. "Oh, yeah? That's cool with me because the Swedes have themselves some good porn movies."

"We'll make an exception," Alvin says. "Crazy white boys who don't shower can have Kansas. We'll keep you around for bodyguards or maybe sanitation."

Wolfie says, "You black dudes cut too many deals."

Alvin points out that the locker room's already segregated, blacks in the corner, big ugly white boys next to the shitter.

Wolfie examines the locker room, grinning, "Sweden, huh? That don't sound so bad."

Morning mile kicks my ass on a regular basis. I start out the day dog-tired, sleep through most of my classes and when I take the field for our warm-up laps, my legs crack and burn after the second lap and I fade to the back of the pack with the fatties and shitheels. Coach U starts questioning my heart, asks me if I'm in love or some fucked-up crap like that.

And he's right because I'm sick about what I've come to call the Heather situation. Homecoming and all that jazz, how I've got to go home and face Heather when Kate and everything else have nearly erased her from my memory. Lately her phone calls have been getting worse. A lot of cooing and "Do you miss me?" and "I can't wait." Other guys are going through the same thing. Even Whigger's beginning to have him some doubts about his pubic-hair-posting Norma Jean Ramey.

——————

"Too many fishies in the pond," Whigger tells me one day after morning mile. "You've got to creep the dorms, homeslice. Get the word out to the women that there's a real live football stud living two floors above them, below them, around the corner—available and open for business."

I tell him about Kate and then some about Heather.

He says, "Sounds like you've got to choose or lose, my friend."

Even Napalm's getting him some from this little Jewish chick named Annick, who calls herself a JAP. She goes about four foot ten (heels included), two inches of dark curly hair and this voice that I swear to God could peel paint.

"It's a covert operation," Napalm says. "Lights out and doors locked. Mum's the word and all that shit."

"Nickname?" I ask, knowing he's got to give her one.

"The Cheesegrater?"

"The voice?"

"That and some other things only a heart should know," he says.

I imagine big Napalm careful not to crush her and say so.

"She likes it when I lie on her," he says. "Says it adds to her pleasure to have a big fat goy lying on top of her. She's got a mouth like a sump pump and when I come to her room she greets me with some phony Shakespeare quote like 'Here comes my sweating lord' or 'Take you me for a sponge.' I don't even know what the fuck she's talking about half the time."

"Sounds like you're learning all kinds of new words," I tell him.

"It's called culture, Riley," he says. "Get it while it's hot like pussy instead of sitting around worrying about the world."

"Is that what it is?"

"Ask that Kate chick when you see her," he says.

"I don't even know where she lives."

"Riley, you've got to capitalize on the fact that you're a stud ball-player, a Stones fan, and my best friend."

"Is that what you're doing?"

"The Cheesegrater about wet her pants when I told her I played ball. That's what it's about, Riley, like it or not you're a ballplayer. I mean look at you, you're too fucking big to be anything else. Chill out and play the game."

I tell him I want to.

The State game comes and goes. We rout them as expected, send their sorry second-rate fans packing back north. In the locker room, after the game, I snag two game jerseys and shove them into my duffel bag. Then I walk past Hart and give him this big shit-eating grin that I can see just burns him up.

We win without joy now, practice in the cold rain, going about our laps and drills like prisoners on a chain gang while the coaches try to inject a little gravity into each day, mentioning future opponents, feared tackles or trick plays. We grow numb to it because winning is tradition here.

The Shed tells me after practice one day (sleet, extra sprints) that this is the beginning of the middle of the end.

"What the fuck are you talking about?"

"The season," he says. "It's over but we have a long way to go. If you want to become an old dog like me—you've got a long way to go."

I trot off to the shower, mulling the Shed's words, thinking, the sonofabitch has his moments.

Then there's what we call the Routine or the Grind.

Seniors who rip through every practice with grim determination are called Grinders. Robeson says you become a Grinder when all the crap the coaches spout finally rots your brain and your body goes on autopilot, like those dudes on assembly lines or crack addicts.

In my lit class we read *Heart of Darkness* and I can't stop thinking about when Kurtz says, "The horror! The horror!"

Instead I imagine him saying, "The Grind! The Grind!"

And like Kurtz I feel that if I start looking too deeply into any of this that I'll lose my mind. A slouching dread somewhere in my gut tells me that I've given up on the football dream and all that's left for me is to go out fighting or find some other way to endure without becoming a Grinder. Better to sit back and catalog the events, note the idiotic coaches and their small victories, watch guys play hurt. For what? So they can make me a man? Show me what it means to be a player or a Wolverine?

I chug through every morning mile, pushing the Heather thing around my head. What to do? How to do it?

I have resigned myself to the fact that I will hurt her, cut a college gash in her heart, ankle-deep, Michigan-wide. I comb *Meditations* for strength and when I don't find what I'm looking for, I pull out *Notes from the Underground*. I can't get over the opening, something about the words keeps me up nights, rolling them around my tongue.

"I am a sick man . . . I am a spiteful man. I am an unattractive man."

Then there's this other passage that I copy down inside my playbook.

It says:

"I say, in earnest, that I should probably have been able to discover even in that peculiar sort of enjoyment—the enjoyment, of course, of despair; but in despair there are the most intense enjoyments, especially when one is very acutely conscious of the hopelessness of one's position."

That's it exactly—freedom in being fucked up. I wonder if any of the other guys ever feel this or if their brains are too full of depth charts and dreams of playing in front of one hundred thousand people screaming their heads off for football. I have dreams where I look up from a three-point stance and there's this guy across the line from me, slobbering, ready to kick my ass and when he does he whispers something in my ear that I can't make out.

Then I run into Kate.

After training table on Thursday, she follows me into the elevator. She's dressed in a long-sleeved black shirt, army pants and thick-heeled work boots that clonk on the elevator floor. Her lips look kiss-swollen. I take one look at her and this tiny shaking starts under my rib cage and I feel my breath catching in my throat.

"You live here?" I ask.

"No," she says, laughing. "I'm here to see a friend."

The minute the door dings shut she gives me this crazy look and smacks the emergency stop.

Breathe, I remind myself, throat tightening, blood pounding in my ears as if she's wrapped her hands around my heart and is squeezing.

"What happened to your nose?" she asks. "It's all healed."

"How come you didn't tell me you're Coach Treller's daughter?"

She looks away. The emergency buzzer sounds like it's inside my brain.

"You never asked . . . does that scare you?" she says.

"Makes things tricky."

"Would it help if I told you I never see him, that he left the family when I was ten?"

I tell her I don't know and she makes a so-what face.

"What happened with us wasn't that big of a deal. We kissed or don't you remember?" she says, watching my face.

"That's your secret?" I ask.

"It can be—if you want it, but no. I meant my father."

I let out an uncomfortable laugh and snap the emergency alarm off, waiting for the elevator to start moving again, and when it does, I feel better. The elevator slides to a stop at my floor and I step out and look back.

"I live over on Elm," she says. "1250, apartment 2B—come visit me sometime."

The door shuts then, pinching her face off from sight, and she's gone.

I trot down to my room, not really sure what just happened, only that when I saw her I couldn't breathe and I was sweating.

When I tell Napalm about meeting Kate, he warns me again. "She sounds fucked in the head," he says. "And she's Coach T's daughter. You haven't forgotten that, have you?"

"They were divorced," I say.

"But still," he says. "I remind you—she's a coach's daughter."

"She told me where she lives."

Napalm lets out a sigh. "Sounds like you're in some good trouble, then. But while I think about it, read this and tell me what it says."

He tosses me *Survival at Auschwitz*.

"That's it for advice?" I ask. "Read a fucking book about people getting tossed into ovens?"

"I told you I needed a minute or two to think this out. That's a favor you're doing for me," he says, pointing at the book. "The Cheesegrater says I need to have it read before we go any further. She gave me that and some book called *Zen and the Art of Motorcycle Maintenance*."

"Further . . . meaning?"

"Meaning, I don't know," he says. "Meaning maybe I'm fucked."

Suddenly I begin to feel maudlin, with the whole five-hour Greyhound to Cleveland, rented tux, the words I have to say to Heather. Napalm and I have talked the whole matter to death, how I need to sever all ties, how the sharpest knife hurts the least. How I'm not being fair to her, holding her back from her destiny: fat, pregnant and mar-

ried to some assembly line bozo who's nuts for the Browns, his riding
lawn mower, and chili mac.

Then I say, "I've been stealing shoes and jerseys from the locker
room."

"You're what?" he asks.

"Lifting stuff, you know like shoplifting?"

"Let me get this straight," he says. "Not only are you thinking
about fucking Coach T's daughter, but now you're stealing?"

I nod.

"Do the words self-destructive behavior mean anything to you,
Riley?"

"I've got it under control," I say. "All I do is shove it in my bag,
give it to Jimmy . . ."

"Jersey boy—have you lost your mind?"

"I'm not hanging with the motherfucker—I'm making a little
money is all."

"There's a lot of crap going on, Riley. I don't know if Jimmy
would be my first choice for point man, but who am I to say? I
thought you wanted to talk about this Kate thing."

"I do," I say. "I just thought you ought to know about the scam—
maybe you want to get in on it."

"Riley, the motherfucker's a dumbshit, just watch your back—then
you can worry about this Kate and Heather crap."

"Yeah, but what about them?"

Napalm sits up, rubbing his face and fingering his eyes until they
make this moist sound. "Go home—do the deed and come back a
better man. That's my advice about Heather."

"That's it?"

He nods and I start to feel sick again, my throat tight, palms sweaty,
brain a little cottony.

"Now, Kate's a whole other matter," Napalm says. "Sort of an
unknown quantity you might say."

"Back there in the elevator, she had me—I mean I could hardly
breathe."

"She sounds like a head case."

"Maybe, but mostly I think she likes to keep me off balance, mess with my head."

Napalm says, "I'd say she's squashed your brain, Riley. I don't get it—Heather's twice as hot and she don't fuck with you."

"That's not the point."

"Then you have to ask yourself, why bother? She's nuts and she makes you feel nervous? Gee, Riley, sounds like the basis for a solid fucking relationship. I say marry her, have kids, buy the farm."

"What do you mean?"

"I mean this is the kind of woman who hands your heart back to you in one of those shrink-wrapped meat trays when she's done with it."

I flip him off. "I can't help it—it's like that feeling you get when you see an accident on the freeway."

"Come on, Riley, we're talking about a coach's daughter."

"No, man—I mean you know how it is when you see an accident, you don't want to look but you have to—that's what she's like."

Napalm rolls out of bed. "Not bad. I never thought of it that way."

"In a good/bad, wonderful/horrible way."

"Car crash . . . I like that," he says.

I nod.

"The Cheesegrater's no car crash," he says. "She's a parked car."

I pick up the book, what can I say? But Napalm's not waiting for an answer.

The day before I'm to hop a bus to Cleveland, I call Stork after practice and tell him I'm coming home for the weekend.

"Whatever the fuck for?" he says.

I tell him about Heather.

"I wondered when that was coming," he says. "I ran into one of her girlfriends and she drilled me about you."

"It's not like that. I'm just sorting things out is all."

"It's okay, Riley—you're becoming," he says.

"What do you mean?"

"Just some shit this Jesus freak keeps telling me. I thought it sounded pretty good."

Then we agree to meet down at the lake behind the high school after I do the deed.

FOURTEEN

On Friday, after the traveling team's jetted off to Iowa for a game, I board a Greyhound headed for Cleveland. The bus driver, a large black man, with loose Jeri-curl hair and a gold tooth, nods at me. "Hey, chief," he says. "Welcome to Greyhound."

I take a seat next to this Amish woman who keeps covering her ankles with her long white underskirt and watch the scenery whip by. Farm to suburb to city.

The bus driver announces each stop in the same, deep, flat voice, staring down the bus in his mirror before snipping off the air brakes and rolling back out onto the road. I slide the window open a crack and get a frown from Miss Amish, which I take to be a good thing.

The bus sneaks through Cleveland's West Side.

The smell gets me first, then the gray chemical-looking lake and the Terminal Tower looming over the city like some concrete syringe. Out on the water, gulls dive for dead fish as the bus trolls through rows and rows of broken-looking buildings with hunchbacked men standing in front of them in greasy work clothes.

Heather meets me at the station and wraps her strong arms around me, pushing my face into her hair. I want her to keep on squeezing until it hurts.

"You look so different," she says, feeling my arms and touching my crooked nose.

I hug her back.

"Harder," she moans. My blood runs cold when I smell her neck.

We get to her car and there are the requisite presents: tapes with her favorite songs, chocolate chip cookies, and tongue kisses. I look out the window at this rail-thin bus porter who stands there shaking his head and waving his arms like he's trying to warn me about wasting all that woman.

"What's the matter?" Heather asks.

I shrug, stare out the window and say nothing, wanting it to rain or snow, for the sky to get dark. Instead, sun shoots through the curled clouds as we drive along the lake.

"Tired is all," I say after we've passed the M. L. King overpass.

"Tell me everything. What about Napalm and his girlfriend? They sound so interesting—not like my boring friends."

"What about what?" flinching the minute I say it. I look over as she pouts, her hands tight on the wheel.

A few minutes later, "I just wanted to know."

"She's not his girlfriend," I say, thinking of the book he gave me to read for him, for her. Nazis and starving worked-to-death Jews, fighting over bread scraps and how it's a horrible book to test someone's love with.

Then I start thinking about all of the novels I've dumped on Heather and how they've rolled right off her like water. Everything except maybe a little Gatsby and broken-nose Myrtle.

Back to Napalm and his woman.

"Then what is she?"

"Who?" I ask, thinking for a minute that Heather's somehow asking about Kate. My stomach drops and I check the rearview mirror for a pothole or dip in the pavement and everything turns to shit, the skyline, nasty-looking lake, and skid marks. As if there's some big snake riding my tail, eating up all the good I leave behind.

"The girl," she says.

"She's just a girl."

Heather bites her lips, suddenly understanding what I mean.

I fill up the time with nervous talk. Nothing about feelings, just facts to keep her wanting more, half hoping she'll turn to me and call me remote and distant. Maybe she'll tell me how she's sort of seeing this guy in her math class and how the distance with us is just too much, that it tears her heart out, makes her cry herself to sleep. I continue with the fantasy all the way through Wickliffe and Eastlake, imagining little things, like the way she holds her shoulders all stiff or the hitch in her speech, as signs that she's sick of me and ready for some new simple guy. We hit another dip in the road and I'm back with her voice and her questions, her asking about football and me telling the truth, watching it scare her.

"It's not what I want," I say, not going into any more detail, half-surprised at myself for uttering the words out loud, wanting to take them back somehow. But I can't because it's one of those truths that've been slinking around my head and heart, waiting to escape.

Her lower lip trembles as she stares out over the two-lane blacktop. There are children on the lawns and massive pin oaks framing the sky in front of us. Then we hit a strip of road where the houses give way to shops and bars with old men out front on cement stoops, pool cues in hand, their breath fogging out of their lungs like departing souls or cigarette smoke.

I'm thinking despair and intense enjoyment—*I am a sick man . . . I am a spiteful man.*

She steps on the accelerator—*I am an unattractive man.*

Faster, I think, I don't want to think this now. Save it and say it later.

"What do you mean?" she asks.

"Football, you know, it's not exactly what I thought it was going to be."

"Oh," she says as if she knows I'm just talking to make her feel better.

The radio plays some stupid, sappy song that makes the words stick in my throat and for a moment I get that my-life-is-set-to-music feeling. The streets around my house don't help much either. Two months and I'm a sentimental sucker and I feel like a phony coming home to break up with her, pretending that I'm some big-time ballplayer for my parents.

Mom gets up from the front porch when Heather pulls the car in, and starts waving. Heather looks at me, runs some last-minute directions by me about the dance; when and how I'm to pick up my tux, what to bring and when to call her. Instead of hugging me she squeezes my hand and I look at her throat, the skin a soft ale brown even now in autumn and now that something's breaking.

Then she runs through the I-love-you stuff again, right in front of Mom, who does her level best not to stare with disapproval. I clench my jaw and mumble a few things (not enough) to her.

At dinner, Mom stuffs me with pot roast, creamed peas, and rhubarb pie while we wait for Dad to get off shift. Every once in a while I get this feeling that I've never even left. Even as Jay pumps me with questions and nobody says a word about Heather or Dad.

I mention the letter about Dad not feeling good and she shrugs and says, "He's excited to see you."

Jay stares down at his plate, then out the window.

The house looks smaller somehow, run-down in a hard-used family way. There are tread marks on carpeting, cracks in the linoleum, and thigh-high stacks of newspapers and magazines.

At six o'clock Dad opens the door, lunch pail tucked under his arm, his skin a sick honey yellow.

"Hey," he says, and I give him a shake. He doesn't squeeze back.

His voice is flat and his skin seems tighter on his skull, eyes deeper set, hair more gray than I remember.

What's wrong with Dad is not entirely clear. There has always been in our family a slow turning away from the facts. A grim determination to look the other way. It's what men in my family do. His old man, a sonofabitch slag worker who drank highballs and never said a word about his job, only that he worked.

Dad sits down at the table, drops his work coat on the chair next to him and sighs. Mom shuffles around in the kitchen, clanging plates, the fridge door chattering open and shut.

He smiles at me, places his hands on the table and folds them to stop them from shaking.

"You look bigger," he says. "That or I'm getting old."

"Maybe a little," I say.

He nods. "Nothing's changed around here, except maybe the Vikes winning a few this year."

Mom comes in, plate in hand, and gets a shot of father-son crap and starts beaming. She sets the plate in front of him, pours a glass of beer and drops a stack of pills by the glass. He looks at her, smiles, this faraway look coming over him as he swallows the pills then the entire glass of beer.

"Doesn't he look good?" Mom says to him from the doorway, tea towel over her shoulder. The kitchen light catches the dish suds on her forearm and for a minute they seem to glow. Dad nods, pushes his food around some more and then stops to stare at his shaking hands.

"You getting along okay?" he asks.

I lie about how things are great and it's okay because my old man knows what it's like to pretend it's all good, no matter what, and make the best of it even if you have to lie through broken teeth. Just like he's not going to tell me what's going on or how old he really feels or how he's worked himself raw and sick. Mom comes out of the kitchen to watch us, pulling a cigarette out of her apron pocket and rasping a lighter to it. Then she blows the smoke up into the ceiling fan where it's chopped up and sent sprawling across the room.

"Did you see the garden?" he asks.

I shake my head no. He points out the kitchen window, at the garden plot, gleaming under the security lights.

"Frost," he says. "Got everything, even the begonias on the front porch."

I clear a few dishes and then go outside with the old man and walk around the backyard in the dark.

"You all right, Dad?" I say.

"I've got terrible headaches," he says, pausing to stare at the ground. "Back hurts pretty much every day and I swear it feels like the muscle's rotting. All the doctors do is tell me I'm tired and toss pills at me."

"My neck's been bothering me," I tell him.

"Hope you didn't inherit your old man's body," he says. "God-damn thing is falling apart on me."

"What if I did?"

He pauses, looking out over the backyard. "Then you've got to know when to stop. My old man never taught me that and I don't ever remember telling you."

I want to ask him what he means, instead I say, "It's okay."

He nods and walks out ahead of me.

"Look at this mess," he says, pointing at the garden. "I should have gotten out here sooner."

I look at the ruined garden and I know something's not right. There are too many full-fruited plants in the garden: rows and rows of pepper plants with frozen peppers hanging to tan stalks, gray and blackened tomatoes, shriveled beans, rotten caved-in squash, and cukes that lie on the cold ground like exploded grenades. He stoops down, pulls off a frozen pepper and mushes it between his thick fingers, shaking his head.

Then it hits me, what's wrong. It's not the frost, but the fact that the garden hasn't been picked since late summer. There are weeds in his normally neat rows where the mulch of dead leaves and grass clippings should be.

"Let me ask you something," he says.

"Go ahead," I say.

"What do you think of me?"

I pause. Only twice have we ever talked like this and it's scaring me.

"I don't know."

"No really, because I'm falling apart and your mother's worried."

"You mean work?"

"Whatever—no, just basically having a hard time keeping it together."

"I think maybe you should quit the plant. If that's what you mean."

"Can't do that, son. Can't do that."

"You're scaring me," I say.

He just flaps his hands at me. I watch him work his way through the row, hoping for one of those moments where he says something that makes the world seem gin-clear and we can head back to a well-lighted house that is warm and safe and smells good.

"I just want to tell you that I'm going to be okay. They aren't going to make me quit before I get the full pension—you can bet on that. Even if they have to haul my cold body to work and prop it in front of a machine."

A dog barks as he steps out of the garden. He stares at me for a moment before speaking. "Just be glad you're going to school. Look at me and learn—my old man never told me that neither. There's a lot of things he never told me. So if you got questions, now's the time to ask."

"Maybe we should go back inside," I say.

"I guess you don't have any questions."

I shake my head and we walk back into the warm food smells of the house. When we get inside he slumps down in front of the television and starts clicking through the channels with the remote. And that is how I leave him.

I find Jay upstairs with his headphones on, nose in a *Rolling Stone*.

I click off the stereo.

"Dad?" he says, as if he's been waiting for this question all day.

I nod and sit next to him on the bed.

"I just had this weird talk with him," I say.

"He came home like that about two or three weeks after you left. Just stopped talking, except for these lessons he keeps trying to tell me. Did you see the way his hands shake?"

I nod.

"It's up here, I think," Jay says, pointing to his head. "Like one minute it's normal old grumpy Dad, then he goes to work and . . . I'm telling you it's like *Invasion of the Body Snatchers.*"

"He told me he was going to a doctor."

"You know how Mom is with that stuff. She don't tell me shit."

"Did he?" I ask.

Jay nods, "He must have, because I checked the pill bottles—head doctor, I think."

"Well, we just had what passes for a heart-to-heart out in the back-yard."

"He's got five years before he can draw his pension. You know that, stop acting like you've been gone a long time."

"Seems that way," I say.

"I wouldn't worry about it. I bet he's just like all of the others now," Jay says, lurching around the room like Frankenstein's monster.

"So that's it?" I ask, wanting more of an explanation.

Jay stops.

"It's not so bad, sort of like he's lost a speed or two. You get used to it, you'd be surprised. It's a lot quieter around here since you left."

"I can't see him like that," I say.

"Then don't. You're busy becoming one of those big-shot jocks, remember?"

"Don't be such a smart-ass," I say. "I mean it, about Dad."

"He'll get it back. Mom calls it a breakdown or spell when she's talking to her friends as if someone's done this to him and one day he's going to snap out of it. You think he's bad, Ryan Callahan's dad got arrested down at Edgewater with a thirteen-year-old boy in the back-seat of his car."

"Get the fuck out of here."

Jay just smiles. "Scout's honor. So our old man's a zombie, at least he ain't hitting on little boys."

I laugh and we make a few jokes about it. Then I tell him about Heather and how I'm going to break up with her.

"She's going to hate you for the rest of her life," he says.

"I can live with that," I say.

"You have to."

I go to bed thinking of what I'm going to say, how I'm going to say it. Napalm's words about the sharpest knife bounce around my head. Below, I can hear Dad shuffling around the house, the late night creak of floorboards and chatter of water glasses.

The poor bastard's pacing, I think.

But then it's back to Heather and how I'm about to take out a tidy little hate mortgage. No easy way around it. Tears will be spilled. I'll tell her straight, maybe following the dance, after she's had her tainted moment in the sun, parading me around the dance in front of her chittering friends with their wanna-be boyfriends.

I pull out the Dostoevsky quote and read it until I drop off to sleep.

In the morning, after three cups of coffee and a handful of pills, zombie Dad looks like old Dad. The color is back in his face like a ripe cherry. He has his hair slicked back and his hands are bomb-diffusing steady, ready for the killer Saturday half-shift. Mom gives him the war bride send-off and for a moment I feel mildly patriotic watching the old man saunter off to work.

Someday, I think. Someday that won't be me.

"Get out of Cleveland," I tell Jay after Dad's left.

"No problem," he says. "I've got plans."

"Yeah?"

"I'm going to be a rock star, date movie hotties with Barbie doll bods and prime rib tans, get my face on TV."

"You'll finish school, Jay," Mom says, as if she's heard this one a million times before and it's her job to inject a little midwestern reality into Jay.

"I'll buy you a house when I'm rich, famous, and on *Entertainment Tonight.*"

Mom gives him this look and points at his breakfast plate.

"I'll settle for you taking your plate to the sink."

On Sunday, after the dance, I meet Stork behind the concrete wave wall where we used to go when we ditched class. The same collection of old men sit on five-gallon buckets fishing for carp and sheephead, even in the cold gray wind blowing off Lake Erie.

Stork's still in his work clothes, sipping coffee from a Styrofoam cup. "Hey, Bigtime," he says.

We do the shake and hug thing, his hands feel thick and woody. Several of the old men shoot us looks as if we might somehow scare the fish.

"How was it?" he asks as we watch this dude with huge purple lips and long greasy hair spring his pocketknife on a slimy-looking carp that's wriggling for its life on the cold cement.

I shrug, blow on my hands. My eyes feel like match holes in carpeting from lack of sleep. Every smack and bruise I imagine coming back to get me for breaking up with Heather on her big night.

"Textbook," I say.

We walk down the shore and watch gulls tip and sail in the air.

"How much blood did you spill?"

"From door to dance my this-just-isn't-working-out speech took six hours," I say.

"Six hours?"

I nod. What can I say? Every heart breaks the same way. And Heather went down easy. I told her after the group slow dance. I'd put a few drinks away and finally I just came out with it. She knew it was coming. I'd been a sullen bastard all night, rude to her friends and short when their dates pumped me with what's-it-like questions about Michigan.

In the end, after a solid hour of me steadfastly refusing to provide any explanation other than It's over, she copped the wronged-woman role, called me an asshole at least twice before giving me one last tear-soured kiss on the lips.

I left her at her door, watching as she stumbled under poor porch light, looking back at me in the car, hating me more intensely than she ever hated before.

I tell Stork all this, even the driving-around part afterward, listening to the radio.

"That's key," he says.

"What?"

"Driving around, listening to the radio—a must for all heart-breakers. At least you can beat a retreat back to Michigan," he says. "Stick and run—float like a butterfly and sting like a bee."

"I wish I felt like that."

"You getting a conscience on you, El?"

I shrug my shoulders.

"Don't," he says. "They're worse than your fucking pecker."

I laugh and we walk back up the jumble of cracked concrete blocks until we get to what passes for sand and a beach.

"You want to get some Biaggio's?" Stork asks.

I nod and we walk up through an empty lot, smell the road, hear the cars, both of us a little stiff, not knowing what exactly to talk about. I mean I've done my homework, smashed Heather's heart, confirmed that my old man has gone around some sort of midlife bend he may or may not come back from, and assured myself that Stork contin-ues to live and breathe and that he is Cleveland.

The counter lady coughs into her sleeve after taking our orders. She looks tired in a been-out-late sort of way. But Stork flashes her that killer smile of his and melts the old girl's wrinkles, putting a bounce in her step.

We sit with coffee and fresh pizza bagels.

"The job's not so bad," Stork says. "All I've got to do is push this red button, make the press go, fish out my product and try to think of something else.

"What about you?" he says.

"It's a lot of bullshit." Then I tell him about the Grind and how somedays it's enough just to make it through practice, take off my helmet, and cut the tape from my ankles and wrists.

The bagel goes a long ways toward filling the Heather sleep-deprivation pit. I wonder if this is some shade of what my old man feels all day.

I tell Stork team stories for an hour and two more cups of Biaggio's burn-the-walls-of-your-stomach coffee.

"But how come you guys always look so wholesome on television, All-American this, political science major that, enjoys fishing and reading? I mean come on, you're even starting to look like one of them—you've got that no-neck look going and you've put on weight."

"That's game day. Just bullshit for television. The only hobby I've seen is beer drinking and groupie screwing."

"Don't sound too bad," Stork says. "Some people pay good money to have that kind of fun. What did you think it would be like?"

"I didn't think. I went along for the ride. They get you with that we're-going-to-make-you-a-man crap. It feels as if I'm starring in some fucked-up movie called *Local Boy Makes Good.*"

"And you're making good?"

"I'm still waiting, that's what it feels like. I didn't know it would be like this. Does that sound corny? I mean you get sort of tracked into thinking football is the be-all and end-all, the Alpha and the Omega, and all that other crap. But it isn't. I know that—fuck do I know that now—the problem is how to get off the merry-go-round without copping out."

"I'm sure you've got some philosophical bullshit for that," Stork says.

"That's just it—I don't. I really don't know what I'm going to do."

"What about the other guys?"

I laugh. "Far as they're concerned this is the first step on their way to the NFL. They all think they're going to be stars."

"And?"

"Not me," I say.

"You sure used to play like you did."

I shake my head and sip some more coffee. "What about you?"

"It's not so bad," he says. "I knew what I was getting into with the factory. But I got a plan, remember? I've been socking away a little out of each paycheck and I'm going to invest some of it next year."

That's when I tell him about my old man, how he's walking around like he's got voodoo on the brain.

"It happens," he says. "It's called old-timer's disease. By the time you get your pension, you're all used up inside. It's working with machines that does it to you. They take and take and take."

"We sound like old men," I say.

Stork shoves his hands in front of my face.

"What the fuck can you do about it?—shit, my hands are numb already. And I been on the job—three, four months maybe? My mom cooks my meals. The guys at work call me Stretch. I think I'm better than them. I mean I walk around the plant all day looking down on these dudes, the way they walk around all stiff and shock-eyed, the missing teeth and fingers. Total fucking shoprats, rambling about the lottery, football, pussy, and who's got the cheapest liquor. Last week I chipped into the lottery pool and it was like I joined some sort of club and I'm one of the guys. But I don't feel like one of the guys. I'm still hooked on the black girls and that's not the sort of thing you tell your fellow shoprat."

"Why not?"

"Riley, this is Cleveland. Remember? They'd tell me I was diluting the white race or else the Bible thumpers would start heaving Scripture at me about mud people."

"Who's she this time?" I ask.

Stork's hands begin to shake. "She works at McDonald's. Her name's Jane."

"What happened to the name thing?"

He shrugs, "Jane, you mean? I know, I know, not much of a name, but you should hear the way she says Quarter Pounder. Breaks my heart. I go there at lunch break just to hear her take my order. It's like this secret thing with me. But one of these days I'm going to ask her out."

"Then what?"

"Then what? My mom'll hate me for the rest of my life and my old man will probably want to kick my ass. But I'm getting my courage up. Matter of fact that's what I do all day—sit at my workstation thinking, What's it going to be, Stork? When you gonna make your break? The other guys, I swear to God, they don't think at all. It's like they've got these trick brains, the minute they punch in, their brains just go blank."

"What about going to college?"

"There's got to be a better way. You tell me?"

I toss my hands up in the air.

"Riley, by all accounts, you're on the fucking yellow brick road. I mean, even if you fuck up, you'll get a job selling Fords or life insurance—it's what ex-jocks do."

"That's the problem," I tell him. "I've got so many options it's killing me."

When I return home Mom fusses and tells me that Heather's called three times already. Dad gets up from the La-Z-Boy with television-ray eyes. I can hear his bones cracking, brain creaking as he squints at me.

"You know what you're doing?" he asks.

I nod, not sure what the hell he's asking about. His hands start shaking again and Mom covers them with hers just before Jay comes bopping into the room.

"I told Heather you were going back today," Mom says, reaching out to touch my hair. "Are you all packed to go?"

I push her hand away and she smiles while Dad just stands there giving me one of his who-the-hell-are-you stares. I want to ask him what happened, but I'm afraid he might answer me and I won't understand.

"I'll get the keys," Mom says.

I ask her why she's dropping me at the bus station.

"Your father's eyes hurt him, honey," she says. "He needs to relax."

Dad looks away and I go upstairs for my bag.

In the driveway there's this awkward moment where words don't seem to work. The family's never been big on hugs or kisses. We're a handshake-and-peck-on-the-cheek-for-Mom family. But this time Dad slaps my hand out of the way and gives me this leaning hug, like he's going to whisper some life-or-death stuff in my ear. Only he doesn't.

Then he pulls away and goes back to the house without looking at me. Jay gives me a soul shake. "Take it easy or don't take it at all."

"Is there any other way?" I ask.

Jay just flashes me one of his smart-ass smiles.

We get in the car and go, Mom driving like the KGB's trailing her, gas, break, g-force curve, and plenty of horn.

I get on the bus and Mom waves.

When the bus clears the city, the clouds break again, and the Heather Pit opens up. I feel like I could be on a bus anywhere as I look at my reflection in the glass, reminding myself that I'm too big for all of this sensitivity crap, that the good man is a bad man.

FIFTEEN

Back in Ann Arbor, the streets have that postriot feel and the minute I see my first block-shaped M and GO BLUE sign, the dread sets in, as if I've somehow crossed back into Jockdom. I realize that I forgot to watch the game on television and, for some reason, the fact that I don't know who won and don't really care makes me happy.

Heather seems a million miles away, although I keep seeing her naked body: her warm breasts, her smell, which last time I saw her (face red from blubbering, wrinkled satin dress) smelled of tears.

And that's it, I think. Where was football? I wonder if the game ever leaves the heart of somebody like Himes or Wolfie, or if it's like this rumbling down in the belly that they were born with.

Not me, I think. Not me. I like it gone.

I buy one of those fold-out maps of the city at a gas station and find Elm Street and start walking, thinking of what I'll say to Kate when I see her. Her house is an old brown duplex with aluminum storm windows and a high-pitched roof. The street is full of trash, broken beer bottles, ripped-open leaf bags, fast-food wrappers, and yellowed newspapers that scuttle across the cement walk. On the front door there is a bell system for the four apartments and a rusted wind chime that lets out this weak ting when I bump it. I press the button for 2B and listen to the buzz as I check my reflection in the glass. Inside, I hear a door open and then the sound of footsteps on stairs.

Kate comes to the door in a long T-shirt, thick wool socks, and mantilla wrapped around her head, which gives her this art student/terrorist look.

"What took you so long?" she says, a little Mae West in the tilt of her hips.

"I would have called . . ."

"But you didn't have my number," she says. "Come in."

I follow her up a narrow set of stairs to her apartment. The room is small and L-shaped with a view of the city from the one window. A white curtain filters the light. There is a small ratty-looking couch in one end and a bed under the window. To my left is a chipped end table filled with photos and half-burnt candles.

"There he is," Kate says, pointing at a picture of her and her father, Coach Treller. I pick up the photo and stare at it. She is a little girl, maybe thirteen or fourteen, and Coach T is smiling. I put it back with the others.

"No roommate?" I ask.

"Of course not," she says. "My father helps with the rent as long as I stay in school. But what he really wants is to keep tabs on me."

"When I first met you, I thought you lived in the dormitory."

She rolls her eyes at me and unwraps the mantilla from her head, letting it fall to the floor. "I can't stand the dorms."

"I have to," I say.

"You have to do a lot of things, I suppose."

She reaches up and touches my face like Helen Keller and smiles. The whole room smells of incense and baby powder.

"What was that for?" I ask.

"Phrenology—you don't look so good."

"That's the skull, not the face."

She frowns, moves her hand across my hair. "Once, when I was little, some older girls took me down into a dark basement, told me to stick my hand into this bowl filled with brains. It was right after we'd done the Mary Worth thing in the mirror. But it was just oysters and I grossed everybody out, because I liked the way it felt."

I laugh and sit on the couch. She sits down next to me, folds her legs under the long shirt, and looks at my duffel bag.

"Going somewhere?"

"I just came back from Cleveland," I say.

"Oh," she says. "You want a beer?"

I nod and watch as she goes to the fridge and extracts two bottles of beer for us. Judging from the looseness in her legs I don't think it's her first bottle of the night.

"What are we doing?" she says. "You do something bad in Cleveland?"

I stare at her, the dark shadows under her eyes, swollen lips, slightly canted eyes catching the light from the overhead bulb, making it look brighter.

"Do you know what I'm asking?" she says in her dumb-jock voice.

"I think so—all that crap about your father being a coach. And you know what?"

"What?" she says, moving closer until I can smell her.

"I don't care. Not one bit, unless you do."

"But I already told you—"

"Told me what?"

"That I swore off dumb jocks, remember? They give you brain cancer and sleep disorders. That or they end up becoming like my father."

I tell her about Heather and the walk back from the bus station. When I finish there are tears in her eyes.

"It's so sad," she says. "It's good though."

"Good?" I say. "I feel like a jerk."

"You're not responsible."

"What do you mean?"

"Everybody has to have their heart broken at least once. That way you learn. In fact, it should be mandatory."

"Mandatory heartbreak?"

"That's right—broken hearts for everybody. This place is full of girls who think that some prince is going to come along and take them away. Only it doesn't work that way."

"How about you?"

"I gave up on royalty a long time ago and I've had my heart broken a few times. That's why I swore off jocks."

"Just jocks?" I say.

"I've got daddy issues," she says.

"What if I told you I'm only pretending to be a jock?"

"You mean like an undercover jock?"

"Something like that," I say.

"Well then, you're doing a pretty good job." She laughs and leans into me, her beer spilling on my shirt.

A couple of loud bangs echo through the room, followed by a door slamming several times.

"Thin walls," I say.

"Field hockey players," she says. "They're always fighting and slamming doors. If you ask me, I think they're in love. Think they could make a movie about it?"

"Field Hockey Players in Love?"

"Need a better title—something like *Chicks with Sticks.*"

I laugh.

She goes to the door, slides the dead bolt, and lights a large green candle before turning off the light.

"Close your eyes," she says. "And no more about this ex-girlfriend."

I close them.

When I open them she's sitting on the edge of the bed, naked, beer bottle pinched between her knees, the candlelight flicking shadows all over the place. I rise and pull off my clothes, the room feels cold and far away.

We slip into bed and she curls herself into me. I smell her hair, run my hands down her shoulder and cup her ass. She moans.

"Yes," she says. "I can feel her on you. It's bad and you need to let it go."

I don't say a word as she presses her skin against mine, until she pulls the blanket over our heads and the only thing I can hear is her breathing. She's different from Heather, more delicate, like moth wings. She puts her hands on my face and then pushes me down to her breasts until I can feel the hardness of her nipples pressing against my eyelids.

"So you're an undercover jock?" she says. I lift her and set her on the bed.

"Yes," I say, spreading her legs.

"There," she says when I push into her. She begins rocking, her skin floating across mine, eyes shut tight. I can hear voices coming through the walls. And for a while there are only our voices asking questions.

When we finish she pulls back the blanket and stumbles out of bed, wrapping herself in the thin white gauze of the curtain until she's tangled in fabric and candlelight. I get us some more beer and throw a T-shirt on.

From the curtain Kate says, "I know what you're thinking."

"No you don't," I say. "And when you do it's over."

"Ooh, an ultimatum," she says as she unravels herself from the curtain and grabs the beer. "My dad's really into giving me ultimatums. You sure you're cut out for this, big boy?"

I nod and go to her in the curtain and press myself against her.

On our way to practice I tell Napalm about Kate and Heather.

"Get the fuck out of here. I don't believe it," he says.

"Which part?" I ask.

"The whole thing. You dump Heather, then you go and fuck this

Kate chick, who—I need not remind you—is Coach Treller spawn, the fruit of his loins."

"Yeah?"

"Hello, Riley," he says, knocking me on the head. "Anybody home?"

I tell him it's not like that, then I try to explain to him the way she wrapped herself in the curtain.

"I guess you had to be there," Napalm says. "What about Heather?"

"She's been calling six times a day."

"Brutal."

"Get this," I say. "Phil tells me last night when I get in that he can hear the phone before it rings."

"What?"

"He says he knows when she's calling. He gets this rattling sound in his head and then the phone rings."

"You sure it's not the rocks in his head?"

I shrug my shoulders. "At any rate I feel pretty good. I've got the buzz back again."

"What the fuck does that mean?"

"I don't know, I guess it means I'm going to make it through another practice—I'm going to be okay. How about you?"

"I look and feel like shit," he says, pulling at his eyelid until the pink shows. "And to top it off the Cheesegrater says she's getting 'feelings' for me."

"Feelings are no fucking good."

He nods. "And she called me 'mansuetude.' "

"What does that mean?"

"I don't know, I'm afraid to look it up."

"Stay that way," I say. "It's probably French for pussy-whipped."

———————

It takes two days of bust-ass practice for me to lose the buzz. Coach U's all over me, screaming and yelling, like a man with his hair on fire, telling me that someday I might be worthy of a starting position, but I've got my head up my ass and it's his job to pull it out.

"Riley," he says, "I'm the best head-out-of-ass surgeon around."

"My neck's been hurting me," I say.

"What's this, Riley—you taking a dive on me? If it's bothering you then go see the trainers and get some pills. Other than that I don't want to hear about it, because your neck's not the problem, your head is, try concentrating."

"I will," I say. Coach smiles, slaps an arm around my shoulder. "That's my boy."

When he leaves Robeson walks over. "What's the matter with you? Reasoning with Coach U's about the dumbest thing I've heard of."

"What would you do?"

"I already told you that—options, motherfucker, before you get old like me and start thinking you might want to stick it out."

"What's wrong with that?" I ask.

"More importantly, Riley, what's wrong with *you?*" he says.

After a little things-have-been-turning-up-missing homily that makes me feel sick, Coach Roe introduces the words Rose Bowl to the team and every awful platitude about roses and thorns gets preached our way. We've got zero losses, but so do three other teams and our schedule's been pretty candy-ass. We are number four in the country with an outside chance of a national title. But first we have to beat Ohio State, go to Pasadena, win, and hope everybody else gets smoked.

The sad thing about Coach Roe pumping the Rose Bowl hype is that it works. Nearly every guy on the team goes around fantasizing about a trip to Pasadena, bowl gifts, beaches, Disneyland, and national television.

Roe calls it the Road to the Roses, as if it's Mao's Long March.

On Wednesday, Napalm goes down hard. I don't see it happen, but we all hear the scream, followed by whistles. O-line drills stop long enough for me to watch Napalm get dragged off the field, by trainers who look as if they're abducting him to some Third World country for medical experiments. They work on his ankle, pads and shoes flying out of the huddle, the zip of scissors, then the call for ice.

"I heard it pop," Jerry Q says, cracking his knuckles for effect.

Everybody gets to stand around in their funereal faces for a minute, watching Napalm get dragged offstage, before Roe blasts us back to the Grind with his whistle and bullhorn.

After practice and another lecture from Roe on the virtues of study table and how attendance is mandatory for all freshmen, I visit Napalm in the training room.

He gives me the Tylenol Four with Codeine thumbs-up, his leg iced like Hitler's brain. All around me trainers do the ragpicker scurry, collecting tape balls and bloody Ace bandages from the floor. Waste cases stumble in, pointing at swollen knees, busted fingers, spasmed backs and all kinds of fucked-up rug burns, begging for ice, drugs, and sympathy.

I look at Napalm's ankle and there's only one way to describe the purple bruise mushrooming around the joint and squirting up onto his shin—angry.

"Does it hurt?"

"I feel like that guy in the song "Heroin." Like I know every raindrop by name," he says, humming the tune.

"Come on, man, does it hurt?"

"What the fuck do you think?" he says, pointing at the ankle as if it's not part of his body.

"I say it's past hurt and into Alaska-sized pain."

He nods.

"Is it broken?" I ask.

He mumbles something about going for X rays with Doc A, and I reach out to touch the plum-colored mass that used to be his ankle. Even with all of the ice it is still burning hot.

Just then Himes stumbles in, mouth open, tape dangling off his wrists, like prayer beads. He looks at Napalm's ankle. "Oh, man," he says. "Looks like you busted your wheel pretty good. What is it with you offense guys?"

"Not now, Himes," I say.

Robeson walks up to us. "Himes, leave the man the fuck alone," he says. "Go find your buddy Bates or something."

Himes looks Robeson over.

"Leave who?" he says.

"The man's injured, can't you see?"

"Shit, Robeson, sometimes you act like a goddamn grandma," Himes says. "I'm just busting balls is all. Could happen to me, could happen to you."

"That's the problem," Robeson says. "We don't know what could happen—do we?" He holds his ground, staring Himes down, until Bible Boy comes in to say a prayer over Napalm's leg.

"Amen," Bible Boy says when he finishes.

"You okay?" Robeson asks Napalm.

"They got me pretty iced-up," he says. "Looks like I might get the gimp vacation."

"You guys ever hear about the Painless Career-Ending Injury?" Robeson asks.

"Here we go again. I ain't sticking around for this crap," Himes says, shaking his hands and walking back to the locker room.

"All I know is this ain't it," Napalm says.

"Maybe," Robeson says.

"What are you talking about, Robe, you can't have a Painless Career-Ending Injury?" I ask.

"Not exactly painless, but let's just say there are a few guys who take some measly knee injury or something and it doesn't heal right or maybe they fuck it up again. You know what happens then?"

Napalm says, "What?"

"They get to keep their scholarship—that's what happens. Thing of beauty, matter of fact I've been trying to have a Painless Career-Ending Injury find me for quite some time—kick back, go to school and learn something besides how to run a Double Bogey Blitz."

"You mean you're not quitting," I say.

"Exactly, Riley. Football quits you. You get to keep your dignity and all that good stuff."

"Goddamn, Robe," Napalm says. "Don't put any ideas into my head."

Robeson shrugs. "The other side of the coin is you keep your scholarship, but you're a gimp for the rest of your natural fucking life."

"I could handle that," Napalm says. "I could definitely handle that."

Before Robeson can say anything else, several trainers push us out of the way and help Napalm off the bench and into a wheelchair. Just as they are about to haul Napalm off into one of the blue vans, he gives my arm one of those I'm-dying-here grips and says, "Tell the Cheesegrater."

I nod and head back to the locker room. Phil flaps up to me, towel wrapped around his bulging belly like some kind of bandage that's holding his guts in.

"Heather called," he says.

"Phil, we're in the locker room. She can't call."

"The rattle," he says, pointing at his head.

Fuckhead, who's standing behind him, points at Phil and says, "I think Phil's developed a case of ESP."

Phil stands there looking at me like some idiot child cursed with second sight.

"Sounds like someone's rattling a chain," Phil says. "I want it to stop. You've got to tell her about it. I'm worried about my studies. Come on, Riley, have mercy."

"This too shall pass," I say cryptically.

Phil throws his arms up into the air and that's how I leave him.

"How hot was it?" Kate asks after I'm done telling her about Napalm's ankle. "Was it this hot?" she says, placing my hand on her stomach.

I shake my head.

"This hot?" My hand goes to her breasts. She smiles, biting her tongue.

"Not even close," I say.

"This hot?" This time she jerks my hand over a burning candle until I smell burnt hand hair and jerk away. She puts my fingers up to her mouth, licking the red spot until it cools.

"Sorry," she says. Then she pulls up her sleeve and shows me a track of small raisin-shaped bruises dotting her arm.

"That's from where you touched me. I bruise easily."

I can't take my eyes off of them.

Then she says, "You should see what my back looks like."

She pulls her sleeve back down and we sit on the couch again. While she puts on music, I look at her fruit crate of books, the spines of each marbled with white cracks, *Portable Nietzsche, Erotica Universalis, The Diary of Anne Frank, For Whom the Bell Tolls, Wiseblood, The Postman Always Rings Twice, Day of the Locust,* and a food-stained hardback of *The Joy of Cooking.*

Before I can make sense of them, she plops back down and hands me a short water glass of whiskey. We clink and drink.

I can't stop thinking about the line of bruises blooming up and down her arm, wondering if her insides are as delicate.

"Drink," she says. "If you're thinking about the bruises—stop. It's normal for me."

"That wasn't what I was thinking about," I say.

"What then?"

"Football."

"I thought you were an undercover jock?"

"No," I say. "It's not like that. Sometimes I feel like I don't want to be doing this."

"Doing what?"

"Football."

"Okay, what about football?" she says.

I tell her about the long practices and how I hate the games, all the standing around on the sideline.

"Boring," she says. "What's with you guys? You think you're special or something just because your biceps get more blood than your brains. I know my father thinks that."

"What about you?"

"I'm with you, aren't I? And what's with this quitting stuff? Look at yourself, Elwood—you're six foot six, two hundred something pounds. Even if you could quit, what then? Do you think they'd leave you alone? It's like your genetic destiny—get big, play ball."

"Maybe I want to go to school."

"You are in school."

"No, I mean really go to school, learn something besides another team's offense or how to avoid getting yelled at by Coach U," I say. "I got out of Cleveland, I mean I've made it this far."

"You know what my father would say?"

"What?"

"Nothing—you'd be persona non grata in a heartbeat."

"That's the tricky part," I say. "I'm acing all the classes Coach Roe forbid me to take. I don't act stupid all the time, so half the guys think I'm weird and I don't know what I want."

She looks at me and takes a long drink of her whiskey, teeth clinking on the glass.

"You really thinking of quitting?"

"Something," I say. "Maybe more complicated than that. I don't know what the fuck I'm going to do. Robeson says they'll yank my scholarship."

"You know what I do when I'm thinking things over?" she says.

"What?"

"I go for walks, real long ones, and try to get lost, that way when I find my way back everything looks better and for a while I'm happy just to be in the same place I started."

"Let's go for a walk, then."

"No," she says, pulling my hand. "Let's get lost."

I follow her around the room, slip my jacket on, and go to the door.

"For warmth," she says, grabbing a small pewter flask.

We head down the street and I imagine people staring at us, with some sort of hungry feeling in their guts, the way people stare at couples when they are sad or lonely. Kate takes a nip off the flask, tosses it back to me and makes a drinking motion.

The campus is full of students darting around in the darkness, their bodies bathed in the bright headlights of parked pizza delivery cars. Kate fits her small hand into mine. As we walk, the dead leaves on the trees rattle in the breeze.

On the diag we come across a group of frat boys dragging wooden crosses on their backs, dressed only in underwear.

Kate looks at them. "Sheep," she says.

Then she leads me up behind some old building I've never seen before. There is pigeon shit everywhere and the wind stops the minute we turn the corner and Kate's face is bloodred from it, her lips almost blue. As she pins me up against the wall, a shout echoes across the diag causing the crows perched above us in the bare trees to caw.

"Kiss me," she says.

I lean forward and she wraps her cold hands around the back of my neck, her mouth warm and full of bourbon.

Then she pulls me back over a ventilation grate and hot air blasts over us, smelling faintly of sewage and rusted metal, and for a minute I could be anywhere—I want to be anywhere.

"I want to tell you a story," she says, air whooshing in my ears like blood.

"Now?" I say.

"Why not?"

I nod and she leans back against the wall, closing her eyes.

"About how I was obsessed with this older guy," she says.

"How much older?" I say.

"Married, older. But I lived in a small town, you know, so what else was there to do?"

"Where did you live?" I ask, making my hand into the state of Michigan.

"U.P.," she says quietly as if she's remembering some detail about the town. "And don't ever do that thing with your hand again or I'll break your finger."

"Promise?" I say.

She smiles at me and continues. "This man, he had a wife and I was still in high school. It was a bad thing, but I walked around thinking I was special, like I had something over the other girls my age. If you want to know the truth, I didn't know what I was doing—it just felt dangerous, so I did it."

"What?"

"Slept with him, even though I knew he was married."

"Did your father know?"

"That's not what I want to tell you—let me finish."

I nod and take the flask from her.

"So one day he meets me at the IHOP and tells me it's over and I cry and all that. This was just after my dumb-jock stage, which was after my bad-boy period."

"I can't imagine you in high school," I say. "Let alone this guy."

"I was just a screwed-up kid. Anyways, I went and bought some lighter fluid and one day, while he was at work, I went over to his house, walked right in the back door while his wife was sitting in the front room watching television and squirted the lighter fluid all over the clothes in the laundry room. Then I lit them on fire."

"Get the fuck out of here."

"I never lie, Elwood—you should know that about me."

"What'd you do?"

"Well, then I called him at work, something he had forbidden me to do, and told him that his house was on fire and that he'd better get home."

"Was anybody hurt?"

She smiles. "I was—don't you see?"

"I meant in the fire?"

"No, I knew what I was doing, the wife just threw the clothes out into the snow. Then she cried."

"You did this?"

"Yes," she says, pulling me tighter. I press my face into her shoulder and wonder if the story is why she brought me out here.

We drink some more until I realize that she's pretty drunk from the way she staggers off the ventilation grate, warm air blasting her hair straight up into the night.

"Come on," she says, running off into the dark. "Let's play follow the leader."

And I follow her.

I wake in the morning, not quite sure where I am, the sheets warm and moist, sunlight cracking through the window. I catch sight of the gauze curtain and I realize I've slept through morning mile. The room is quiet and as I move my hands under the blankets they come up damp and cool in the morning air. Carefully, I pull back the sheets while Kate mumbles in her sleep and rolls, putting a hand to her face.

When I step out of the bed I see a dark spot in the sheets and puzzle over it. The sharp acidic scent of urine filling my nostrils. I watch her sleep and note that the wet spot is on her side of the bed.

Fuck it, I think. Not a word, pretend it never happened and walk away. Something sticks in my chest as I look back at Kate, her hair pooled around her neck and shoulders and the dark stain on the mattress.

I walk straight back to my dorm room.

Phil's up when I key the door to our room, his eyes ashy and bruised.

"Heather called," he says.

I ignore him.

"Heather called, did you hear me?"

It takes me a minute before I realize that he's actually getting in my face, puffing out his chest. Then I remember the chains rattling around in his head.

"I'll take care of it," I say.

He sits back down on the bed.

"And," he says, "Coach Hart was by, wondering where you were this morning."

He cracks a smile and for a minute I want to jack him one in the face, but I don't. Instead I sit at my desk and stare out the window wanting to be lost again or out in the dark wandering around.

SIXTEEN

For missing Hard-on Hart's morning mile class, Coach U informs me that I'll run with Hart the rest of my natural frosh life. An honor, he says, bestowed on only two other unfortunate fuckups who eventually got shitcanned from the team.

Hart busts my stones through the last two weeks of the season, calling me a nonconformist as if it's some sort of ultimate insult.

"I know you're up to something, Riley," he says.

Little by little I've been tagged by the coaching staff as someone who won't quite go with the flow. So I make it my mission to bag at least one pair of shoes a week and after a while it's just something I do. A little fuck-you to Hart.

But then things start going to shit.

Coach Roe has a little heart-to-heart with me about responsibilities.

"Get a haircut," he says. "The least you can do is look like a ballplayer, son. What would your parents think?"

I shrug.

"That's it, Riley? You're going to sit there and shrug your shoulders at me?"

209 · IF I DON'T SIX

I say nothing and he gives me the there's-no-I-in-team speech, which I know by heart.

When we beat Ohio State and get the Rose Bowl bid, Phil's parents have a dozen roses delivered to our room. He walks around all day beaming with Rose Bowl pride. Every time I come into the room and see the roses I just shake my head because the bowl game means practice through the holidays and extra conditioning in the indoor unit with the heat jacked to mimic California sun. I try telling this to Phil.

"We're going to get Rose Bowl rings and watches," he says.

"So what?" I say. "It's not like we did anything for them."

"We practiced, Riley—that counts for something."

I shake my head and leave him standing, because it strikes me that it doesn't count for anything. Some of the seniors actually cry when we're officially extended the bid. Three-hundred-pound guys who can bench 425 pounds twelve times, and drink forty beers at a sitting, break into tears. It's an ugly sight. Even Bam Bam breaks down and starts hugging Bates until Bates smashes him into a locker and runs off to the weight room.

On campus, students I've never met before congratulate me and wish me luck, some even try to slap me five and say stupid shit about kicking ass in the Rose Bowl.

The next day, as I'm walking back from classes I see Jimmy from Jersey hanging outside the dorms trying to talk to some girl. I try to walk by without him noticing, but he yells out and waves me over. The girl looks relieved. She has loose blond hair and narrow blue eyes that make her face looked pinched.

"Be ready," he says.

I look at him. "Huh?"

The girl rolls her eyes at me and sighs.

"You heard me," he says. "Be ready."

He rubs his fingers together and I smile. "Know what I mean?" he asks.

I nod and listen as he goes back to talking with the girl.

"Now, Little Stevie," Jimmy says. "Good guitar player, but he decides to split the E Street Band, right?"

I leave them and head back to my room.

Later that night I wake to a sharp pain in my ribs and Jimmy's fat face mooning over me. He jabs me one more time before placing a finger to his lips to quiet me.

I get up, rub my face, and look over at the sleeping lump that is Phil. The whole room smells of old chewing tobacco.

"You ready?" Jimmy asks.

I ask him for what.

"The mother of all scams, you dumbshit," he whispers.

Phil stirs, mumbling something in his sleep that sounds like a Hail Mary.

"Come on, motherfucker—we on or off?" Jimmy says.

It takes me a minute to figure out what he's talking about, but remembering the scam I nod. He gives me this caper face and tells me to dress warmly, before slipping out the door.

When I come out of the room Jimmy pulls himself off the wall to give me a silent high five. Right away, I'm thinking I don't like this fucker and how if I tell him I don't want to go along with him that I'll be pegged as one soft sonofabitch.

The dorm's stone-quiet, just the empty sound of water trickling through pipes as we walk down the hall.

"In one shot we'll get enough stuff so we don't have to be shoplifting all the time," he says.

I think about it for a minute as we hit the stairwell.

When I don't answer he says, "Don't go chickenshit on me, Riley, or else I'll go get Whigger, that boy's got himself a reckless pair of balls."

"Is that how you do things in Jersey?" I ask.

Jimmy punches the panic bar on the door and frowns at me. Outside, the air is so cold it hurts my lungs. Something in his challenge bumps me up to the occasion and I want to show him how reckless I am.

"Fuck it," I say. "We going to make any money off this?"

"We're meeting somebody first," Jimmy says. "We'll see though."

I follow him down this house-encrusted side street. Trash scutters along the curb and the bare trees look beautiful against the black sky. Then I catch my reflection in the window of a parked Honda and wonder what the fuck I'm doing and how I should get back to the dorm.

But then this car creeps down the street and flashes its lights at us. Jimmy waves me forward and when I get close enough to the car I recognize Cheswick behind the wheel.

"Poker boy," Cheswick says.

We shake, his nose looks better than the last time I saw it wrapped in a tea towel spouting blood. He and Jimmy mutter between themselves while I crawl into the backseat.

"He cool?" Cheswick asks, pointing at me.

Jimmy nods and we drive down the back streets in silence. Cheswick parks the car behind the football facility on an old practice field, covered with bright orange pylons.

Cheswick kills the lights and turns to Jimmy. "Same thing, same way?"

Jimmy nods, grim-faced, and then goes on to explain how they've been creeping Dumpsters outside the equipment room.

"They're always throwing stuff away. Perfectly good shoes, old jerseys. You believe these people?" Jimmy says as he pulls a wad of black garbage bags out from under the seat and tosses a few into my lap.

"Frat boys will buy anything," Cheswick says. "But tonight . . ."

He displays a single silver key under the dull glow of the dome light. "Ta-dah—the key to the kingdom."

"How did you?" I ask, staring at the key.

"People owe me favors," Cheswick says. Jimmy lets out this retarded henchman-type chuckle before popping the door open. I follow them out of the car, Cheswick keeps coughing loudly and every time he does I get this nervous sinking feeling that we're being watched. But the fact that there are fans out there willing to pay cash money for any genuine Michigan gear follows me over the rough brick wall behind Cheswick and Jimmy.

The practice field looks different in the dark. The goalposts cast long harpoon-shaped shadows in the moonlight and the oak tree which I've run around a thousand times looks bare and lonely as we creep across the field to the back entrance.

"Do the Dumpster first," Jimmy says, pointing at the large steel square next to the equipment room door.

Halfway to the Dumpster a bright security light clicks on and I step back a few paces.

"It's nothing," Cheswick says. "Motion sensitive, half the time the fucking raccoons trip it."

Unfazed, Jimmy goes over to the Dumpster and cracks open the lid as I look back over my shoulder at Roe's coaching tower standing dark against the night. Above us clouds skitter across the sky with that black movie-time speed.

"Take a fucking look at this," Jimmy says.

I pad up to the lip of the Dumpster and peer down into the scrawl of garbage, most of it tape and torn-up hip pads, thousands of crushed Gatorade cups, half-melted ice bags, and bloody Ace bandages, but sprinkled in amongst the trash are a few pairs of shoes, older models with flat heels and faded white piping.

"They're old ones, but they'll sell just fine," Cheswick says. Jimmy tips himself into the Dumpster and shoes begin sailing out behind him, landing on the cracked asphalt.

"Christ, Riley, pick the fuckers up," Cheswick says. "I'm the brains of this operation and you—*mon frère*—qualify as labor."

I stare him down for a minute until he looks away, before gathering the shoes into the garbage bag.

"Got 'em," Jimmy says, tipping himself back out of the Dumpster.

"Stop staring at the field," Cheswick says to me. "What's a matter, you miss this place?"

Jimmy says, "He's sprouting pussy hair. Come on, Riley, stop pissing down your leg and get with the program."

I shake him off and heft the bag of shoes a few times, half hoping they'll call it a night and head back to the car. Instead Cheswick pulls out the key and presses it into my palm.

Jimmy looks at me. "We've never done this before."

"What do you mean you've never done this before?" I ask.

"Inside," Jimmy says.

"It's called B and fucking E," Cheswick says. "All I want to know is if you jock sniffers are up to it?"

Jimmy does a little air guitar jump and says, "I'm Born to Run, Ches."

Cheswick rolls his eyes.

"Well goddamn, Riley, slap some hair around that keyhole and shove the fucking key so Bruce Springsteen here can do his thing," Cheswick says.

I look around one more time at the dark and empty field before keying the door. Both Cheswick and Jimmy stand back a few feet to watch, looking over their shoulders nervously as I turn the key and pull open the door.

It's the same hallway I've walked down a hundred times before, helmet in hand, thinking about the warm hiss of the showers and training table. I look back at Jimmy and see that it spooks him a bit too as he whispers something at Cheswick and points at the equipment room to our right. The whole place smells and feels as if at any minute taped and padded players are going to come roaring out of the locker

room. I tap Jimmy on the shoulder, pointing at one of those phony
Eye of Michigan paintings on the wall. The words ACCEPT WITH-
OUT PRIDE, RELINQUISH WITHOUT STRUGGLE written
underneath it.

"Fuck the Eye," Jimmy says.

I don't know why, but I flip the painting off. Jimmy snickers and
does the same.

Cheswick tries the equipment room door and it swings open.

"That Dumpster shit's Puppy Chow," Cheswick says, waving us
into Rotten Bobby's lair. "Now this . . . this is the whole fucking
righteous enchilada."

Both Jimmy and I creep forward into Bobby's room, holding our
breath and letting it go in slow uneasy sighs as we pass his paper-
encrusted desk. Several tit-shaped paperweights hold down piles of
invoices and in the corner, next to the filing cabinet, is a stack of porn
mags.

"Lights?" Jimmy asks.

"Don't be a fuckwit, Springsteen," Cheswick says. "Just show me
where they keep the helmets and jerseys."

I point to the back of the room which is obscured by tall blue-
painted shoe racks on top of which sit old helmets. Shoelaces hang
off the fluorescent light fixture like tinsel and Cheswick parts them
and walks to the back of the room, disappearing into the black-
ness.

I turn to Jimmy. "If we get caught we're fucked."

"You're a genius," Jimmy whispers.

Even in the half-dark of the room I can see the shadows on his face
as he nods just as Cheswick emerges from the back with an armful of
jerseys and two helmets swinging from his fingertips.

"Cha-ching," Cheswick says, pumping the helmets over his head.
"Some asshole will make a lamp out of these."

"Let's go," I say nervously.

"You guys done holding hands?" Cheswick asks. "If so, bring me some of those garbage bags and go get some more helmets so we can get the fuck out of here."

Both Jimmy and I wade into the back room and slide helmets off the rack, slipping them into our garbage bags where they thud against the shoes.

After we've filled our bags we walk out into the hallway again. Cheswick clinks the equipment room door shut behind us and gives another thumbs-up before pausing and staring at the line of pictures on the wall—every All-American who has ever played for Michigan.

"You guys gonna get your pictures on this wall?" Cheswick asks, his head twitching ever so slightly.

Before we can answer I hear his teeth begin to rattle, then I see the shaking in his hands.

Jimmy looks at me. "Cut the shit, Cheswick."

I step closer just as Cheswick hits his knees, his body doubling over. A thin choking sound escapes his lips as he drops the garbage bag.

"Stop fucking around," Jimmy yells.

I push Jimmy aside and kneel over Cheswick, who is now on the floor, his legs and arms thrashing.

"What the fuck?" Jimmy says.

"Must be a seizure," I say.

"What do you mean a seizure? There's no fucking way this can be happening."

"Hit the lights," I say. Jimmy looks at me a minute before running his hand along the wall, groping for the switch. Suddenly, the hall is flooded with a fluttering light. I stand over Cheswick's shaking body, his legs bumping into mine.

"What the fuck are we going to do?" Jimmy asks.

"Hold him down."

Jimmy drops his bags and leaps on Cheswick as if he's covering a hand grenade.

"Careful, motherfucker," I say. Jimmy slides off him. "Just hold his arms down, that's all I want you to do."

I grab hold and steady Cheswick's head, preventing it from slamming into the floor as I look into his egg-white eyes.

Jimmy looks at me. "What now?"

"His tongue," I say, pointing at Cheswick's tightly clenched jaw.

"That's right, that's right," Jimmy says. "He might swallow it or bite it off."

"We need something to put in his mouth."

Jimmy gets this worried look on his face as Cheswick's shaking speeds a little.

"Get something," I say. "Now."

Jimmy scrambles back to one of the bags and comes back with a shoe.

"No fucking way I'm sticking my fingers in his mouth—that's your job."

"A shoe?" I say. "We can't put a fucking shoe in his mouth."

"You got any better ideas?"

I look around and consider sending Jimmy into the locker room for a mouthpiece or roll of tape, but instead I wave him off and attack Cheswick's jaw, prying at the seizure-hardened muscle around his lips until it parts and his teeth start chattering again.

"Now," I say to Jimmy.

He looks at me a moment before plunging the toe of the shoe into Cheswick's mouth. I let go and Cheswick clamps down. We roll him over to his side and I tell Jimmy to sit on him.

After what seems like forever, the shaking stops and Cheswick's body goes slack as if someone's pulled the plug on him.

"He dead?" Jimmy asks. " 'Cause if he's not I'm going to kill the motherfucker."

I take the shoe out of Cheswick's mouth and check his breathing by putting my hand under his nose. Finally his eyes flutter open and he shakes his head.

"You all right?" I ask.

It takes him a minute or two of staring around the room before he knows what happened.

"Shit," he says. "Shit, shit, shit."

He sits up and looks down at the wet spot on his crotch.

"The motherfucker pissed his pants," Jimmy says.

I reach out and shove the stupid bastard against the wall, causing a few of the All-American pictures to swing back and forth.

Cheswick hops to his feet. "What are you fuckers staring at?"

"You, man," Jimmy says. "Pissing your pants."

Cheswick looks at the shoe on the ground and points at it. "You stick a shoe in my mouth?"

I nod.

"We saved your life," Jimmy says.

"All right, you New Jersey jerk-off, so I had a seizure and you stuck a shoe in my mouth, you wanna medal or am I supposed to hug you?"

I ask him if he's all right and he just shrugs me off, staring at the bags as if he's already forgotten the seizure.

"Pick up the bags and let's get the hell out of here," he says.

"I thought you were messing with us," Jimmy says.

A smile creeps across Cheswick's face. "I was—then I had a seizure. You think that's bad. I had one when I was screwing this chick."

He laughs, pointing at the bags again as my heart slows down and crawls out of my throat. Before we leave, Jimmy corners Cheswick and says, "Don't ever do that again or I'll kill you."

Cheswick yawns at him. "Whatever you say, Bruce."

By the time we get back over the wall and into Cheswick's car the sky seems lighter in the east. Flecks of traffic flash by in the distance, reminding me to look at the sky again for stars through the windshield. There are none. So I just sit there listening to the plastic crinkle of the garbage bags and Cheswick chattering about our haul. I want to take it all back, key the lock again and place every helmet back on its shelf, even throw the shoes back into the Dumpster where they'll be hauled away with the rest of the trash. I start thinking about Kate setting the man's house on fire, the accident I caused on the overpass, the look in my father's eyes after the eight-hour-shift shuffle has turned his brain into oatmeal, the feel of Cheswick's plugged-in body. It's one of those moments where everything is like a car crash and I'm seeing things 20/20—what I should have done, what I could have done—what I might do.

"Somebody staple your fucking tongue?" Jimmy asks. We're almost back at the dorms and Cheswick has let Jimmy slip *Darkness on the Edge of Town* into the tape deck and he's back to his heavy-browed self again, thinking about money; Cheswick's seizure a thing of the past.

I tell them I'm tired.

"Sure you are," Cheswick says. "Just remember you were right there with us and you shoved a shoe in my mouth. You think I'm gonna let you forget about that?"

"I know," I say.

"Don't worry about him," Jimmy says. "He's cool, he'll keep his mouth shut. You can take him to the bank, besides you're the motherfucker who was the liability tonight."

Cheswick ignores him and says, "All I'm saying is he plays poker for shit, how do I know he's not gonna run his mouth or get a conscience?"

I ask him how his nose is and that shuts him up.

At the dorm we get out and amble toward the light without saying a word, the gear stashed in Cheswick's car, nothing about money mentioned. I feel sick and cored out and can't stop thinking about how the air felt when I pushed the door open, the way it dropped down into my lungs like dry ice and started to burn.

The next night I take Kate to Wolfie's Rose Bowl party and Napalm drags the Cheesegrater along. Napalm uses this fake taxi money he gets for being a temporary team gimp and the minute we climb into the slick vinyl seats Kate pulls a handful of small airline bottles out of her purse and hands them out saying, "Gin, vodka, and bourbon for the boys."

I twist the top off of mine and drain it in one swallow. Napalm does the same and tosses the empty bottle out the window. "Kind of like little alcoholic snacks," he says.

"No drinking," the cabdriver says. "You want me to let you off right here?" All I can see of the driver is his swollen nose in the rearview mirror and I imagine him poking at blackheads in it when he's all alone, waiting for the next fare to crackle over the radio.

"You wouldn't do that to us—would you?" Kate says, leaning over the front seat.

He manages an ugly smile and shakes his head no, asking her the directions again.

When we arrive at Wolfie's house the party's already out of control. Half of the team stands huddled around the keg, staring at it with plastic cups in hand and beer-reddened faces. Kong has seized control of Wolfie's cobbled-together stereo system which consists of two dozen car speakers nailed to the wall, all wired into one receiver. He's playing AC/DC as loud as he can. Girls with bottle-blond hair and short, fuck-me skirts work their way through the crowd whispering, "Is he one?" to each other as they point at broad-backed guys in letter jackets and tight jeans.

Kate takes one look and smiles. "The Promised Land," she says. "Do I look like a groupie?"

Napalm looks at her. "Not yet."

"Fuck you," Kate says, punching him on the arm.

"There you go," he says. "That's the attitude."

"Your hair isn't big enough," I say, pointing at a trio of besweatered groupies who are standing by the doorway eyeing Kate and the Cheesegrater enviously.

Napalm whips his crutches into a corner and stumbles to the couch with the Cheesegrater dragging behind him, while Whigger attacks us with plastic cups of beer.

"The brothers are here," Whigger says.

A beer bottle shatters against the wall behind me, followed by another. The Shed comes over and pushes Whigger away with a flip of his thick forearm.

"Brothers?" I say.

"It's a Rose Bowl party," the Shed says. "You know, team unity."

Whigger bounces back between us. "Hey, Shed," he says. "Why you got to play me like that?"

"Because I can. Got a problem with that?"

Whigger smiles and slaps Shed's exposed belly, which hangs out over his belt buckle like a bag of wet cement.

"You might want to cover that up," I say.

"Fuck it," he says, slapping his gut. "I look good."

I pull Kate into the kitchen and see a few of the black guys actually hanging with the loud grinding music, drinking Martell out of water glasses, and wearing shades.

Whigger follows us in saying, "See, see?"

I introduce Kate around. Kong comes over from the stereo and does the brontosaurus lean into her face, flashes his fucked-up teeth and says to me, "Not bad, Riley. You're doing okay for yourself. You got any more where this came from?" Talking as if Kate's not there.

I go through the elaborate shake deal with Ant, Big Money, and Slope. Jimmy from Jersey walks into the kitchen all beery-eyed, frowning at the brothers, who smile back at him until he spots me.

"Hey, El," he says. "I'm still waiting on Cheswick, you know?"

I look over at Kate and ignore him.

"You want your money, don't you?" he asks, his broad face somehow making him look thoughtful. "What's the matter—nobody knows what the fuck I'm talking about."

I nod and he slaps me on the shoulder and leers at Kate before looking at the brothers in disgust and stumbling back into the living room to stare at the keg.

"This is fun?" Kate asks after we've toured the house. "I don't know—you want to quit this? I mean come on."

"Be quiet," I say. "I'm supposed to be one of the fellas, remember?"

The Shed bumps up to us and stands there staring at Kate, his nostrils flaring.

"Where's Wolfie?" I say.

"What do you want Wolfie for?"

"I don't want him, it's just a good thing to know where he is."

The Shed smiles and nods toward the stairwell. "He's with the Dishwasher."

I nod. "Oh."

"She's giving out party favors," Shed says, winking at Kate. I push him away and he just laughs, draining off the rest of his beer as he ambles off into another room.

"Where's Robeson?" Kate asks.

"Not really his sort of party. Besides, he's been keeping a low profile lately."

We drink our beer and watch as Bam Bam runs his line of bullshit at this mousy-looking girl who looks as if she's been attacked by the mascara wand. Bam Bam dips his head down over her shoulder and pinches her under the arms. She squeals, turns to face him and touches his considerable triceps, giggling as she looks at him over her beer cup.

"Pathetic," Kate whispers as she watches Bam Bam flashing his bowl rings at the girl.

"Do you do this?" Kate asks.

I shake my head. "I hope to someday though."

"Hey," she says. "You're with me."

Whigger comes up to us again and hands us two glasses as Ant yells out to him from the corner, "Hey, Whigger, you Oreo-cookie motherfucker, stop handing out liquor to white people."

Whigger ignores him and raises his glass at us.

"Drink," he says, winking.

Kate eyes him a minute before tipping the glass against her lips and wincing. I do the same.

"What was it?" I ask.

"Everclear with a little Martell for flavor," he says. "You like?"

Kate nods and Whigger produces a flask, pours.

We drink. I feel the skin inside my mouth peel off as the liquor fans itself up into my nose. I look over at Kate, then around at the guys and for some fucked-up reason, I want to show her how I get along with them, how I fit in, like it's all some secret club and I'm her escort.

Kate finishes her shot and stands staring at the glass.

"Shit, that burned," she yells.

"Goddamn," Whigger says. "She drinks too."

We go back out and sit on the couch with Napalm and the Cheesegrater, who sits curled up on his lap like a ferret.

"Exciting, isn't it?" Napalm asks Kate.

Kate nods. I can see Whigger's Everclear is doing the two-step on her brain, which, I figure, may not be a bad thing, because I hear grumbling about the keg kicking. Himes pushes the keg crowd out of the way and starts sucking on the plastic tapper until Jerry Q karate-chops him on the neck several times.

Himes pulls off, belching in Jerry's face, beer foam running down his chin.

"Rich," Kate says, shaking her head with disgust. "You call this a party? It's like day care with alcohol and whores."

"That's right," Napalm says. "Watch people drink, score groupies, and try to get someone drunk so you can fuck them up."

"What about the music?" Cheesegrater asks.

"Oh yeah," Napalm says. "Listen to music real loud and nod your head. If we're lucky somebody will start fighting over it."

"Don't forget the puking," I say.

"I've heard so much about football player parties," Cheesegrater says.

"What did you expect?" I ask.

Cheesegrater watches as Himes and Bates stand in the middle of the room with their forearms pressed together, side by side.

Napalm nudges Cheesegrater. "Watch this."

A dark-haired girl with deep-set eyes and scabs on her elbows stands next to them dragging on a lit cigarette.

"You ready?" she asks Himes as she dangles the cigarette above their pressed forearms.

Bates growls and nods, his lank hair falling across his face. Without so much as flinching the girl places the lit cigarette in the soft fold of their forearms. The tang of burnt hair drifts across the room.

"What are they doing?" Kate asks.

I tell her it's a game of chicken, then roll up my sleeve to show her my scars from it.

"That's sick," Cheesegrater says.

Sweat rolls down Bates' face as he struggles to keep his arm pressed against Himes'. Several other guys look on, bored by the spectacle as the girl lights another cigarette and stares off at one of the speakers on the wall.

After a minute or so, Himes lets out a shriek and rolls his arm away. The cigarette sticks to Bates' raw arm until he brushes it off like a wasp.

"Why the fuck would anybody want to do that?" Cheesegrater asks. She punches Napalm on the shoulder. "Would you do that?"

"No," he says. "But why? Because they can—that's the only reason."

Cheesegrater calms down, watching as Himes and Bates laugh about the whole thing, rubbing their arms and toasting each other by slamming beers.

"They make a cute couple," Kate says, pointing at Himes and Bates.

Jimmy comes into the room and sees us sitting on the couch. "Elfuck, I thought you left."

"Does it look like I left?"

"Follow me," he says, curling his finger at me.

I get up to go and Napalm shakes his head at me. I follow him out onto a small porch overlooking an overgrown backyard. The thigh-high grass is littered with empty beer cans, rain-sogged pizza boxes, and several rusted-out barbecue grills.

"You want your money, right? Cheswick says he wants to do it again and I already told him that if he has another fit I'm gonna kill him and throw his body in the Dumpster."

"Where's Cheswick?"

"Don't worry, he's here—just take a fucking look," he says, pulling a wad of tens and twenties from his pocket. He peels off a bunch of twenty-dollar bills and slaps them into my hand. Part of me wants to tell him to keep the money, but I slide it into my shirt pocket.

"Keep your hole shut," Jimmy says.

"Next time, I'm out," I tell him.

"What do you mean?"

"You heard me." And I walk back into the party, leaving him on the porch. He shouts something at me and I can hear him kicking the door.

When I return, Kate says, "You missed a fight."

"Really?" I say. Napalm waves his hands like it was nothing.

The Shed lumbers in, shakes the keg. "It's ready to blow, man."

There's talk of taking up a collection, and a crude argument spoken mostly with hands and grunts follows. Kong grabs a dirty-looking baseball hat off of some guy's head and walks around sticking it in people's faces.

We drop some folded bills into the hat until he grunts, lumbering over to a group of sophomores who are telling war stories to a couple of sorority-looking girls. The girls listen, flipping their hair and punctuating every other word with an "Oh my God."

Somebody passes a bottle and we drink, the liquor tastes like drugs or rubbing alcohol, I can't tell which, and Kate puts her hands in my lap and I start getting one of those perfect-moment feelings, like the world's rushing by and I've got my head stuck out the window, inhaling.

"I'm smashed," she says. "I'm really, really smashed and my teeth hurt."

"Never fear, it's Everclear," I say.

Napalm and Cheesegrater nod in slow motion and point at Whigger, who's curled up under the window, his body shaking as if he's freezing to death.

"He's having some sort of reaction," Cheesegrater says. "Shouldn't we help him?"

"How?" Napalm asks.

"Get him some water. I don't know—something."

"It happens," I say. I am too drunk at the moment to get off the couch and see if he's all right. I feel like telling her how it's not part of the Fella Code to show mercy.

Napalm says, "He'll sleep it off. It's his own stupid fault—he's lucky nobody's taken his clothes or pissed on him yet."

Then somebody starts throwing a football around and nobody's sober enough to catch it. I slouch down in the couch cushions and watch as it takes out a window. Bates picks up the ball and heaves it into some guy's face I've never seen before. The guy doesn't even flinch. Instead he keeps drinking for a minute as blood runs down his nose and splashes into his drink.

"Wouldn't be a party . . . ," Kate says.

Then Bam Bam trounces into the room with the mascara girl on his back, topless, whooping as if she's on some sort of ride. Not to be outdone, another girl lifts up her shirt and runs squealing through the party and into the kitchen. We take this as our cue to leave.

"It's just getting interesting," Kate says. "Can we stay for the orgy?"

"You really want to stay and see them pull a train on her?" I ask.

"I was joking," she says.

"I'm not," I say.

"What's a train?" Cheesegrater says.

"If you have to ask," Napalm says, "you don't wanna know."

Others are leaving the party too, even the sorority sisters, who walk past us with their pointy chins held high in the air as they head toward their burgundy Saab.

When we get outside, Napalm stares at the road. "I'm so fucking drunk," he says, "I forgot to call a cab."

"I don't feel like I've been anywhere," Cheesegrater says.

"You want to go back?" Napalm asks.

"No, baby. I want to be with you," she says.

I shiver because something in her voice tells me she really means it.

Napalm looks over his shoulder at me and makes a gagging motion. We stagger with a certain drunken choreography, shoulders bumping shoulders, voices too loud then slurred until Kate hops on my back.

"Giddyup," she says, digging her heels into my sides.

Later, after Kate and I have made love in her apartment with the lights on, I wake up, the Everclear tearing through my stomach like Drano, and put my clothes on.

Instead of heading back to the dorm, I walk down the side streets to the party. I remember the money and every so often I take it out of my pocket to look at it.

I spot this overpass, draped in GO BLUE banners, cars creeping across it. I head toward it, my thoughts clearing in fits and starts as I scramble up the grass incline. The lights of the city blink and glare behind me as I walk across the span, spitting over the edge at the cars whooshing by underneath. When I get to the middle the wind stops and I stand there for a minute, trying to remember things: how the woman screamed, the blood in her hair, the sound of Heather's figurines meeting concrete, the bottle I dropped on Donald, the way he looked at me when he slid me the Bible and how I dumped it. This time though I wait until the cars have passed underneath to take the money out of my pocket and toss it over the bridge. It flutters a few moments, dipping and swooping like wing-shot birds before it is out of sight and I feel better, like something in me has turned. To my left is the darkened football facility. When I turn to go I don't look back. I wonder who'll find the money and what they'll think.

What's left of the party when I get there are lots of large bodies lying around the floor in beer comas and puddles of vomit. Bates and Himes are punching holes in the wall—Himes with his fist, Bates with his head—while Kong looks on from a broken-down couch, thumbing through an old *Hustler*.

I spot Bam Bam and weave through the sparse crowd to him but Kong grabs me and stares into my face saying, "You know anything about a fag on the team? I'm asking everybody."

This is the third time I've been asked about this and like all rumors on the team (Coach Roe quitting and going to the NFL, Kong's steroid use, hidden cameras in the locker room) it has to run its course like the flu.

"I just can't believe it," he says. "I mean fags can't play ball. You ever hear of one?"

I decide to provoke him. "Ahmad Rashad?"

Kong shakes his head. "He's a nigger. Shit, brothers don't even eat pussy because they've got this fucked-up theory about how you might be indirectly sucking some guy's dick, which if you ask me is fucking retarded."

"Jack Lambert?" I say.

Kong sucks in a breath. "Jack fucking Lambert—what's wrong with you, Riley? Everybody knows Jack fucking Lambert was a motherfucker. Christ, Riley, if one of the linebackers heard you say that, your ass would be grass. They'd make an example of you."

I tell him I'm joking.

"This ain't no joke, Riley. I'm not talking ancient NFL history— word is we got a butt pirate on the team. What would that do for morale? I mean with the Rose Bowl and all."

"Maybe it's one of the skill guys, you know ball handlers?" I say, knowing that linemen are willing to believe anything about the speedsters and ball handlers.

"There you go. Now you're starting to make sense. Just keep your eyes peeled. I don't want no fag checking me out in the shower, know what I mean?"

"Maybe it's already happened."

"Still, if I knew," he says, losing his thought, his booze-gray tongue lolling out of his mouth.

"What about those two?" I say, pointing at Himes and Bates.

"Himes—I don't know," Kong says. "But Bates—it don't matter because that would be the least of his problems. If I was you, Riley, I'd keep my mouth shut."

"You need a drink," Bam Bam says as he hands me a glass of something. He's so drunk his swollen bottom lip keeps snagging his teeth when he speaks. "Did Kong tell you about the fag hunt?"

I nod.

"Good," he says, as if he's discussing a matter of national security. "We need to get this out in the open. Find out if there's any truth to this matter—you know, like an internal investigation."

I look at him and sip my drink. The sting of alcohol ripping up into my sinuses as the room takes on this gauzy look.

"That's the last of it," Bam Bam says, pointing at my glass. "All tapped out."

"Then what?"

He looks at me. "Then we're going to play a joke on Mary after she gets done blowing Chernak."

Wolfie leans in and says, "Did you tell him about Mary?"

"He's up to speed," Bam Bam says.

I look between them, fairly confused. Fuckhead comes stumbling down the steps holding his crotch.

Wolfie points, shakes his head with disgust. "These frosh, they can't handle a fucking hummer."

Fuckhead spots me and begins sputtering about how I should go upstairs.

"Third door on the left," he says. "It's like *Let's Make a Fucking Deal* up there. Even Revlon's getting him some."

I nod and wave him off, not wanting to hear any more.

Then Wolfie starts fucking with me, calling me one of them refined motherfuckers who think they're better than everyone else. I ignore him because this is his normal trip right on down to the race bullshit he talks with the brothers even though, if you put a gun to his head, I'd bet money he'd say he was just joking.

Mary stumbles down the steps, her long hair pulled back into a tangled knot. I can see the rumples of her undone bra pressing against her shirt. Ackley intercepts her with a hug, tells her to sit down and winks over his shoulder at us.

"I want another beer," Mary moans. "Mary wants another beer."

Bam Bam shakes his head in disgust. "Take a fucking look at her. She shouldn't drink. Some people—they just don't get it."

Then somebody asks if we're ready and I nod, not knowing what the fuck anybody's talking about, half drunk, half full of myself for hanging with the fellas as we form a loose huddle around the fridge. Wolfie produces a bottle of beer. "It's the last one," he says, holding the bottle aloft like a trophy or a severed head.

"And it's got Mary's name on it," Bam Bam says.

When Wolfie unscrews the cap, drains half the beer and unzips his pants, I realize what's up and try backing away from the fridge but Kong clamps one of his meathooks around my head and says, "Where you going, Riley?"

I look up into his beer-shot eyes, knowing that resistance is futile.

"Time for a Whiz Quiz, fellas," Shed says.

All of us watch as Wolfie centers his pee hole over the lip of the bottle and squirts a little juice down in with the remaining beer. The bottle gets passed around, each guy adding to the brew until it comes to me and I stand there with the now warm bottle in my right hand.

I open my mouth to say something, but Kong cuts me short. "Don't even bother, Riley," he says. "We don't wanna hear none of your bullshit, just do your duty and be a fella."

Kong's words are seconded by several meaty yeahs.

But it's the part about being a fella that gets me, as if they somehow sense why I've hung around the party so long, sidling up to them, drinking like them and watching fucked-up shit happen without so much as a shrug of my shoulders. I'm numb when I pull out my dick and fill the bottle right up to the rim.

The Shed gives me a welcome-to-the-club slap across the shoulders. Wolfie screws the cap back on the beer and in my Everclear/beer fog I start to laugh. I look around at the fellas and realize that tomorrow we'll be out on the field looking like clean-cut All-Americans as we play step-and-fetch-it for the coaches.

I follow the group out into the living room where Ackley's baby-sitting Mary.

"Look what we've got for you, Mary," Wolfie says, doing the game-show-host display with the bottle as Ackley shakes her shoulders. Her head rolls from side to side, hair sticking to her sweaty face and neck.

"Beer," she says. "You guys are so good to me—I just love you."

Even the Shed winces when he hears this and we all look at each other, waiting for someone to stop the joke. But Wolfie doesn't, instead, he shakes the bottle up and cranks the top off for her saying, "Look at how fresh that is. We want you to have the last one."

Mary swats at the bottle, swinging it to her lips, some of the guys look away, but I watch as her throat works the beer down. She pauses after her first swallow and says, "It's too warm. Hey, Riley, is that you?"

The Shed shakes my shoulders. "She likes you, buddy."

Mary gets down two more long swallows before she begins to retch and the crowd scatters.

"You fuckers," Mary screams as she runs into the kitchen, stumbling on the linoleum, still retching, realizing, even in her beer haze, what's happened.

I follow her in and watch as she heaves up the beer. She tries to say something in between shudders as her hair slides around the dirty floor, drifting over the foam of vomit like willow branches.

I feel this pit open up in me and it's all I can do to force myself to watch. I go to her and try putting an arm under her shoulders but she shrugs me off and continues to shake and retch as some sloe-eyed groupie shuffles into the room, her makeup all undone, smelling like sex. She takes one look at us, shakes her head and pads back out into the living room. The Shed comes in and pulls me into the other room where the guys are sprawled all over the dirty floor laughing, as Wolfie imitates Mary.

"It's Riley, Mr. Good Fucking Samaritan," Wolfie squeals in his Mary voice.

I flip him off.

"She'll pass out and sleep it off," Shed says. "In the morning—"

"In the morning she's going to wonder who the fuck pissed in her mouth," Ackley says.

"Wouldn't you?" I ask.

The fellas turn to me.

"We're just trying to have some fun, blow off a little steam before the bowl game," Bam Bam says. "She won't even remember it. Besides she sucked Chernak's paste, what's worse, our piss or Chernak's jism?"

"That's fun?" I ask.

"What the fuck are you talking about, Riley?"

I shrug my shoulders and tell them nothing and wait until the Shed goes into the kitchen, returning with Mary under his arms in a clumsy hug. He places her on the couch and puts her feet up. She brushes the hair out of her eyes, smiling at him as if it's the sweetest thing anybody's ever done for her.

Then Kong puts on some more music.

"See?" Bam Bam says. "She loves us."

"That's great, Bam Bam," I say.

"You know what you need, Riley?"

"What?"

"Why don't you go upstairs and see if there's any scrap pussy lying around, maybe it'll lighten you up a little."

Instead, I wait a few minutes before slipping out the door.

The next day, nobody says jack shit. Napalm humps it down to practice and sits in rehab, while I tape up and strap it on before filing into a team meeting.

Robeson wanders by after having his knee taped and says, "Heard you been anointed, man."

"You heard shit," I say.

"Easy, my man. Just checking to see if the fella machine got to you."

I sit and listen to more blather about the Rose Bowl and how we've got to stop the run. Roe lays out the rules of the trip, says we're going to be locked up tighter than Mother Teresa's snatch. Says we're not out to have fun, but that we're out in sunny California to kick some Pac-Ten butt.

"But first," Roe says, "it's been called to my attention that things have been turning up missing."

Everybody stiffens in their seat, listening as Roe gives his standard trust speech, how we're one big family and if you can't trust your family, well then who can you trust? Followed by an abbreviated version of the one-bad-apple-can-spoil-the-whole-bunch speech.

For a moment my hangover thrums back up into my brain and I sneak a look over at Jimmy, who's sitting wedged between Fuckhead and Reems with this tuned-out television expression on his face.

"I've assigned Coach Hart here to look into this problem," Roe says. Hart steps forward out of the bank of coaches, tipping his hat at us like he's some kind of jock-sniffing Jack Webb. And I swear the fucker gives me the once-over as his gaze sweeps the room.

"We've got to run a tight ship, men," Roe continues. "Keep an eye out for any hinky stuff and remember that above all else we're Michigan men and Michigan men comport themselves with honor, dignity, and pride."

A weak sigh of rah-rah stuff goes up in the room before we're dismissed into our position meetings.

Coach U fist-fucks us about some lousy practice film from the previous day's practice. Kong catches the worst of it, gets called dog-ass, lazy, and the world's first three-hundred-pound pussy.

"I ought to call *The Guinness Book of World Records,*" Coach U snorts.

And Kong takes it, because it's the unwritten rule of team meetings that you have to take, swallow, and smile about any abuse tossed your way by a coach.

Outside, on the warm-up lap grind, Jimmy motors past me and gives me a slight shove before shooting me the eye. I answer back with a forearm shiver, just enough to let him know I'm cool. Then I start thinking how the idiot likes the secret agent bullshit, like he's somehow matching wits with Roe and Hart.

Practice happens, bodies flying everywhere on the hustle and double time. I take a couple of hits in scrimmage that make my arms go numb and my fingers tingle.

Coach U gets in my face. "What's the matter, Riley, you take a shot in the pussy?"

"Burner," I say, pointing at my neck.

"Get back in there, then—shake it off," he says.

I bop back into the huddle.

After practice, Jimmy from Jersey approaches me as I'm about to step into Harkens Land for my workout.

"We cool?" he says. "They don't know shit."

I tell him I'm still out of the deal and he does his best soul-searching stare at me, which on his broad ordinary face comes across as utter confusion with a little Chet Baker stupor thrown in. Then he adds, "If I six, you six."

"Let's hope that doesn't happen, then," I tell him.

SEVENTEEN

Two weeks before the Rose Bowl game we hop a plane and fly West, dressed in our team-issue blue blazers and solemn as pallbearers. There is no in-flight movie, instead, we have position meetings to discuss game strategy.

When we land and walk out onto the cement tarmac there is a reception line of Lady Blues waiting for us, who pin roses to our lapels.

We stay in a hotel with real palm trees and three different pools where the coaches' wives loll around on sun chairs, tanning their pale midwestern skin a lobster pink. All of them look soft around the edges, former Homecoming Queens or Miss Cherry Festivals from small towns. Now they're just the sort of average women you'd see anywhere. But something about their faces spooks me, the boredom of living week to week, season to season.

Napalm gets stuck with the gimp brigade in another section of the hotel and I pull Smitty as my roommate, who snores like a goddamned chain saw and talks in his sleep.

Curfew is at 8 P.M. and the only fun we have is a canned trip to Disneyland where Bates decides he's going to grab Snow White's ass and give her a kiss.

"Ever since I was twelve I've had a crush on her," he says, edging closer and closer to the stage.

He gets the ass part okay, but when he goes to plant one on Snow White's Pan-Caked cheek some guy in a Goofy costume comes out of nowhere and tries to separate Bates from Snow White. Then Himes runs up on the little stage and starts pounding the Goofy guy in the head with his forearm until its nose is smashed. With his best Prince Charming imitation, Bates manages to lick Snow White's face, his tongue cutting a dark pink swath through her makeup, before two muscle-bound security guards take him away. The coaches get involved, start arguing and flipping complimentary tickets around to nervous-looking middle management types in bad suits. A little later, Himes and Bates emerge from some secret back room and flash the thumbs-up sign as they take in our hoots and cheers.

Himes gets confined to his hotel room for the duration of our sunny stay; he is let out to practice and attend meetings like some sort of furloughed zoo animal. Bates receives a good talking-to and some penalty workouts, but with the big game coming down the pike he gets the let's-not-do-anything-rash-he's-a-starter treatment.

It takes two days before the guys start grumbling about the heat blisters and sunburn we get from practicing on this hard little junior college practice field. Roe bars the press from our practice compound, picking up where he left off, screaming hell and brimstone, telling us how we're not prepared and if we're not careful we are going to get our asses handed to us on a Rose Bowl float on national fucking television.

Coach Argent teaches us USC's plays and fight song and we go about preparing the first team for the big game. During the first week, I get three burners that shoot down my arms like a soldering iron, leaving me feeling light and airy. The trainers walk me around under the pepper trees, waving smelling salts under my nose until I can count to ten forward and back.

Himes staggers by on his way to the water cooler and says, "What's a matter, Riley? You finally discover what it means to hit?"

I tell him to fuck off.

Argent sticks me back in, even though I tell him I can't turn my neck.

"You don't need to, son. Just line up and hit somebody."

The burners start coming pretty regular and something about the sun and heat suddenly makes me acutely aware of every ache and pain, as if I've reached some critical mass.

At night the coaches check us into our rooms and give us the countdown to showtime. With us frosh it's more of a someday sort of thing, hang in there and make the guy in front of you better, and all that team-effort bullshit.

I go to bed with ice bags Ace-bandaged to my neck and wake when the water trickles down my chest. I can't feel my arms anymore and I spend the rest of the night listening to Smitty rattle the window with his snoring.

Two days before the game I catch Robeson out by the whirlpool reading the newspaper.

"Read this," I say, tossing him my copy of *Meditations*.

"What is it?"

"Just read it. You'll like it."

"How's that neck doing? Ant tells me you've been getting burners."

"It's nothing," I tell him.

"Remember Darryl Stingley?"

"Yeah?"

"Well, he thought he was a bad-ass, now he's totally fucked up," Robeson says.

"That's not a Painless Career-Ending Injury?"

"No, man, that's called a roll of the fucking dice, besides he wasn't looking for it—it just descended on him and fucked him up good."

"How about you?"

"I'm making it and if you want to know the truth, this sun ain't half-bad, kind of melts the antiestablishment b.s. right out of you."

"As long as you don't hop the fence and become a fella," I say.

"No need to worry about that," he says. "No need. I've got my eyes on the prize."

"What's that?"

"Riley, if I don't six, I've got one more year, then I'm out of here with my degree. Maybe I move my black ass out West and look for a job."

"Sounds like you've got it all figured out," I say.

"Maybe," he says, tucking the book under his arm. "Maybe I do."

Before I know it game day swings around and we board a bus that barrels through the city, trailing a police escort. When we arrive at the Rose Bowl there's the normal fan litter: tailgates, small pods of screeching fans, alumni, boosters, and drunk students burning up their Christmas breaks on Rose Bowl junkets.

In the locker room we get the same speeches, the same nervous pad pounding and huff and puffing, and pregame chatter like how we're going to kick ass, take names, shove the ball down their pansy Californian throats. I sit there amazed anybody gets up for this bullshit anymore. My neck feels rotten and now with all the hype and glory going on I admit to myself, in the company of my teammates, that the game no longer matters to me and all I want to do is get out. On cue the guys come to life and we take the field with a polite roar from the crowd. Bob Hope toddles out to the fifty-yard line to crack some lame jokes over the PA system, before the national anthem.

Kickoff.

And we *lose*.

21–17.

I watch from the sideline, and oddly enough, I feel nothing, just this strange poolside detachment. I look around at the other guys as we stream off the field and that same look's smudged across their faces, knee-deep in the spectacle, mute with the end near.

Afterward, in the locker room, Coach U tells us Roe's too steamed to offer any postgame talk and has asked him to fill in.

"We sucked pond water today, men. We got beat by the better team—our heads handed to us," he says. Blah, blah, blah. "But it's been a helluva season and in the end, as Michigan men, we must hold our heads up high."

The bus takes us back to the hotel.

We get three days with no curfew to spend bowl money per diem while the coaches take their bored wives and scrawny kids sight-seeing.

The only thing that stops us from totally pillaging Southern California is our lack of transportation. Only the seniors are allowed to rent cars. So they blow their money on Firebirds and Trans Ams and cruise Sunset Strip looking for bars and hookers. Most of us frosh are reduced to begging for rides or else taking taxis.

At night the guys gather around the pool to replay who got fucked, drunk, arrested, assaulted, or kicked out of a titty bar for grabbing the women.

Rope cops a blow job off one of the room service maids while Vezio records the whole thing on his camcorder, narrating.

"Goddamn sword swallower," he says.

The video quickly becomes a team favorite. Sometimes as many as twenty guys crowd around a television to watch Rope get sucked off by this cleaning lady who looks like someone's mom.

Lousma and Reems get nicked for DUI in a rented minivan and spend their last day in court where they lose their entire bowl per diems on fines to the state of California.

Napalm and I mostly sit by the pool and grumble about our teammates although on our next to last night, Napalm works it so that we can get a ride into town with Jerry Q and Childers. We spend the evening wandering around broad palm-lined streets drinking peach schnapps until Childers starts booting out the window. We make it to only one bar, the Red Onion, and watch a cheesy lingerie show hosted by this loudmouth deejay who keeps telling the crowd, half of which are Michigan football players, to "Check it out, gentlemen."

Before I know it we're back in Ann Arbor, the cold biting into our suntanned skin the minute we step off the plane. A small crowd of well-wishing boosters and parents has assembled and cheers us as we come off the bus with WE STILL LOVE YOU and THERE'S AL-WAYS NEXT YEAR signs.

I step out of the small reception/pep rally being held in the indoor practice facility. Nobody sees me go and it feels good to be walking up the hill to the dorm by myself.

The dorms are nearly empty, except for a few losers with no holiday plans. So I slide out of my clothes and go to my desk and start writing in the notebook all the things I hate about football. Then I stare at the calendar and the single month before winter conditioning begins, followed by spring ball, which I hear is a diseased bitch of a time, because it's when reputations get made and positions won. From here spring ball looks like hell done up in a new dress.

Then Kate gets back from break and it's high old times again.

"I saw the man," she says from the curtains where she's wrapped herself. I reach down, rubbing semen into my stomach.

"Who?" I ask.

"The man with the wife. The one who told me I was smart and beautiful—the one whose house I lit on fire."

I nod and tell her to come back to bed. Instead she untangles herself from the curtain and pours us drinks. It's Saturday, the day before winter conditioning, and every bone in my body hurts. I can hear the snow batting against the windowpanes as if it wants to come in.

"To him," Kate says, holding a glass of bourbon out for me. "The sonofabitch who made me what I am today."

"Why?" I say, not wanting to hear the story again.

"You're not listening to me, are you, Riley?"

"No."

"Well, I've got this theory about what he did for me. Wanna hear it?"

"What's that?"

"He broke my heart and gave me life. That's my theory," she says. "It was a good thing, because I was just a kid, you know—you wouldn't have liked me."

"That doesn't sound like a theory," I say. "It sounds like fact."

"I'm not done," she says, crawling back under the covers. "My theory's that everybody has to get totally screwed over at least once in their life."

"Sort of like losing your virginity?"

"Exactly, only much more important. Anybody can lose their virginity. What I'm talking about is like this Real-World Cherry you've got to break and if you don't, you become one of the innocents."

"You mean you've got to be tough—a Michigan man," I say in my best coach's voice.

Kate squeals and rolls under my arm.

"Yeah," she says. "Not like you, mister."

"Leave me alone. I'm actually starting to feel okay for once."

"Even the neck?"

"There's still something wrong there, but if I tell anybody about it I can forget spring ball."

"Kiss me," she says. "Kiss me hard."

We kiss.

"So now you think you're tough?" I say.

"Hard, bulletproof heart," she says.

"And what about me?"

"I don't know," she says. "But I'd say you've got a lot of potential heartbreakers on the horizon."

I stare at her.

"Don't look at me," she says. "What you've got coming is big and bloody."

"What do you mean?"

"Football. You can't fool me, Elwood Riley. Remember, I'm a coach's daughter. You don't want it like the other guys do."

"What other guys?"

"Like at the party."

"What am I going to do?" I ask.

She looks at me, her black hair falling in front of her face. "I don't know, you're kind of stuck in the middle."

I roll away because I know she's right—I am in the middle and it's a cold, cruel place, that my body wants to be in, but my brain won't let it.

Winter conditioning starts without the graduating seniors, and everybody, even now, seems to be fighting for positions. Harkens makes us run until the insides of our thighs rub raw, blister then bleed. When we fall down, he tells us to get up. Then he straps fifty-pound weights to our backs and tells us to run some more.

The afternoons are full of meetings where the new offense and defense get drilled into our heads with film and chalk talk.

Napalm has his cast sawed off and begins physical therapy which he claims is like being a hamster. All day he pedals arm bikes, does leg raises, ultrasound, and sit-ups followed by hours of ice therapy.

In meetings Coach U slots me in the running for a starting position, while on the other side of the ball, Himes platoons with another guy.

We run the plays in shoulder pads and shorts waiting for the official start of spring ball and the chance to hit again and stop beating up on ourselves with weight lifting and running.

Coach U's on my ass twenty-four-seven.

"Riley," Coach U says, "I've got to be honest with you—I think you're going soft or something. I mean if you don't want this chance to show me what you've got just let me know."

I tell him I'll be ready.

Then he slaps an arm around me, pinches my neck and shakes me. "You'd better," he says. "Or I'm going to shove this shoe up your ass and you'll spend the rest of your college career trying to get it out." He laughs and looks at me as if I'm supposed to laugh too, even though I feel like telling him to fuck off (a move which would seal my fate and forever banish me to scrub status). I don't. Instead I close my eyes and see my father's zombie stare, telling me to stick it out, no matter the cost, even if I have to wade through shit up to my nostrils.

At night in the dorms, everybody lets on similar stories, how they're a cunt hair away from snagging a starting position. Even Whigger thinks he's got a shot. We're no longer tackling dummies and drill bitches for the first string.

A week goes by and we're into spring ball full tilt, bodies swollen and full of the requisite aches and pains. I spend ten minutes every morning snorting water in the shower until the clots of blood and snot in my nose loosen and I'm able to breathe. Fuckhead tells me to try snorting vodka mixed with Vaseline. It feels like hornets have lit up my sinuses, but it works.

Word on the team is that Roe's tightening down, blaming the Rose Bowl loss on lack of discipline. Problem is that all anybody does is toss around a lot of yes sirs and maybe we jog to stations a little faster. It's one big suck-up fest, with Hard-on Hart running around like some sickdog drill sergeant.

He gets on me about my hair, which now hangs out of the back of my helmet, and at least once a week he grabs a gob of it and says,

"Better watch out or someone's going to grab hold and give you a good bitch fucking."

I snap his hand away and keep walking.

"You're a fuckup waiting to happen, Riley. The only problem is somebody thinks you're going to be a starter one of these days."

I just nod and flip my arms at him until he finds somebody else to pick on.

During warm-up lap on the second week of full-pad spring ball, the rumor that Jimmy's been tossed off the team percolates through the ranks. Coach U follows us around the inside of the track, screaming and yelling at us to pick up the pace while I keep looking over my shoulder hoping to spot Jimmy lumbering somewhere behind me.

During grass drills I scan his group and don't see him.

Whigger bops up to me. "Did you hear, did you hear?" he says.

I shake my helmet.

"Fucked up," he says before stumbling down the sideline to repeat the same thing to someone else. I look around and everything's as it should be, bodies colliding on whistle blasts, yelling, the odor of sweat and wet turf, Roe above us in his tower like a sniper. I start thinking about the way Cheswick's trembling jaw felt in my hands, how Jimmy freaked out and the fact that I was right there alongside him, stuffing helmets and jerseys into my garbage bag.

Several other guys file by on their way to the water cooler and mention Jimmy's name. I get this light feeling in my throat and go about practice on super gas, hitting and sticking as if the enthusiasm is somehow going to save me.

After training table I track down Napalm, who with his rehab-boy status is privy to the best gossip on the team.

"You heard?" he asks.

I nod.

We walk past the grease-filled kitchen doorway and head straight for the elevator and go to his room. He sits on the bed, pulls the sock off his bum ankle and begins wiggling his toes.

"Come on, motherfucker," I say. "I can't wait any longer."

He smiles. I can see he's rifling through his brain wondering where to start.

"Seems our boy got caught red-handed. One of the trainers said the whole deal went down right before practice. Cleaned out his locker and expelled him from school."

"How did it happen?"

"All I know is that Hart had something on him. That and he tried to sell a pair of shoes and a couple of jerseys to this undercover guy."

"Cop?" I ask. I start sweating as I run through the possibilities, hoping Jimmy kept his mouth shut.

"No, are you kidding me?" Napalm says. "They got some kid is all I know and had him ask Jimmy about buying some stuff."

"That's it?"

"Far as I know. The trainers told me that Hart had been looking at him for a while."

"I'm fucked," I say, pacing the room. "Totally fucked."

"I thought you stopped."

"I did."

"Well then, you've got nothing to worry about," he says. "Hart got his man, Roe dropped the ax and now things will get back to normal—blood's been spilled."

I shake my head. "He's going to rat me out."

"Did anybody say anything to you today?"

"Hart said I was going to get bitch-fucked."

"That's just his homo fantasy," Napalm says. "Did anybody say anything to you about Jimmy?"

I shake my head no. "The whole team's talking about it though."

"Chill then. I'd say you have until tomorrow. If you don't get the knock-'n'-roll in the morning you're in the clear."

"You think?"

He nods. "I told you Jersey boy had rocks for brains."

What can I say? I don't even know why I did it in the first place or even why I stopped doing it. Maybe a little of it was the money, the extra ten or twenty a week, peanuts compared to what Jimmy was skimming.

"I'm doomed, FUBAR—ass-fucked," I say to Napalm, who's still busy picking the crud out from under his toenails.

He pauses, looking up long enough to let a smile cross his lips.

"You think this is funny?" I ask.

"There's nothing you can do, El," he says.

"Except sit back and wait for the fucking."

"What's the worst that can happen?"

"I get booted," I say.

"Precisely my point. If it was going to happen you'd be packing your shit already. They didn't mess around with Jersey boy. It was like a surgical, fuck-with-us-and-you're-gone kind of deal. I heard they even got a few of those lunkheads from the weight room to help him pack his stuff."

"Okay," I say. "I get it."

"My guess is that nothing will happen and you and me will be at the party this weekend same as usual."

"I hope you're right," I say.

"Bet on it. But then again you'd be eagle-free if they were to shit-can you."

I tell him I can't even imagine what it would be like.

"No more of this crap. You'd be a regular guy. Imagine that."

I tell him I know, pacing around the room a bit. Then, "But—"

"I know," he says. "Not the way to go—you'd have to face your parents?"

I tell him I can't.

"Then deny—deny everything."

EIGHTEEN

I make it through the next day of practice.

No morning knock-'n'-roll out of bed and Phil asks me about Jimmy as if he suspects something. I tell him to fuck off.

"Touchy, touchy," he says, opening a can of Vienna sausages, one of several his parents send with alarming regularity.

"What do I care?"

"He deserved it," Phil says, drinking off a little of the sausage brine before fingering one of the gray tubes out of the jar.

For some reason the urge to crack him with a little chin music rises up in me but I manage to quell it as I watch him shove another sausage down. Instead I stomp out of the room and go see Kate.

I come clean and tell her about how I broke into the building with Jimmy, even how it felt to look at the Eye of Michigan while we walked past it, our arms loaded with bulging garbage bags. Then about Cheswick's seizure and how we shoved a shoe in his mouth.

"But you quit," she says. "I mean how long ago was that?"

I tell her that it still doesn't make it right.

"Screw the football team. Jimmy got stupid and that's what happens, Riley. Don't you get it—you don't seem like the stealing type. If you want I'll talk to my father."

"Don't you ever," I say.

"Okay, fine. I was just . . . ," she says, recoiling.

I tell her I know and say I'm sorry.

"It's just part of it. I mean when I'm presented with the prospect of quitting to save face or getting booted, I don't really give a fuck, except for this tiny piece of me that says I should hold on and stick it out even though it's the last thing in the world I want to do."

She smiles and pushes me back on the bed and sits on my chest. "They aren't doing you any favors—you bitch enough about it. So the worst is you could've gotten kicked off. So what? You can't be a dumb jock the rest of your life."

She leans down to kiss me, her hair falling across my face. I get this flash of feeling that I don't love her, that I can't love her. Then I start thinking how I'm perhaps incapable of it—too caught up, too selfish, too—I don't know what.

"So what? So then what? I mean where does that leave me?"

She kisses me again.

"It leaves you where it leaves you," she says in between kisses. "Sort of like this big storm that just picks you up and drops you in the middle of nowhere, like Dorothy in *The Wizard of Oz*."

"What if I don't want to be picked up?"

"Then do it yourself, El."

"What's that supposed to mean?"

"It means you've got to find a way out, because I can tell this is driving you crazy. I mean look at you. You actually go to class and get decent grades—you're not one of them and even if you wanted to be they wouldn't let you—they'd find a way to break you. That's what they do."

I go to kiss her, but she turns away from me.

"Are you listening to me?" she says.

"What can I do? My neck feels terrible and I no longer like to hit. It's like I don't have any options."

"Of course you do," she says.

"What?—I quit and go back to Cleveland—then what? Get a job at a factory like my father? It's that or I become one of the fellas and beat myself to death for what—a game? Basically I'm fucked because I wish I could be like the other guys and get all starry-eyed about playing in the NFL, but I don't give a rat's ass."

When I finish, I realize I'm practically yelling. Kate stands up from the bed and says quietly, "Well, you have to find a way. That or you just walk away and get lost."

Later that night Napalm and I decide to get drunk so we head out to a keg party celebrating the midpoint of spring ball and the departing seniors. The whole thing's been put on the q.t. because of all the spring-cleaning fervor the coaches seem so full of.

The party is in high gear when we get there. Dope smoke floats in the air. Guys are punching holes in the wall and throwing Chinese stars at a picture of Coach Roe. Ant and Rope sit around a table scraping their jersey numbers into their arms with nails until the numbers are bloody smears. When it heals they'll have raised welts and be numbered forever.

Bam Bam cruises up to us and slaps an arm around me.

"Hey, El," he says. "Your buddy Jimmy got a one-way ticket back to Jersey."

I tell him it's too bad and do my best to look disinterested.

Kong leans his face into mine. "Fuck him. He got what was coming to him. He was a thief and a liar and I didn't like the sonofabitch."

Bam Bam pulls a plastic flask from his pocket and dumps what smells like whiskey into our cups.

"Here's to being done with this bullshit and to the frosh who have to suck it up and drive for four more years," Bam Bam says, raising the flask.

"And here's to Jimmy," Napalm says.

Kong stops, looks at Napalm. "I ain't drinking to that dumb bastard, that's his bad luck. What's wrong with you, Napalm—all that rehab and codeine rotted your brain?"

For a minute I think he might swing on Kong which would be pure uncut suicide. But he doesn't, instead Bam Bam biffs Kong on the head with the flask and says, "What are you, some kind of angel? The guy fucked up. Just chill, it ain't worth throwing down over."

Kong shakes his head and shoots the liquor down. "I don't have to be nice. My ass is out of here and I'm going to get paid for playing now."

Bam Bam, who won't be drafted, looks at us and rolls his eyes. "Mr. NFL Bigshot."

Then Yo Joe stumbles in and starts rambling about how Kong should play for the Denver Broncos. Kong just looks at him and says, "Who the fuck are you?"

Yo Joe deflates and slinks away.

Napalm and I wander around the party watching as the others go about the mayhem laughing and toasting each other. We drink beer until I can feel it bubbling around my head.

Vezio cruises up to us all smiles. "Follow me," he says.

"What the fuck is it, Sleazio?" Napalm asks.

"You guys drunk?" he asks.

We nod.

"Then shut the fuck up and follow me."

We trail Vezio through the living room to a narrow hallway pinned on either side with heavily painted doors. I can hear voices coming from one of the rooms up ahead as Napalm taps me on the shoulder to tell me he's drunk.

"You gonna mug us, Vez?" I ask. "If so, I should tell you that I don't have any money."

He looks back at me. "Better than that, El, much fucking better."

When we reach the last door on the hall Vezio turns to us.

"You guys ready?"

We nod.

"Good," Vezio says, cracking open the door to the room. A blast of sweaty beer-laden air comes tumbling out of the room and I can hear the tinny strain of a clock radio playing somewhere in the room. It takes me a minute for my eyes to adjust to the darkness.

When he sees it, Napalm pinches my arm, pointing at the single bed in the middle of the room. On the bed is a small dark-haired woman with deep slits for eyes and this sleepy look on her face. At the foot of the bed I recognize Himes with his pants down around his ankles, eyes closed.

"Meet Kim Ho," Vezio says, spreading his arms toward the bed. "Never mind Himes, he's having some plumbing problems. Ain't that right, Himes?"

Himes looks up from the bed. "What the fuck are you talking about, Vez?"

Smitty sits slouched in an armchair looking at us with glassed-over eyes, nodding to the music. In another corner I make out Fuckhead's face, his gaze fixed on the bed and the now moaning Himes.

Vezio leans into us. "She likes it."

I wince and notice the way her arms flop over Himes' broad back and the slight jog of her head when his pushing increases. She is out-of-her-mind drunk, and she looks small and helpless as Himes moans something to her.

"This is fucked up," I say. "She don't want this."

"Who's next?" Vezio asks the room, ignoring me. "Himes—you're about to lose your turn if you don't blow or go."

Fuckhead steps forward out of the shadows and raises his hand to signal his place in line.

Before I can say anything else Himes flips her onto her stomach and grabs a beer bottle off the nightstand.

"Pour it on her snatch and let Fuckhead eat it off," Smitty says from the armchair.

"She likes it—don't you, baby?" Himes says, steering the stream of beer down her back until it is empty. Then he places the empty bottle in the crack of her ass and begins wiggling it back and forth as she gropes blindly up and down her body with her tiny hands. I step forward to put one of the blankets over her but Vezio punches me on the arm. "What the fuck are you doing?"

"She's drunk," I say.

Fuckhead looks at me and continues pulling his jeans off as Himes stands up from the bed.

Napalm whispers in my ear, "Just leave it, Riley."

The girl looks at me, her dark brown eyes focusing on me for a minute.

Vezio laughing, "Go on, El, you wanna go next? I think she likes you. Last party she passed out and had sixteen fucking guys. I think that's some kind of record—she so hawny."

"Let's just go," Napalm says, grimacing at Vezio.

Himes steps between us. "I'm not done yet, Riley—back the fuck off," he says.

On the bed Kim Ho rolls back to her side and I catch sight of her eyes and for a moment I imagine my face reflected in them even though it's too dark to see anything.

Himes pushes me away, grabs the beer bottle again and lowers it at Kim.

That's when I punch him in the ear. He lets out a short shriek, dropping to one knee as Kim lifts off the bed and starts screaming, her hands clawing at her hair and face. Somebody jumps on my back and I hear Napalm shouting and the thump of somebody hitting the wall. Himes gets up to his feet and comes at me grinning, blood running from his ear.

I see the bottle in his hand before I feel it smack against my cheek. Glass crumbles down my chest and the room lights up for a second. I go down to the ground. Himes hits me again and it is all I can do to crawl toward the bed and the tangle of blankets and clothing. There is more shouting, but it comes to me in short unintelligible bursts before the darkness.

When I wake I'm still in the room and my head feels like a hollow rattle that hurts when I move.

"Hey, hero," I hear somebody say. I look around the dark room to see Napalm sitting in the armchair, holding his mouth.

"I think I lost a tooth," he says.

I rub my head and look around the room some more. Kim is still on the bed, asleep or passed out—I can't tell which. I walk unsteadily toward the sound of Napalm's voice, burners shooting down my neck and into my shoulders. I touch my cheek and it comes away sticky, the rich tang of blood spreading across my tongue. I try to clear the buzzing in my head, but each step seems to bring all of the aches and pains roaring back into my body.

"We got our asses kicked," Napalm says. He has a plum-shaped knot over one eye and his lower lip is fat with blood.

I go to the bed and pull Kim's limp body into a sitting position.

"This is fucked up," I say. Napalm grumbles in agreement. "What the fuck was Himes thinking about?"

"That's a stupid question," he says.

When I bend to move her off the bed she mutters and rolls into me as I pull on her shoulders, her hips stirring as if I'm another guy wanting to jump between her legs. I can smell the gin on her breath and when I shift her head back against the headboard her eyes flutter open a moment. My hand brushes against her cold breast but her nipples remain flat and lifeless.

I tell Napalm to find her clothes and after a minute of rummaging through the debris on the floor he tosses a beer-soaked dress at me.

"Find something else," I tell him.

He goes to a plywood chest of drawers and hands me a large blue sweatshirt and a pair of shorts.

I manage to pull them over her body by leaning her into the arm-chair, her thin frame bending under my grip and then sagging as I work the shirt down her torso.

"How come they left us?" I ask.

"Riley, Himes creamed you with that beer bottle, remember? Then shit started to fly and I think I caught a trophy or something to the head, then my tooth—in a word they kicked our asses."

"You mad?"

"No, man. The whole thing's fucked up. I don't know what's wrong with Vezio—and Himes' got shit for brains. Let's just get the hell out of here, my ankle's hurting again."

"What about her?" I ask, pointing at Kim in the chair swaddled in the too big clothes, smelling of beer and sex.

"I suppose we'd better get her out of here too, before the second round starts," Napalm says.

And I know that he's thinking about all the abuse we're going to take from the guys walking out of Taylor's party with a passed-out girl over our shoulders.

I nod and sling Kim over my shoulder. Her stomach brushes my swollen cheek and for a minute the hot sizzle of pain shoots down my neck as the blood oozes from the cut. The soft heft of Kim's uncon-scious body across my shoulders only sickens me in some way I can't begin to describe.

When we walk out into the pulse of the party the hooting starts. Hands reach out to grab Kim's ass and I do my best to push them away as Napalm walks behind arguing when somebody grabs him and tries to stop us. People call us faggots, homos, pussies, etc. Several tired-looking groupies stare at me blankly then at the load slung across my shoulders and raise their eyebrows as if to say that she got what was coming to her.

At the door Vezio steps in front of me, pushing his face into mine.

"I don't get it, Riley. What the fuck's wrong with you? Himes is fucking deaf—all this over a gook whore? I mean come on, Riley—she liked it and don't you say different."

"No, Vez, she didn't—in fact she's drunk," I say. "What's wrong with you?"

I shake Kim at him, push past and walk into the night with Napalm in tow.

The next day at practice I have a hard time getting my helmet over my split cheek and I'm bleeding before we hit warm-up laps. Himes pounds up to me, threatening me a few times while others talk behind my back. None of the coaches say a word about the star-shaped cut on my cheek and I don't give them any reason to, hitting and throwing my body into pileup after pileup until the burners are coming on in one long ribbon of pain.

Above us, Coach Roe bullies out orders from his tower, blowing the whistle when we screw up or he thinks we aren't giving it our all. Napalm and the rest of the gimp squad sit along the sideline pedaling arm and leg bikes. I step back from the huddle and notice that the whole big machine's clicking along just as it's supposed to. It's the clicking-along part that gets me, as if all of the events of last night have been forgiven and cleansed.

Robeson comes up to me at the water cooler. "Heard you did the right thing last night."

"Maybe," I say.

"Remember that book you gave me in California?"

"What about it?"

"Some bad shit," he says. "But that Stoic crap don't hold water around here. If I was you I'd be looking for some other way of life. Know what I mean?"

"What do you mean?"

"The fellas are going to be gunning for you," he says. "Just watch yourself."

He clomps me on the shoulder pad and walks away.

After practice we hustle in and out of the shower and jump into our street clothes before a quick position meeting. Himes gets in my face just as I'm ambling down the hall with ice bags strapped to my neck.

"My ear," he says. "All you had to do was wait your fucking turn— maybe that's your problem, Riley, you need to get laid."

I just nod, push past him, walking down the hall and into the O-line meeting. Coach U glares at me and I know it's the gash on my cheek or some blocking assignment I've blown at practice today. Without Kong, Bam Bam or the Shed to scream and yell at he's picked up his tirades against us, venting his spleen about our lack of balls and unwillingness to absorb the new plays.

After Smitty's shuffled in and taken a seat in the back, Coach U hits the lights and starts the projector running. We watch the first play twelve times until every tiny inconsistency has been addressed and guilt accepted with the promise of doing it right the next time.

We watch a Red Right 46.

I barely make a block on Reems and Coach U lets me know it.

"Piss poor, Riley," he says, running the play back again and freezing it on my near miss. Then he directs his attention to Smitty, who all but falls down on the play.

"Son," Coach U says. "Un-fucking-acceptable."

We watch the play a third, fourth, and fifth time. Each time Smitty's flailing block looks worse. He sinks into the seat, covering his face with his hands. Coach U gets to his feet, pacing the room as far as the projector's remote control will allow, screaming about how we're looking at a .500 season if one of us doesn't come through on O-line. The whole room groans and we watch the play ten more times, Childers catching it for pussying out on his slant block.

After ten minutes we've reviewed only one series of plays and Coach U's worked himself into a neck-bulging frenzy.

Then comes a play that I can barely watch. A simple blocking scheme where I blow my call and let the fullback get stuffed by a stunting Himes. We watch the play in silence a few times, Coach U clicking the projector back and forth, pausing on my stumble and the ensuing tackle by Himes.

I slouch down in my chair and wait for the tongue-lashing to start. We watch it maybe six more times, until Coach U turns in his seat and looks at me.

"Pa-fucking-thetic," he scowls. "What were you thinking about, Riley?"

I don't answer him, even though every guy in the room's watching me, half smiling, glad that it's my ration of shit and not theirs. As Coach U runs the play back again I finger the cut on my cheek which aches the way a rotten tooth does: deep and fine.

Coach U sticks the play on pause again, freezing my image in mid-stumble.

He repeats, "What were you thinking about, Riley?"

I don't answer and to tell you the truth I don't know what I'm really thinking about. And when I look up, Coach U is standing over me.

"That just ain't going to get it done. Blocking like that is going to get someone killed—*you hear me, Riley?*"

What he wants is for me to mumble something or nod brightly, tell him I'll do better no matter what it takes—even if it kills me.

Instead I stare at myself on the screen, somewhere between falling and getting back up, my arms outstretched, helmet down, Himes flying by me.

"Son," Coach U says. "You'd better come up with some kind of answer or your ass is going to be riding the bench for e-fucking-ternity and then some. I mean, my God—you call that a block?"

When I don't so much as move, Coach U raises his arms and smacks me with an open palm. I'm not ready for the blow and it sends me stumbling out of my chair. The gouge on my cheek breaks open and blood runs down into my shirt.

For a minute the room is dead silent. Getting hit by a coach out on the field is one thing, but this is something different—an event with consequence—and every mother-loving guy in the room knows it, even the phony Eye of Michigan painted above the door seems to be looking at me as I push myself off the floor.

I do nothing as Coach U stomps back up to the front of the room and hits the lights and tells us to go to training table and call it a night. He doesn't look at me. My head hurts like hell: hangover, practice, the fight last night. When I get up to go I take my sweet old time, letting the blood flow down my neck and the buzz come into my ears.

A couple of the guys whisper amongst themselves about what they've just seen. A few of them even pat me on the back and tell me it's fucked up.

At the door Coach U calls out my name.

"Elwood Riley," he says, still unable to look me in the eyes. "Come here."

Only I don't.

In that very second with the football machine meshing gears again, revving back to normal, something quits in me as I look around at the broad-body-filled hall, at the tired faces streaming out of meeting rooms on their way to training table.

"Riley," he says again. "Come here and talk to me."

I wipe the blood off my cheek and in the moment it takes to walk past Coach U, I can already see myself strapping on the pads tomorrow and walking out onto the field. After warm-up I'll line up across from Himes and feel the grass under my knuckles and the coil of my body. I will feel large and capable of great things. Then I'll spit on him, ask him if it was the bottle because he couldn't get it up. I'll call him a homosexual or rapist.

Then the whistle blast. I'll rise up from my stance, drop my arms, stick my my neck out and wait for Himes to plow into me, wanting the impact, rolling the dice. The burner will come and I imagine going down to the turf, Himes stepping over my body on his way to the quarterback, pain rushing in and then another whistle to kill the play. There will be a stretcher and maple back board to lash my head and arms to before they wheel me to the sideline. Robeson will be there shaking his head, so will Napalm asking, "Where does it hurt?"

And me saying, "All over."

ACKNOWLEDGMENTS

Thanks to my agent and friend, Gordon Kato, who believed, prodded, and slogged through countless drafts of this novel. Also thanks to Bill Thomas for his conviction and commitment to making the best book possible.

The following people must be thanked for support, guidance, and inspiration: Eileen Pollack, Nick Delbanco, Phil and Karen Moore, Charles "Coach" Baxter, Caroline Kim, Mark Janosy, Mike "Black Rain" Paterniti, Carol Houck Smith, Andrea Beauchamp, and especially Alyson Hagy for sticking with me and being patient.

Thanks also to Keith Taylor for not being coy and letting me browse and talk books at The Shaman Drum Bookshop. Thanks to John Doris for drywall and philosophy. The same for M. Loncar and his jazz, bourbon, and Berryman. Thanks also go to Leah Stewart for short sentences and friendship. Many thanks to Ilena Silverman for letting me in the door and showing me how it's done. Thanks also to Adrienne Miller for saving me from the slush pile.

I owe part of this book and possibly future children to Rob Depalma, who was there and who let me sleep on his floor.

Most of all thanks to my parents for believing and to Jeff and Ellen for putting up with me.